ESCAPING CAPTIVITY

HUMAN PETS OF TALIN, BOOK 2

Warning: Author is dyslexic as hell.

Beta reading team: Mary Alegre, Martha Collins, and Lauren Meghoo

Professional editing: Amanda Brown Edits, LLC.

And, as with many writers, your reviews on Amazon, Goodreads, and/or Kindle help immeasurably, even if it's just clicking on the stars.

Thank you to all my readers!

CONTENT WARNING

-There is talk of past torture and trauma by both main characters.
-There are scenes of violence and fighting including the death of characters on page.
-There is a threat of rape.
-Characters are kept in cages in several scenes.
-Characters are forced to wear collars and Lakin is restrained hand and foot in one scene.
-There are several scenes of graphic, consensual sex.
-There is a character with Down's Syndrome in the bonus chapter at the end.

GLOSSARY

Adultlette: When Talins reach a human equivalent age of between 17-19 years old they graduate from the cresh and return to their families to start their adult education and decide on a career.

Artificial wombs: Talin women cannot get pregnant if they don't "scent bond" (see Cresh) with their partner. When scent-bonding started going out of style (and eventually became illegal), Talin started using artificial wombs to have children. Once live births were outlawed and only artificial wombs were used, it was expected that each Talin couple would have exactly two children, one male and one female, unless the government requested more to make up for a population imbalance.

Common/Universal: One of several universal languages used both for speaking and writing adopted by many species as a second language. The Talins don't bother learning it because they consider their empire dominant in the universe.

Common Units (Also referred to as a Unit): This is a universal time-keeping framework used by most species. It's based on a ten-unit day with each unit being the equivalent to about two hours of Old Earth time-keeping. Most species divide up a day into a five-unit working cycle and a five-unit rest cycle.

Cresh (plural - creshes): It became fashionable not only to have a child produced in an artificial womb but also to have them raised by specially trained professionals. Children spend their lives in the cresh and only leave when it's time for them to train for a future career under the guidance of their family.

Ending (clinically referred to as Collapsed Scent Disease): If scent-bonded partners are separated for too long, they can suffer and die. The length of time partners can go without each other depends on the individuals, but most can only last ten or so days apart before they start suffering. It's a painful death, and one of the reasons that an ancestral Talin monarch started encouraging his people not to scent bond.

Fading (clinically referred to as Catatonic Withdrawal Disease): This is a disease that can strike a Talin at any time in their life but is most common when they're in their prime breeding years. Without a scent-bonded partner to help stabilize them, they can fall into a deep depression. They stop eating, moving, and eventually die. It's considered a shameful disease among the Talin, and those that suffer from it are often hidden away by their family.

Identification Cubes: Often called simply an Ident, these devices act as a combination of communication device, locator, identity verifier, recorder, and method of payment, among other things. Most species have moved to using small Information Squares instead of the awkward cubes, but Talins refuse to give them up.

Information square: These can range from the size of a human hand to the size of a human torso. They look like a square of glass but are embedded with electronics. They can store data, record, access UniBases, store wealth, and act as a form of identification. Most species use these instead of the older, less versatile Identification Cubes.

Inner-cranial translator (also known as an INT): This is a small bit of tech that almost every hearing species has implanted in their head. It only works with verbal or gesture-based languages; it can't translate written words.

Marks and Stikes: Talins don't use Universal or Common Units. They have marks and strikes. 1st mark is at sunrise, and 13th mark is at sunset. Strikes are used at night and go from 1 to 13. Each strike and mark on Talarian is the equivalent of 45 Old Earth Minutes. Each mark is made up of 100 sub-marks. Each colony has to divide up their strikes and marks differently depending on the length of their night/day rotations but Talin ships and space station will keep the same time as Talarian.

Mattil medal: Awarded to soldiers for acts of bravery. At best, most soldiers only win one in a lifetime of service.

Scent-bonding: Talins have oil-secreting glands in their cheeks. Each Talin produces oil with a unique scent, and they can become addicted to their partner's smell. The lack of oil-producing scent glands in humans is why it's believed that Talins can't become scent-bonded with humans.

Talin Government Basics:
- **Monarch:** The monarch and Apogee Assembly work together to lead the Talin people. Although the monarch doesn't serve on the Apogee Assembly, they have the power to challenge any laws the assembly wants to pass. They can also unilaterally disbar an assembly member, but this is considered an extreme action and rarely done.

-**Apogee Assembly**: This is the major law-making and governing body. Other government programs are overseen by this assembly. The members of the Apogee Assembly are referred to as Servant Citizens and are elected by their Clan Assembly to their position. (It is expected that a monarch's grown children, called Prime Son/Prime Daughter, will serve on the Apogee Assembly. There are always two positions set aside for them, although it's rare that both will serve at the same time.)

-**Clan Assemblies**: Talarian, the Talin homeworld, is divided into provinces. Each province has a Clan Assembly made up of a representative from each clan in the province. Those that serve on Clan Assemblies are called Assembly Citizens. These Clan Assemblies will pick one of their members to serve on the Apogee Assembly.

-**Colony Assemblies:** Most colonies don't have large clans or are made up of a few families starting a new clan; therefore these assemblies are comprised of whoever the citizens of that colony believe will do the best job of governing. Most homeworld Talins look down on colonies as being made up of upstarts or new clans.

Talarian: Name of the Talin homeworld. Their capital city and seat of centralized government is Moravi.

UniBase: This stands for a universal database that most species keep and allow free access to for all their citizens. Often ships will have a copy of their specie's UniBase but might restrict access to only the members of the crew that are the same species as the captain or owner.

DEDICATION

To the other half of Writers Synonymous, Martha C. You've never failed to be enthusiastic and encouraging. I can only hope I'm as helpful to you as you are to me.

CHAPTER

1

Lakin

The small cage they've shoved Lakin into is so tight she can barely move. Everything hurts, and the way she has to curl up inside the confined space puts pressure on her injured shoulder, but she isn't about to complain. No one can touch her while she's ensconced in the too-small cage, and that's a good thing.

She's not sure how long she's been locked in the tiny crate. When they first stuffed her in, she was heavily drugged and in so much pain she might have blacked out. For a long time she drifted in and out of consciousness, hearing muted engine noise and the clatter of a ship around her.

Now, fully awake, she waits as the cage sways with the movement of a vehicle. She can hear muffled voices talking but can't make out what they're saying. She's in no shape to fight or flee yet, so she's going to need to pretend to be docile when they finally open the crate.

Assuming they don't just leave her in here to die of dehydration and hunger, that is. Her life has taken so many bizarre twists and turns over the years she wouldn't be surprised to end up dead because they stuck her crate somewhere and forgot about her.

Someone, decades from now, might uncover her desiccated corpse and wonder how a human ended up boxed up and stored with bolts of cloth. Or ammunition. Oh, she likes that idea better— she wants to be stored with ammunition or bombs.

That makes her dream of all the things she could do if she could just get her hands on some key components. She could make so many weapons with just a few ingredients. Images of all the trouble she could cause make her smile and help her ignore the pain.

A sudden burst of movement pulls her out of her thoughts as the top of the box is literally ripped off. Overwhelming brightness makes her eyes water and hurt, so she shuts them, having only been able to make out the outline of a figure standing over her.

Massive hands close over her and lift her out. Even though the hands are gentle, the pressure on her injured shoulder and abused body sends a wave of agony through her. She tries to be silent, but a little groan escapes her lips.

"Easy, little one," a voice murmurs as she's set down on something soft. She grits her teeth and breathes through the pain. "You're safe now. No one's going to hurt you here." The urge to laugh at those words is strong. She's heard it all before. Safe isn't in her vocabulary anymore, just survival.

Distracted by the pain, she doesn't notice the man has let go of her until she hears him addressing someone else. Forcing her lids open, she blinks through the discomfort as her eyes adjust to the bright daylight. Once they stop watering, she takes in the scene around her as three of them argue about her, or more specifically, about the crate she was shipped in.

They're a tall species, and all three of them are wearing what she's come to think of as their uniform—loose trousers gathered just below their knees, a wide, thick belt with a pouch and an Ident Cube dangling from it.

That's everything. No shirt or shoes. No jewelry. Well, the belts might count as jewelry. They seem to be pretty ornate. But other than the pants and belt, they're remarkably bare of adornment.

By the look of their feet, which she can see well from the low vantage point of the soft bed she's lying on, they have a good reason not to wear shoes. Their four-toed feet are covered in hard calluses and look like they could handle just about any terrain. That makes her feel vaguely envious.

How nice it would be not to need to worry about foot coverings. In fact, by the looks of them, those digits might even be opposable, allowing them to grab things like a hand. That would make climbing through maintenance corridors so much easier. As an electrical systems tech, she's climbed into some tight spots, so having feet like those would make her job so much easier.

Why is she staring at these guys' feet? Giving her head a little shake, she tries to focus.

Idly, she continues to examine the arguing males. They have hard natural plating on their upper chests and shoulders as well as down their backs. She knows from watching her original captors that the back platting running down their spines can move a little, and they use it to make a variety of sounds. Their faces don't have the mobility to be expressive, so they convey emotions by either rattling their back plates or making rumbling sounds from deep in their chests.

Right now, one of the males is facing off against the other two, his body language aggressive and his back plates rattling quickly and making a sound similar to an angry swarm of wasps. The other two are making soft rumbling sounds from deep in their chests. The rumbles make her think of distant thuming of a bass drum. She thinks those rumbles are meant to be apologetic or maybe concern.

"This is unacceptable! You contacted us a full rotation ago. Has she been in this crate the entire time?"

"She was fighting and unmanageable, and it was the only shipping container we had."

"Didn't it occur to you to sedate her? She could have permanent damage from being forced into an unnatural position for so long!"

That comment makes her check her own body for numbness. Everything hurts but seems to be mostly working. Her two biggest issues are her right shoulder and her feet. The limited range of motion in her shoulder is bad, but if she doesn't move it there isn't much pain. The bigger issue is that the soles of her feet are hamburger . Not only do they hurt like hell even now while she's laying down, the damage will hamper her escape attempts.

The three are still arguing and don't even seem to notice when she sits up to look at her feet. They're covered in blood soaked and crusty bandages. Lovely.

"We've never dealt with humans before. We didn't know what medications might hurt her, so we didn't give her any." She wants to call them out on that lie—they medicated her before shoving her into the crate—but there's no point. Jailers aren't interested in what their prisoners have to say.

"And it didn't occur to either of you to even provide her with food or water! Everyone knows how delicate humans are. You could have killed her!" His rattling increases in volume, and changes to a loud clacking making both men take a step back. "You'll be lucky if I don't tell the commandant about this. All of you are idiots. No wonder you're assigned to the cleanup crews. You're not fit for anything else."

That insult doesn't seem too bad to Lakin, but the argument suddenly turns violent so it must have been a whopper of an insult in this culture.

These guys are of the same species the Leemron sold her to. She has no idea what this species is, but she knows one thing; they're a mean, sadistic people. The Leemron updated her intercranial translator with these guys' language before handing her over, but understanding what they're saying didn't keep her from being tortured.

It probably made things worse because she could hear and expect everything they planned to do to her. Every insult. Every nasty comment. And now she gets to listen to them argue.

As the men near her shove at each other in agitation, one man turns partially away, allowing her to see the armor extending down the back of his head all the way down his neck and spine to disappear under the waistband of his pants. Those armor plates are moving too fast for her eyes to follow and making quite the racket.

When a fourth man walks up and joins the conversation, things get even louder. One of them even goes after another one with claws fully extended. Huh. She hasn't seen that before. She also notices they have quills on their forearms. They must have been flat against their arms before, which is why she didn't notice. The bristling quills and claws look wickedly sharp.

Again, she envies this species for their natural weapons. Wouldn't it be nice to be something other than a soft, weak human? But then again, she's damn clever and has kept herself alive and free so far. This current captivity is just a blip. She'll be free and in space again soon. She's sure of it.

When the blood starts to flow, Lakin grins. Not that she likes to see violence and bloodshed, but this level of distraction is helpful. The more time they spend arguing and hurting each other is less time and energy they'll put into paying attention to her.

She takes this opportunity to examine her surroundings. She's in some kind of square enclosure about the size of her captain's quarters on her last ship. Most of the enclosure is made up of metal bars. Running over her head is a type of metal mesh. It looks weak and easily torn, but she knows better. It's Cadarin netting, light and nearly indestructible. She won't be able to climb out of this enclosure.

They'd set her down on what seems like a nest made from pillows and bedding. Maybe this cage is normally used for an avian type species.

The nest is inside an area sheltered on three sides with stone walls and covered by a domed stone roof. A glance around the opening shows ion generators that would keep weather out when activated but continue to provide the illusion of no barrier.

Within the stone area is a secluded space with a flimsy, old fashioned sliding door. The door's half open and she can see inside is a small area for elimination and bathing. Other than the nest and that room, the place is bare.

A stone bench sits near the front of the enclosure, close to the gate. Soft moss-like green plants blanket the ground, both in the enclosure and on the path outside. She can't see much beyond this except other enclosures. The one side that doesn't border another cage, or the pathway, is blocked by large bushes.

This feels like a zoo. Or a kennel.

The only way to get in and out is through a heavy gate at the front of the enclosure. The display on the gate tells her it's secured with a biosignature lock. Normally it would take her some time to get past that, except the gate is standing wide open.

She has no idea what planet she's on, what this species is, or even which solar system she's in. Escaping before she has more knowledge is foolish. Running before she's given herself some time to heal is idiotic. Sneaking away when the threat outside of her cage might be greater than inside is ill-advised.

Yet, off she goes, silently limping around the men, two now on the ground fighting. They're roaring and rattling loudly enough to wake the dead.

Hers is the last in a row of at least a dozen enclosures, and another row sits across from her row. The area between rows is shaded by colorful tarps stretched between the enclosure fencing. As she casually slinks through the gate, she notices another human with wide eyes watching her leave. Lakin silently pleads with the woman to remain silent.

Now that she knows other humans are held here, once she's free and healed, she can come back and rescue them. But she needs to escape first.

The woman looks equal parts shocked and puzzled. She shakes her head, looking back and forth between Lakin and the fighting men.

"Don't," she whispers urgently. "It's dangerous!"

Relieved that this captive isn't going to betray her, Lakin just gives her a grin, waves, and leaves, doing her best to be quick despite the agony in her feet.

It's no surprise to Lakin when she doesn't get far.

The area around the rows of enclosures is devoid of large plants, decorative boulders, or buildings. With no place to hide, she's spotted almost immediately. A high-pitched fast rattle coming from several different directions makes her stop.

She's in too much pain to sprint, so instead she picks up a stone the size of her fist to use as a weapon. Three males she hasn't seen before step out to surround her, their warning rattle turning to soft rumbles that remind her of Old Earth cats purring.

"Stay back!" she shouts.

"Easy, human, don't be afraid. You're not in danger," one of them says.

Hiding both her pain and her fear, she faces them down. "You're the one who should be afraid!"

Then a fourth male comes running from the enclosures. She recognizes him as the one who pulled her from the tight box and then got into a fight with the others over it. He steps closer to her than the rest, but not so close that he can touch her.

"I'm Keeper Eranan," he tells her. He's not rattling any longer and is purring loudly. "I care for all the humans here. I know you don't believe me yet, but you're safe now. Put down the rock. I don't want you to get hurt."

He holds out his hands to show he doesn't have a weapon. The gesture is pointless. He could hurt or kill her with just his big hands alone.

Scowling at him, she keeps her flat teeth hidden as she talks. "Keep away! I'm venomous. My bite can kill!"

That bluff has worked in the past. With only a few hundred thousand humans in the entire universe, most species she meets have no idea what they can do. When the men around her rumble in a tone that must mean they're laughing, she realizes her ruse didn't work.

"You're no danger to us," Eranan tells her. "And we're no danger to you. If you go back into the enclosure, I'll tend to your injuries. You're covered in blood and obviously in pain. We can take the pain away. Would you like that? Are you hungry? Thirsty? I can get you food and water. No one will hurt you here. No more pain. No more torture. You're safe and will be well cared for."

There's no point in mentioning that's very similar to a speech she's received before. One time her ship was captured. They'd gone into a war zone attempting to get supplies in and lives out. She and the rest of the females in the crew were separated, and she figured out pretty quickly that they were to be sold, even with all their captors' goodwill words of comfort. If she'd believed all the little speeches, she and the crew would've sat tight and ended up as slaves somewhere.

She and the rest of the females kept silent and pretended to be docile. They all waited until no one was paying attention. Then using a stolen bit of broken tool handle, she got them out of there and back to their ship. It was lucky for all of them that the ship was antiquated, and Lakin had worked on a similar one before. It made their escape relatively easy.

And, of course, she also managed to sabotage a few things on the way out. It's been satisfying to watch the ship disintegrate from a safe distance!

They weren't able to rescue anyone on that trip, but they didn't lose any crew members either. Some days that's the best outcome one can hope for.

That experience taught her not to trust what captors say. Right now, standing on the grass surrounded by members of this big species, she realizes she's going to have to pretend she's given in. She throws down her rock and hunches her shoulders, trying to look small and defeated.

"Don't touch me," she warns. "I might not be venomous, but I can still bite you! I have long, sharp teeth that descend when I fight."

Instead of calling her bluff or backing away, Eranan continues to purr. "I won't give you cause to bite me if you'll walk back to your enclosure." His tone tells her he's amused by her.

Moving slowly, partially from pain and partially because she wants to keep her eyes on them, she makes her way back to the cage. None of the men try to touch her. When she walks in Eranan doesn't follow her but just shuts the gate firmly. She hears the display next to the gate chirp as the locks engage.

"I'll be right back," he promises her and hurries off as the other men also walk away, murmuring among themselves. The crate she was pulled from is still in the enclosure. She gives in to temptation and gives it a good kick. It doesn't move, but now the top of her foot hurts along with the bottom.

"Good job," she mutters to herself.

"That was dumb," a voice calls out. She looks up to see the human woman who whispered to her earlier sitting at the very edge of her enclosure watching with a curious expression. "You shouldn't run away like that."

"Had to try," Lakin says with a shrug that makes her wince. Gods, everything hurts. Her body is urging her to settle down on the nest, but this friendly fellow human might be an invaluable source of information. She'll heal whether she's sitting and talking or lying flat on her back on soft bedding trying to sleep. Might as well gather intel while she can.

Walking on unsteady feet, she makes it to the edge of her cage and sinks to the mossy ground. She sits carefully and then tries to smile. It must have looked bad because the other woman flinches slightly. "What happened to you?"

Unconcerned, Lakin waves off the woman's questions. "What hasn't happened to me is probably a shorter answer. I haven't been decapitated yet, so that's nice."

The woman snorts. "My name's Henni."

"Hi, Henni, I'm Lakin. Where are we?"

"You're owned by Commandant Holian," Henni explains. "This is his estate." When Lakin doesn't make any sound of recognition, Henni continues, "On Kalor Colony? Sarista System?"

"Nope, not familiar. What's this species called? I mean, you're human. Right? You look human."

"Yes, I'm human. They're Talins. I'm surprised you haven't ever seen one of them, even if this is your first time in their territory. They've got a lot of political power. Their empire is large, and they have trade contracts with a lot of species, even ones that no one else can trade with. I talked to another human who said most of the remaining human settlements are very far away, but you should have at least heard of them."

Now Lakin nods. "I have heard of them but never saw one before the Leemron caught me and sold me to a couple."

Henni shakes her head. "You're wild-caught, but I hope you adjust quickly."

"That's an interesting expression, wild-caught. I guess I was. Were you born a slave here?"

Shaking her head, Henni frowns at Lakin fiercely, "I was born here, but I'm not a slave."

Now it's Lakin's turn to look surprised. "Uh, so that would mean these are the guest quarters?" she asks as she taps the bars in front of her.

Dissolving into giggles, Henni leans forward until her forehead is almost touching the bars of her enclosure. "We're pets."

"Pets." Lakin tests the word on her tongue. "What exactly do pets do?"

With a look that clearly conveys Henni thinks she's mentally slow, the young woman heaves an exaggerated sigh. "We keep the Talins from dying."

"That's as clear as an infected biosystem," Lakin mutters. Before she can ask another question, a Talin walks down the aisle between enclosures. He stops at Henni's door, making Lakin tense. She worries the girl is about to be abused for talking so freely with a new prisoner, but when Henni sees the new arrival, she scrambles to her feet and launches herself at him with a delighted shout.

"Ianino!"

The Talin catches her in his arms and holds her tightly. Henni wraps her legs around his waist and her arms around his neck. Lakin watches with keen interest as the male Talin rubs his face against Henni's hair. The smell of sandalwood fills the air.

"I missed you, sweet Henni," the Talin murmurs as he carries her over to a large stone bench and sits down with her still in his arms. Lakin shifts a little to better watch them. Her movement catches his eye, and he looks over, rattling when he sets his eyes on her.

"Dear ancestors, what happened to you?" His facial expression never changes, but his voice is full of horror.

"She just got here," Henni tells him and then whispers loudly enough for people on the other side of the planet to hear. "I don't think she was treated well by her former masters."

Lakin snorts in derision. Former masters, ha! She's not calling anyone master. Slaver. Asshole. Dead man walking. Those are the names she uses but never Master.

Although by the look of this place, if she doesn't end up executed, she won't be talking Henni into escaping with her. The woman looks healthy and damn happy. Too bad it's probably temporary. With no say in who can sell or buy them, slaves often find their circumstances shifting dramatically within a single rotation. One moment they might be owned by a caring master and the next subjected to dangerous conditions or death.

Or, like her, tortured for amusement.

"Poor thing," Ianino says, turning his attention back to Henni. "You need to stay away from her. We don't know what kind of contaminants she might have. And she could be violent. My father shouldn't be so cavalier about accepting unknown stock."

It's on the tip of her tongue to insult the guy, but the arrival of Eranan keeps her quiet.

Another Talin follows Eranan, and they both enter her enclosure. She remains still and seated, watching them warily as

Eranan sets a tray of food next to the nest. The other man easily picks up the heavy transport cage by himself and walks out with it.

That thing didn't budge when she kicked it. The level of strength it would require to carry it so casually takes Lakin's breath away. She knew this species was strong; she just didn't know how strong.

Right. She's going to need to be extra careful and very clever when dealing with these Talins.

CHAPTER 2

Lakin

Something significant must be going on because Talins are scrambling all over the place. Lakin watches from the corner of her cage with the best view, which isn't saying much because the enclosures are surrounded by tall ornamental bushes. After limping a circuit of her cage, she finds a small hole in the greenery, probably caused by an animal. It allows her a limited view of the large green area around what looks like a mansion.

The movements of the Talins running around the green space and in and out of the mansion are frantic, telling her that whatever's happening isn't part of their normal daily routine. They must be putting everyone to work because the Talin named Eranan, who promised her pain suppressants, didn't come back after dropping off food. Not that she would've taken any. The last thing she needs is to end up spaced out on drugs.

Moving slowly because the pain is exhausting her, she shuffles over to the nest and drops down next to the tray of food. She doesn't recognize any of it but starts eating anyway. It's probably laced with something, but she hasn't eaten much in the last several days. Worrying if the food is drugged is pointless because lack of sustenance will render her incapacitated anyway.

Although bland, the food goes down well and only causes a pleasant sensation of satiation. Sighing at having a full belly after so long living on so little, she reclines and closes her eyes. She might as well rest for now.

Someone dropping something loud wakes her with a start. Moving faster than she should, she scrambles to her feet and then gives a little moan before falling to her knees as all the pain in her body hits her at once. The pain in her shoulder is so bad she can't lift her arm much at all, and her feet are throbbing in time with her heartbeat. The injuries seem to feel even worse now than when she fell asleep. She hopes they're healing and not getting worse. If she gets an infection without access to a med bay, it's as good as a death sentence.

Of course her shoulder and feet are just the worst of her injuries. The rest of her body is checking in to tell her she's hurt in a lot of other places.

If her tired, aching body had a choice, it would force her to lie back down and keep still until the pain goes away. Too bad she doesn't have the luxury of listening, because while she was asleep someone left her another tray of food.

She's still full from the first meal, so the food isn't what gets her attention. No, it's the long, dull implement with a triangle cross section on the tray with the food. It's some kind of eating utensil, probably for the fist-sized fruit on the tray, but that doesn't matter. What does matter is that they gave her a tool.

Snatching it up, she hobbles over to the gate and inspects it. Her new tool won't help her here. The gates are too sturdy and the locking mechanism too advanced. She'd need either a much bigger tool to smash open the gate or a very slim tool to jimmy open the display and manipulate the electronics inside.

Turning, she does another circle of her enclosure, looking for the spot she noticed earlier where this eating utensil might be effective.

When she finds the spot she's looking for, she drops to her knees and starts working at the soil with her tool. Roots have undermined the fencing at this spot, so all she needs to do is dig out a few stones to get to the soil. Once the stones are out of the way, she grabs one of the bowls from her tray and starts digging. Despite her weakened state, it's not long until she's dug a hole big enough to fit through.

Checking over her shoulder, she makes sure no one's noticed her. Henni and her Talin have disappeared, and none of the other cages around her are occupied. Satisfied no one's going to shout out an alarm, she wiggles herself through the hole, gasping a few times as her many injuries protest her movements.

Suck it up, body, she tells herself. *I know you're tired, hurt, and want to rest, but if we don't get out of here, we might end up dead. Hurting is better than dead.*

Her body doesn't seem to agree because once she's free, she's forced to sit and breathe in ragged breaths as the pain ebbs. She uses that time to look around, trying to figure out a course of action.

The green area she ran to on her first ill-conceived escape attempt appears busy as massive fabric shades are erected and elaborate seats and tables set out. The advantage of the chaos is that now she sees places to hide as she heads across the green.

She's under no illusion. Only because everyone's so busy and preoccupied is she able to make her way undetected. Once she's to the side of the mansion, she ducks behind a planter. Biting back a hiss of pain, she remains still as a group passes by, all of them talking loudly.

"Can you believe it? The monarch herself!"

"Why do you think the trip is so urgent? I know Commandant Holian is important, but wouldn't the monarch normally have him visit the royal compound? She travels so rarely. It must be very urgent that she's traveled all the way out here."

"Who are we to question her? The thing we should ask is if the food will be good enough. We bought out all the local shops, but I don't think we'll have nearly enough and it's all plain."

The voices fade as the group moves away, and Lakin slumps a little in relief. It's nice to know the cause of all the fuss isn't preparations for her public execution. As a bonus for her escape plan, whatever brings the monarch of the Talin people to the colony will probably distract everyone for a good long time.

"Lakin! Where are you? Lakin, you need to respond. You're not well and shouldn't be running around." It's Eranan's voice, and he's closing in on her position. Damn, she thought she'd have more time. Shouldn't he be busy helping everyone else prepare for the arrival of his monarch?

Looking around frantically, she finds there's no direction that isn't crowded. Talins are bustling around everywhere with trays of food, chairs, and bundles of thick cloth. The only safe path is through a door in the wall next to her. She dives inside and then freezes as two sets of eyes regard her.

One set of eyes belongs to a Talin who quickly steps in front of a human female sitting on a tall bed. He doesn't come near her or threaten her in any way. Lakin knows his body language well because she's done the same thing and shielded others from harm.

The woman, just like Henni, looks healthy with no hint of fear or anxiety clouding her features. She makes no objection when the male steps in front of her. She just moves her head so she can still see Lakin around his bulk. This must be a familiar action between the two, him guarding and her being guarded.

Sounds outside make her turn and slam the door shut. She slaps at the display next to the door, hoping to engage a locking mechanism, but it does nothing. It's the same as the display in the cages and not set up to recognize her biosignature.

Another door sits at the far end of the room, but with her injured feet she doesn't think she can make it that far fast enough to avoid the Talin hunting her down. Then she spies a hiding spot.

Ignoring the other human and the Talin in the room, she clambers up onto a counter, knocking a few things onto the floor. Opening a cabinet, she uses the shelves inside to climb up and wiggle herself into the space between the cabinet and the ceiling. The other two in the room don't move or make a sound as she hides.

No sooner is she safely ensconced out of sight than she hears someone slamming open the door.

Eranan's voice is frantic as he questions the two in the room. "Is she in here?"

A voice too deep to be the human replies to his question. "She?"

"A new human arrived this morning. She's gotten out once already while I was distracted. This time I found the impossibly small hole she managed to dig and crawl through. The healer was going in to see her and found the enclosure empty." Eranan's loud rattle echoes in the room—a clear sign of frustration. "We need to find her. She was rescued from a terrible situation. She's traumatized and needs medical attention." Eranan sniffs the air. "I can smell her in here. Are you sure you didn't see anyone?"

They can smell her? That's good information to know. She'll need to take precautions to mask her scent from now on.

"We just got here," the male tells Eranan, making her smile. She didn't expect any concessions from either of them. Hiding was a last-ditch effort to evade. She expected that if Eranan came into the room, the two of them would point her out. But they're protecting her.

"She must have come through here, probably looking for a place to hide," Eranan mutters. She can hear him moving around the room, probably looking for her. "As if the day isn't already hectic enough with a royal visit from the monarch, now I have a wounded and distressed human loose on the grounds."

For the first time the woman speaks up. "The monarch is here?" Her voice sounds anxious and edging toward panic.

"Just arrived," Eranan confirms, still making rattling noises as he slams open cabinet doors. "The front green has been prepared and Commandant Holian and his men are assembling to receive her, but I need to find Lakin before anything bad happens to her."

"Lakin is the human?" the male asks.

"It's the name on her paperwork. Who knows what her real name is." Eranan's tone tells her that paperwork has lied to him before. That's her name, but she wonders what else is on this "paperwork." It probably doesn't include details about the ship she served on or her position as electrical systems tech. And it definitely won't mention her secondary profession, saboteur. That fact would have lowered her selling value.

The sound of cabinet doors slamming shut makes her flinch slightly.

"If you see her, don't try to grab her or anything. Just corner her and call for help. We're going to need to sedate her or she might end up more hurt than she already is."

Biting her lip, she listens as the footsteps leave and the door shuts. She needs to verify that Eranan left, so she gingerly slides herself over until she can peek out from her hiding spot.

She looks out just in time to see the large male stride over to the display next to the outside door and slap a large hand down on it, locking both sets of doors. Unsure of his motives, she remains still and watches him. He looks up at her, meeting her gaze with his own.

"They're locked out," he calls out softly. "I won't let them sedate you."

"We won't hurt you," the woman adds. "I don't know what happened to you, but I was a slave for ten years before the Talins bought me. This colony is very good to us. You're safe here. No Talin would deliberately hurt you."

Lakin debates about being honest with these two. They wait, the woman looking at her with concern and the man standing without any facial expression at all. She's getting used to the Talins' lack of facial expressions, but he's not making any noises either. That's not helping her figure out his mood. Without breaking eye contact with the male, she talks.

"Most of this damage was done by one of his people." She expects him to either declare her a liar or ask what she did to deserve it. Instead, he lets out a low hiss of anger.

"Who?" he demands, his voice rough and furious.

She doesn't know the names of the men who acquired her from the Leemrons or even their ship's name. Those days of torture are a blur of pain. For some reason, thinking about her pain makes her notice the state of the Talin watching her with such intensity. He's not like the other Talins she's seen so far.

He doesn't have the quills on his forearm that all the others have, just a mass of scar tissue and a few nubs. The rest of him seems odd too, somehow misshapen, but she can't quite put her finger on why.

The door opening makes her abandon her visual examination and duck her head back. Footsteps don't come into the room, but she can hear a rattle of agitation and a new voice speaks out clearly.

"Dalt, get Sora to the front garden to meet the monarch," the new voice orders. "You need to be respectful and honest."

"Yes, Master." The woman sounds so scared that Lakin's tempted to come out of hiding to help her. A loud rumble that sounds like a purr starts up. It's not the purr she'd heard from the other Talins, this one sounds like it's coming from a rusty engine. The direction of the purr tells her it's the male with the human woman and not one of the new arrivals.

"We need to come back here after," the man says, still purring. Lakin can tell he's talking to her, telling her he'll come back and help her if she stays hidden.

"You take such good care of me, Dalt," the human woman states loudly. "You would never let anyone hurt a human. Never. I bet you'd die to protect us." Lakin knows that's also for her benefit. Now she knows the man's name is Dalt and the human woman, Sora, wants her to know he's a protector, not an abuser.

The door shuts again and Lakin waits for a beat to make sure no one else is coming in. Unfortunately, when she tries to move from her hiding spot, she finds she's stuck. Trying to move through the pain in her shoulder makes her vision dim and causes her to cry out despite the need for quiet.

She gets herself moved to the edge of the cabinet and looks down. Eranan left most of the cabinets open so she's able to survey the contents. Just under her is a row of vials. Plucking a few of them up, she examines the labels. The contents scroll across the label, repeating in various languages. She waits, hoping she'll see a language she recognizes. Finally, common scrolls by and she finds out the vial she's staring at contains medication to fight infection.

Downing the contents of that vial, she examines the next one. That turns out to be a pain inhibitor, so she swallows that down too. After reading the labels on the third and fourth vials, she tosses them aside. Both are for conditions she's never heard of, so it would be pointless to take them. She settles down to wait for the pain inhibitor to work so she can escape from her hiding spot.

The problem is, she falls asleep while she's waiting.

CHAPTER

3

Dalt

"The female is to go to the monarch. You are to stay here," the guard instructs. Dalt tries to rattle but makes no sound. Hard to rattle when you don't have any armor plating to rattle with. Unable to make negative noises, he settles for putting force into a one word sentence.

"No."

"Let her down, Dalt," Holian orders him. "The monarch isn't going to hurt her."

Sora is his responsibility. Where she goes, he goes. He can't fail her again. It might be the monarch waiting for her, but that only makes him more worried, not less.

"No."

Holian goes quiet and then leans in close to him and Sora. "Put her down and let her go to the monarch or I'll send Eranan and a dozen guards to the medical room. I'll have them pull Lakin out from where she's hiding on the top of the cabinets and forbid them to use any sedation."

The commandant's words send a bolt of anger through him.

For the first time since returning from the wars, he wants to hurt the man he's served loyally for so many solars. That little human is hurt and scared and the commandant just threatened to make her life even worse.

Grimly, Dalt realizes that Holian must feel deeply concerned and perhaps even threatened by the monarch's visit to resort to such tactics.

"You know I'm good for my word, Dalt. Don't test me on this." It's true. Holian doesn't bluff.

Torn between staying with Sora and protecting Lakin, he bares his teeth at Holian, letting out a ticking growl. The other man doesn't react at all, just waits. They know each other much too well by now. Dalt will yield.

Reluctantly, Dalt lowers Sora to the ground. "I'll be right here," he tells her.

"Everything will be fine," she assures him as she gives his forearm a quick squeeze. Her shaking hand tells him she's not sure if that's true. It warms his heart that the little human wants to soothe him, but that's part of Sora's caring nature. With a last look at him and then at Holian, she walks away, stiff and scared but trying not to display it.

Once she reaches the monarch, he can't hear what they are discussing, but he watches closely for signs of danger. It's obvious when the monarch says something that causes Sora deep distress because she pales and wavers on her feet. He moves to go to her, but several sets of hands grab him and hold him back.

"I'll see to her," Holian declares and strides off. "Hold him back with however much force you need to use," he orders over his shoulder.

Dalt struggles in earnest as he sees Holian grab Sora's arm to keep her standing, but he doesn't walk her away. He keeps her there, facing the monarch and whatever threat is making her so scared she's about to collapse.

The monarch and Sora continue to talk, but when Sora whimpers, Dalt loses what little control was holding him in place. He only vaguely hears Holian's order to "stand down," but he doesn't obey. He can't. His entire attention is focused on getting away from the hands holding him. He has a driving need to snatch up Sora and get them both to a safe place where he can defend them.

More bodies come at him and soon he's on the ground, overpowered but unwilling to give up. Suddenly he's not on Kalor Colony anymore. He's back at the outpost, chained and helpless, listening to the screams of his men and the civilians they're protecting. Sounds of pain echo all around him.

Then Sora is there, kneeling next to him, touching his shoulder. The screaming stops, the war-torn buildings disappear, and reality snaps back into focus, leaving him breathless and shaking.

"I'm going to be safe. The monarch herself is going to keep me safe, but that girl in the infirmary doesn't have anyone. I'm worried about her. Can you look after her? Protect her? She's going to need someone patient." Sora's voice is steady. She's still pale, but her hands aren't shaking and he sees determination in her expressive human face.

Images of the dirty and blood-covered human female fill his mind. She must have been in so much pain, but with force of will she fled what she perceived as danger. That was quick thinking too, squeezing herself into a place no one as big as a Talin would think to look. Unlike Sora, who now seems content to join the monarch, that girl has no dedicated owner to care for her.

Eranan's an honorable male and skilled at dealing with the human pets, but she would be one of many under his care. If Dalt is looking after her well-being, she would be his sole focus. And he can make sure she never comes to harm again.

"She's going to need someone who knows what it's like." Sora's words confuse him, so he sounds a questioning rumble. She gives him a sad little smile. "Someone who knows what it's like to be tortured."

Comprehension makes his rumble go quiet. That poor little female hiding in the med room admitted to being tortured by his kind. How could another Talin do something like that? Not only did they damage her physical person, but they created distrust in her. She probably expects all Talins want to hurt her. She'll be suspicious of all of them.

But she's owned by Talins now, and there's no escaping, so she needs to be handled gently with a lot of patience until she learns to trust again. He remembers how angry he was when he woke up in the ship's infirmary. No armor plating on his back, no claws in his hands, and no quills on his arms. He felt like half a male. He felt worthless.

He felt vulnerable.

Probably exactly how she feels now.

Yes, he understands Lakin very well. He pins Sora with his gaze. "You'll contact me if you need me."

"I won't need to," she promises, and he hears the truth in her voice. Whatever the monarch said to her gave her all the confidence she didn't have before. "Maybe, someday, we'll visit. But now I need to go. Searin needs me." She touches a hand to her swelling stomach. "And I'm eager for his child to know him."

He's long suspected the child she carries was the grandchild to the monarch, but now his guess is confirmed. That explains a lot and why Sora is so sure she's safe now. If the monarch promised her that both she and the child will be protected, it's guaranteed.

"May the ancestors bless your union and your child," he whispers. A single tear falls from her eye and she gives him a human lip press on his cheek, just below his empty scent glands.

"And I hope Lakin realizes how lucky she is," Sora whispers. "Because if it wasn't for Searin, I'd want to stay with you."

Then she gets up and leaves him without a backward glance, eager to leave with the monarch. Eager to leave him behind.

He can't blame her. They both have new lives to see to.

He turns his attention to the guards. "Let me loose," he demands. "I have a task to do."

CHAPTER 4

Dalt

The moment the guards release him, Dalt sprints back to the infirmary. Lakin's scent is strong in the room, but he doesn't relax until he levers himself up and looks between the cabinets and the hard-stone ceiling to find her wedged in there sound asleep.

She doesn't wake up when he touches her hand, and then he notices the two empty vials lying next to her. Picking them up, he drops back down to the ground just as Eranan comes into the room.

"Holian told me the human's hidden in here," he states, looking around. Dalt studies him for a moment and then decides he's going to need the man's help, so he points up to Lakin's hiding space.

"Look. Don't touch," he orders, making Eranan rattle with irritation.

"I'm in charge of the humans, not you," he declares, but when he grips the top of the cabinet and lifts himself up, he only takes a quick look before dropping back down and sounding a bewildered rumble.

"How did she fit herself in there?" he murmurs with wonder. "And she's still asleep. She's been very aware and quick to wake. I'm surprised she still slumbers." Then he notices what Dalt is holding. "Where did you get those?"

"She took them," Dalt grunts and hands them over to Eranan, who rumbles with concern as he reads the labels.

"Well, that explains part of what's going on here," he murmurs. "This one is for plate rot, but can also be used on humans for some infections. The thing is, it acts as a strong sedative for humans as well as fighting infection. If she swallowed the whole vial, she won't wake until tomorrow at the earliest."

"That's probably for the best," Holian declares as he strides in. "I have a more detailed report on her now."

"Was she tortured by Talins?" Dalt asks and feels Eranan tense next to him and lets loose with a furious rattle.

"That's impossible—" he starts to say, only to have his angry tirade cut off by Holian.

"It's true. A couple of Traditionalists picked her up from a Leemron ship. She was under arrest, but the details on the Leemron arrest are missing. The Leemrons were trading with the Talins and included the girl in the trade. Later, the Traditionalists that had her were boarded by a Talin security ship on suspicions of weapons dealing. When the weapons cache was found, they resisted and ended up dead. As the security team searched the ship for other contraband, she was found. She looked so bad the guards panicked, shoved her in a box, and sent her here, the closest Talin Colony."

"They sent her to you because of your reputation," Eranan counters, and Holian dips his head in acknowledgment.

"Either way, she's our problem now. It doesn't look like she was a slave before the Leemron gifted her to the Traditionalists. And now she's been severely abused by our people."

Unsaid is the fact that she can't go free again. A complicated cross section of Talin culture, needs, and resistance to change means the Talins have many laws regarding humans, and one of the most rigid is ownership.

In short, humans can't leave Talin control areas unless traveling to another Talin-controlled area. Humans can't be sold or gifted to anyone but another Talin. And no human can exist as a free, self-governing entity within the Talin Empire.

Holian regards Dalt, sounding a soft frustrated rattle. "Sora begged me to let you care for the new human. Said you were the best one for the job. I'm not sure that's true. I think another human might be a better pick. It's been my experience that wild-caught humans do better with other humans around. After she's comfortable, we can start introducing her to the Talins here on Kalor." He considers Dalt silently for a moment. "But I'll let you stay close to her for now. Here are the rules; she stays within compound boundaries. She stays in her enclosure unless I give authorization. You don't go into her enclosure except for extreme circumstances. I mean it, Dalt. If I find out you went in there, it better be because she was dying. Otherwise, I'll have you exiled off this colony."

"What if she asks for help?"

Sounding a tired sigh of a rumble, Holian rubs a hand roughly over the armor plating at the top of his head. The commandant rarely displays much emotion. That he's not only rumbling more than usual but showing a physical manifestation of his frustration is telling.

"If she asks for help, you can help. If she doesn't ask, you give her space. Do we understand each other?"

Dalt gives a sharp rumble of agreement.

"Eranan will be in charge of her general care, such as food and medication. We don't know how seriously she's damaged yet, but expect a long recovery period if she fights the healing or won't take medication. It'll take her a while to trust us, but she'll come around. There's nothing like being treated kindly to change someone's mind. Now, the two of you get her back into her enclosure and have Healer Vormian treat her while she's unconscious and can't object. After she wakes up, we aren't going to force anything on her. Not even healing."

"What if she becomes very ill?" Eranan asks with an anxious rattle.

"Then it's her choice," Holian replies blandly. "Kalor is one of the only places humans are almost free within our empire.

Freedom means making choices that might ultimately end one's own life."

"It shouldn't be that way," Eranan mutters to himself.

"I would change a lot of things," Holian says. "Including the fact that this poor girl was tortured. But I can't change those things. All I can do is give her honor and independence within the limits of this compound. I will not have my will undermined."

"Yes, Commandant," Eranan says quickly, rumbling out an apologetic sound.

Glancing up at the small area where they can all hear her softly snoring away, Holian makes a sound of incredulity. "And I'd like to know how she managed to fit up there. We're going to need to keep a close eye on this one. I have a feeling she's going to be even more trouble than Sora. I wish you both luck. I have a strong suspicion we're all going to need it."

With those words he turns and leaves, a soft humorous rumble sounding from him as he disappears out the door.

Dalt eyes Lakin's hiding place. "I don't want to pull her out and risk damaging her further."

"I agree. We can empty the cupboards and then pull them off the wall and lower them to the floor."

Dalt rumbles out an assent, and together they pile everything from the cabinets on a nearby bed. It takes both of them straining against the cabinet to tear it loose from the stone wall. Grunting, they lower it onto the countertop below, revealing Lakin's dirty, bloody body lying on top.

No longer squished against the ceiling, she turns on her side with a sleepy mumble and curls up in a little ball. Dalt gathers her in his arms, but she cries out in pain and gets her eyes open for a moment.

"Hurts," she says before her eyes drop closed again.

"I'll make it better," he promises her, trying to sound a soothing rumble. He wishes his chest box wasn't so damaged, but at least he can still make sounds with it, unlike his missing back plates. His soothing rumble might not be as smooth or flowing as others, but Sora told him his unique rumble had a comforting quality, despite its flaws.

It's a quick trip back to the enclosures. Eranan indicates one of them.

"Put her here. I guess I should be thankful that first Sora, and now this one have shown me where all the weaknesses are," the keeper grumbles. "All the solars I've served Commandant Holian, and I've never had a human escape, but now these two are escaping as if it's a competition."

Deciding on tact, Dalt doesn't point out that no humans have ever wanted to escape before, so there's been no chance for weakness in the enclosures to be exploited.

First, Sora was stolen from Searin and given to Commandant Holian under the pretext of a political gift. Then this poor female arrives. Someone brutalized by other Talins isn't going to take captivity among them quietly. On top of that, Lakin appears to be a determined, smart, and tough human.

"She won't wake for some time, correct?" he asks Eranan.

"Like I said, probably not until morning at the earliest. She could end up sleeping for over a rotation."

As long as she's unconscious, Dalt's going to take the liberty of holding her. Sitting down on the soft nest in the enclosure, he cradles her in his lap. Gently, he brushes the hair from her face, wondering what she looks like under all the dirt and blood.

"What happened here?" a familiar voice practically shouts, with a rumble of deep distress. Dalt looks up to find Healer Vormian coming to a halt over him.

"She was hurt."

The rumble of distress turns to annoyance as Vormian kneels and pulls a small scanner out of her pocket. "I can tell that. I've never seen a human so brutalized."

"She was tortured by a pair of honorless Traditionalists," Eranan volunteers.

"I hope they're dead," Healer Vormian mutters as she runs the small scanner over Lakin.

"They are, mores the pity," Eranan states, making both Dalt and the healer look up at him in confusion. Eranan shrugs, "I would've liked to hurt them for a while before they died."

"I think we would all have liked to take part in that," Vormian mutters as she finishes her scans. "She's got several broken ribs and deep bruising everywhere. This shoulder looks like it was popped out of place and then popped back in while being wrenched badly in the process. Her feet are nothing but bruises and lacerations." Holding up one foot, she hisses in a pained sound. "It appears they deliberately abused her feet in particular."

"They didn't want me walking on two legs." A sleepy voice slurs out the words, making all of them move their gazes to Lakin's face. Her eyes are half open but not focused.

"Be at ease, little one," Vormian soothes her, but before the sentence is even finished, Lakin's eyes are closed again and her breathing is deep and even. "She's a strong one," the healer murmurs and goes back to examining Lakin's feet.

"She is," Dalt agrees. How did Lakin move so quickly when her feet were so badly injured? Most would've just lain down and waited for their fate to unfold around them, but not this female. No, she pushed back against her captivity, ready to do whatever was necessary to gain her freedom. Given more time with the Traditionalists, he's sure she would've found a way to either escape or destroy the ship and kill them all. That would have satisfied her little warrior heart, to die knowing she ended the lives of her enemies.

The two of them have a great deal in common in that respect.

One of the healer's trainees shows up with a tray full of equipment, and together they treat Lakin. Once they're finished, the healer leaves several different medications and instructions for the human's continued care.

"I'll be back late tomorrow to check on her. Do your best to keep her calm and off her feet." With that, the healer and trainee are gone, leaving just Eranan and Dalt in the enclosure with her.

"I have to care for the other humans. I've neglected my duties all day," Eranan says. He sounds a frustrated rattle that makes Lakin twitch and jerk in her sleep.

"No rattling," Dalt orders harshly, rumbling his broken, soothing sound to calm her. The men who held her probably rattled constantly as they hurt her. The noise is no doubt a trigger for her now, even in her sleep.

Sounding an embarrassed rumble, Eranan stands up. "It won't happen again. I know the commandant said you needed to stay out of her enclosure, but before you leave, I need you to clean her up." The keeper points to a stack of drying cloths and garments. "When you're done, put her in a clean wrap and leave the enclosure. I've checked this one. It doesn't have any weak spots in the fence or stonework, so it should be secure. I've coded the gate for your biosignature so you can come and go."

"Yes," Dalt grunts.

"Contact me if you need anything. You know my Ident." Dalt gives him another grunt as Eranan leaves.

The enclosure includes a small area for bathing, so Dalt carries her in there. Because he no longer has claws, he works her old, soiled wrap off her body instead of just ripping it into sections. Activating the water, he waits until it's warm and then steps under to sit down so the water's cascading over both of them. His pants get soaked immediately, but he doesn't care. His entire focus is on Lakin.

The water running over her skin clears off some of the dirt and old blood. When the running water stops being effective, Dalt goes to work.

Afraid to even use the gentlest cleansers, he wets a cleaning cloth and moves it delicately over her skin. Most of the lacerations are minor, and the healer used a flesh knitter on the few that were severe so he doesn't need to worry about reopening a wound. Cleaning her skin reveals bruising everywhere. He's not sure there's a part of her that isn't marred by either a bruise or cut.

Turning his attention to her mane, he decides he has no choice but to use some cleansers on the thick, dirty mass. The cleanser helps him to untangle some of it, but he's going to need to use one of the humans' special grooming tools to get it completely straightened out.

Turning off the water, he dries her and then applies the special softening oil to her skin. He marvels at how delicate she is. Even though he's lived with Sora, he never got to handle her this much. Sora let him carry her, and even allowed him to hold her in his lap occasionally, but other than that, they didn't touch. This is the first time he's touched a human so extensively.

Now that she's clean, her human scent fills his nose instead of dirt, blood, and stale sweat. He's not sure how to describe her scent except for comforting. Like walking into a house and being met with the familiar smells of home.

He breathes in deeply as he finishes massaging lotion into her delicate skin. All too soon, every inch of her is cared for, and he has no more reason to keep her naked. He wishes he needed to rub other products into her skin because he's loath to stop.

Unable to put it off any longer, he dresses her in a clean wrap. The deep purple color of the wrap makes her bruising seem all that much worse. Dalt wishes the clothing was just about any other color, but this is the one at hand.

He should buy her more wraps. He's got all the pay he received from his service, including the large bonus they gave him for surviving when so many others didn't. He lives mostly off the land and trades with the commandant's house and other estates on Kalor, so he rarely touches his wealth. That money makes him feel guilty for surviving, as if his wealth comes from the blood of his fallen comrades. But for her, he'd be willing to go into town and spend it.

Maybe he could buy some scented lotions and oils also and a nicer grooming tool for her mane. This one is serviceable, but he's seen Henni use one carved from wood.

A list of items to buy Lakin fills his head as he carries her back to the nest with the mane grooming tool. Laying her on her back, he pulls her hair from under her body and starts working the tool through.

It takes almost a full mark before her mane fans out around her head as it should. The mass is a deep rich brown and is slowly forming into waves as it dries. He can tell that when she stands, her mane will fall appealingly around her shoulders and down her back. It will be soft too, but will she like to have her mane petted or groomed once she's awake?

Even if she enjoys being groomed and petted, would this little human eventually come to trust him enough to let him do the petting?

The thought makes his broken rumble start up again. When a small, half-smile forms on Lakin's face in her sleep, it only encourages him to keep rumbling.

Done cleaning and grooming her, Dalt doesn't have any excuse to stay in the enclosure. Commandant Holian's orders were very clear. Lingering is a fast way to get himself ejected from the property and potentially barred entirely.

After he covers her in a blanket, Dalt leaves the enclosure, locking the gate behind him. Settling down right next to the fence to one side of the gate, he checks to make sure he'll still have an unobstructed view of Lakin.

He watches her fidget in her sleep, her hand reaching for something and her face marred with a frown. Wishing he could go back in and hold her, he automatically starts rumbling to comfort her. The sound makes her wrinkled brow smooth, and she stops moving.

Later he'll go find some bedding so he can sleep here, but for now he'll sit and rumble for the little human, so even in her sleep, she knows she's safe and looked after.

CHAPTER 5

Lakin

Lakin wakes in a rush, but years of training keep her still and her eyes closed as she tries to assess her situation with her other senses. The pain that's been her constant companion for days is all but gone. She's also lying on something soft. This can only mean one thing.

Opening her eyes, she frowns as the sights around her confirm her suspicions. She's back in an enclosure.

"Oh good, you're awake," a male voice says, startling her into motion. Without thinking, she launches herself at the voice, intent on showing strength. As a member of one of the smaller species in the universe, she's trained herself to be aggressive when startled so her small stature isn't mistaken for weakness.

The man goes down without resistance, crying out in surprise. She lands one blow to his face before she's pulled off of him. Strong arms wrap around her, holding her off the ground. The scent of cedar fills her nose. She fights this new threat even harder, landing several blows that make her knuckles hurt but don't stop her from continuing to strike out.

"Lakin, calm down!" The power of the voice in combination with the use of her name throws her off, making her go slack and take in the world around her.

A human male voice shouts with outrage, "She hit me!"

Looking down, she sees a dark-skinned human male with long, straight black hair and beautiful, large dark eyes huddling in the arms of another Talin. "I didn't do anything! She just started hitting me!"

"I've got you. You're safe," the Talin says, picking up the human male with no visible effort. She recognizes Eranan as the Talin holding the human she hit. By the looks of anger and hurt he's casting her way, even though they're both human, he's not going to be interested in being friends any time soon.

Eranan makes that purring sound. "I'm sorry, Nol. I thought this would be a good idea. I'll take you back to your enclosure."

"I'm not hanging out with new humans ever again," Nol retorts, wrapping his arms around Eranan's neck and nuzzling his face against the big Talin. "You can pick someone else next time."

"I told you it might go badly," a familiar voice tells Eranan as he carries the distressed Nol to the enclosure gate. The voice comes from the Talin holding her. He's also the source of the pervasive smell of cedar she finds strangely comforting. It reminds her of a chest her mother kept a few precious old Earth items in. It's the smell of family and home.

"Just keep her restrained until the gate latches behind me, and then you can put her down," Eranan calls back. "I'm going to get Nol settled in his enclosure. I'll return later with food. Thanks for assisting, but remember the rules."

The arms holding her don't relax until Eranan and Nol are out of sight. Only then is she lowered back onto the nest and released. Turning, she sees the Talin who restrained her back up quickly to give her room. "I'm going to leave the enclosure now. Keep your distance, and I won't need to restrain you again."

Knowing he's not intimidated by her in the least, she watches with amusement as he moves to the gate, careful not to give her his back.

He's acting overly cautious, as if she really could hurt him if she tried. That makes her realize that unlike the rest of the Talins she's dealt with, he understands her need to be seen as an opponent as opposed to a victim. She feels badly that she attacked the other human, Nol, but she wouldn't change her instincts. They've kept her alive a long time, even through some dangerous situations.

"No one will come back in without your knowledge or permission," he tells her as he shuts the gate and walks down the fence of her enclosure. He stops at a pile of bedding and sits down, his movements precise and controlled. By the way he moves, she can tell this Talin was a soldier at some point. No matter what the species, soldiers move differently than civilians.

Giving him only a quick nod to acknowledge his words, she looks down at herself and takes stock. She's dressed in the same kind of garment that every human she's seen here wears—a simple, single piece, wrap-around dress that ties at her waist. The fabric is soft and warm, nicer than most of the items she owned back onboard the ship. She wouldn't have picked the eggplant color, but she's the last one to be picky. She's not naked, and that's a bonus.

That makes her realize she's not only wearing new, clean clothes, but her body's been bathed as well. Putting a hand to her head, she finds even her hair has been washed and combed. It was so matted after the first day of torture she was sure it was going to need to be chopped off. But somehow, whoever cleaned her up salvaged it. That must have taken a lot of patience. Her scalp doesn't even hurt, so whoever untangled her hair took their time to be gentle.

She has a strong suspicion the Talin sitting outside her enclosure is responsible for her cleanliness and detangled hair. She's not entirely comfortable with the fact he must have handled her naked body while she was helpless, but she decides to let it go.

No point in getting emotional over being seen naked. She's spent plenty of time wearing either very little clothing or nothing at all. Some ships she worked on had crew members that needed high heat to survive. In those situations, at times she wore nothing but a sleeveless top and underwear. Not to mention the culture on small ships leaves little in the way of privacy.

This Talin seeing her naked doesn't even make it on the scale of things that bother her.

Keeping half an eye on the still and silent Talin, she continues to take stock of her body. Her shoulder feels much better, and with a few test movements, she finds she has uninhibited movement in that arm. She can draw in a full breath of air without pain.

Pulling up one of her feet, she presses a finger into the sole and winces. It's still going to hurt to walk, but at least the pain won't be as intense as before.

"You've been asleep for almost two full rotations," the Talin volunteers. "The healers have seen you several times."

"That explains why I don't hurt too much," she replies, grateful she slept through most of the healing. Some medications or treatments to heal rapidly can be intense and painful. Nice of them to both tend to her injuries and let her stay knocked out for the process.

"You said they hurt your feet on purpose. Why?"

Looking at him in silence for a few moments, she tries to remember his name. This same Talin was with the other human in the infirmary. He locked the others out and promised he'd keep her safe. She's not sure if ending up back in an enclosure strictly fulfills his promise, but at least she wasn't punished for attacking Nol or escaping. Well, not punished yet.

"Dalt?"

"Yes, and you're Lakin."

She eyes him thoughtfully. Can she talk him into helping her escape? Individuals do things for all kinds of reasons. As soon as you figure out what they value, you can often bargain with them. Would his price be credits? Exotic items? Sexual favors?

She doesn't need him to do much, just get her access to an interstellar comm. A few individuals out there owe her favors. If she can make contact, she should be able to arrange for pickup. She might not even need to escape this cage again. She can think of at least one captain who's rich enough and owes her a big enough favor that he could come and buy her. He could even use the money she's saved up herself.

What would be this guy's price for access to an interstellar comm?

"Your clothes are old," she says, using that as a point to start a conversation about his wealth or lack thereof. His response is nothing like she expects.

"Commandant Holian owns most of this planet," Dalt tells her, as if reading her mind. "All traffic in and out of the port has to have his approval. All incoming ships are scanned and often searched."

This information doesn't deter her in the least. Her plan is still a good one.

"Do you live here with Commandant Holian? Is he your superior?"

He ignores her question in favor of his own. "You didn't answer earlier. Why did they hurt your feet so thoroughly?"

Two can play at this game. "What happened to you?" she points at the place on his forearm where his quills are missing. She hopes to throw him off, maybe see how he'll react with her as inquisitor.

"Tortured, like you." His voice doesn't change, and his gaze doesn't waver, telling her he's not likely to be easily manipulated with anger or a challenge. "Why did they target your feet?"

Guessing he's not going to let that line of questioning go, Lakin goes for honesty. Maybe she can build trust between them and use that to manipulate him later.

"They said walking on two legs should be reserved for intelligent creatures. Humans are pets and unworthy of standing upright. They beat my feet until I couldn't stand on them and then ordered me to do things I had to crawl to accomplish."

The memory makes her chest feel tight, and tears prick the back of her eyes. The few days she was held by the two Talins had been the worst of her life so far. Pain and mistreatment are no strangers to her, but their systematic abuse was a whole different level than she's ever known before.

"They're dead now." There's no inflection in his voice, no rattle or rumble either. His silence is mildly unnerving, considering the constant sounds that have come out of all the Talins she's met so far.

"That's too bad," she murmurs, looking down at her feet. "I was hoping to kill them myself."

He rumbles out a sound that makes her think of marbles clinking together in a bag. She's pretty sure that sound is the equivalent to a human laugh.

"I said the same thing." His amused rumble soothes her a little, like a human with an expressionless face finally smiling.

Liking this Talin despite herself, Lakin grins without showing teeth. "I had some basic plans. To get back at them."

"I have no doubt. I'm sorry our military got in your way." Now it's her turn to laugh, which makes her side hurt where several ribs aren't completely healed. She scrunches over, putting her hands on the painful spot. Why does it hurt more now than when she first woke up and jumped on Nol? Human bodies can be so strange!

"Do you need more pain inhibitors?" Dalt asks, starting up that rusty purr of his.

Taking a few shallow breaths to allow the discomfort to recede, Lakin finally answers. "I don't want to go to sleep."

"We have inhibitors that won't put you to sleep. I'll make sure you aren't put to sleep against your will again. But in our defense, last time you put yourself to sleep. One of the vials you consumed was a sedative."

"Damn, bad guess on my part," she says ruefully. "That must have made it easy for you guys."

"We were forced to pull the cabinets apart to get you down. You found a very effective hiding spot," he compliments her. "You must have been in so much pain. It's astonishing you made it so far so quickly. Your will is strong, and your mind is quick."

"Thanks," Lakin says, feeling buoyed by the compliments. She can tell that his admiration is genuine. It's not often that other species in the universe take her seriously.

Humans are rare because after Earth was no longer inhabitable, they had no homeworld or unifying government. Now humans live on the fringe of nonhuman societies, carving out places to live at the goodwill of other species. Sometimes the human colonies do okay, like Lakin's colony when she was young. And sometimes they are hellholes where humans scrape by, their population dropping every year, like Lakin's old colony is now.

All of that means humans are often seen as next to worthless—dumb, inconsequential, and ineffective. But this Talin not only sees her as an individual but also as worthy and accomplished. It's a nice change of pace, especially considering her first introduction to the Talin species.

"I seem to remember someone promising to keep me safe," she points out, interested in gauging his reaction to the accusation. "Not pull my hiding space down to get me out."

"Are you not safe?"

That question makes her pause. Technically, they're treating her well and without reprisal. Yet.

The thing that probably surprises her the most is that they aren't even threatening her with anything. They just keep telling her to stop. Stop escaping. Stop running. Stop hurting herself.

That poses another question: What do they plan to do with her? The first two Talins who held her had one obvious goal—to cause her pain and suffering. What does this new group of Talins want from her?

Putting her hand to her throat, she feels the slim metal collar there, evidence of her captivity and her new status as a slave. Slaves that aren't useful are disposed of, either by selling or killing. If she's their property now, what will they want her to do? They'll probably start her off with menial work. But if she's smart, maybe she can get them to grant her access to important systems, allow her to get her hands on something that will help her.

"What services are going to be required from me?" Her question seems to startle Dalt, who jerks and stops purring for a few seconds.

"You will not be forced to work," he declares with confidence. "You'll be cared for. Your life of labor and pain is over."

Her life of labor and pain is over? What does that even mean? What good is a slave if they aren't put to work?

"I'm pretty skilled with electrical systems," she probes. "I've helped set up solar and wind collection sites. Or I could set up grids. Or—"

"Your job is to heal."

"Right, but after I'm all healed up. I'm also good with machinery. Especially bots." In truth, she's only fixed a few bots over the years. Otherwise, she's pretty much useless at that type of repair. "I don't have any tools, but if you can lend me some, I'll be good to go. And I—"

"I understand now," Dalt says, interrupting her again. He stops purring as he explains. "I've been told this happens to wild-caught or former slaves. You're under the mistaken impression that you must do labor to earn your keep. That's inaccurate."

The memory of Henni saying that humans keep Talins alive surfaces, and Lakin feels more confused than ever.

"So, what's my job? And the other woman, Henni, what does she do? Why do you guys go to such expense to house and feed us?" Looking around her enclosure, a scoffing sound bubbles out of her throat. "I mean, this place is nicer than half the rooms I've rented over the years. Soft bed, clean water, air that doesn't smell like stale recycler." Suddenly she's tired and frustrated and that makes her next words harsh. "What's the point?"

Dalt goes quiet for a bit, not even rumbling now. His unwavering gaze is unnerving. Feeling challenged, she meets his intense eyes without looking away or blinking, but it isn't easy.

"You keep us from Fading," he finally tells her in a voice almost too quiet to hear.

"Fading?"

The strange, struggling purr sounds from his chest again, and Lakin finds it relaxing despite her anxiety. She's half tempted to ask Dalt to come into the enclosure and hold her while he purrs, but she pushes that thought away. She's not ready to have anyone touch her yet, no matter how pleasant he might sound or how much he compliments her.

"You need to rest," he declares, and she knows he's not going to answer her question.

"I'm not—" she starts to say, but he cuts her off.

"Relax for now. Food will come soon and then you can eat. If you feel you can't sleep, at least try to rest."

Those words sound final. Lakin tries to ask a few more questions, but Dalt remains stubbornly silent except for his steady, rusty, misfiring purr. Giving up, Lakin flops back down and closes her eyes. Later she'll work on getting more information, but for right now, a little more shut-eye isn't a bad idea.

CHAPTER

6

Lakin

Waking up, the first thing Lakin notices is the purring.

When she opens her eyes, she finds Dalt is still sitting in the same place. Has he there and purring the entire time she slept?

Carefully sitting up, she looks around, trying to figure out how long she was asleep. The sun's moved, but she doesn't know this planet's rotation pattern. She could have been asleep for a few Units or an entire day. Her side is still tender and a quick flex of her foot causes pain, so that healing isn't much further along. All of it indicates she hasn't been out for long.

The smell of food draws her attention away from her self-assessment to a tray placed inside the enclosure gate, out of reach from her nest. She's going to have to walk to get the food and that's going to be uncomfortable. But there's no help for it because no way in hell is she crawling again.

Oh well, she ran when her feet were worse. She can manage the short distance inside the enclosure.

With a resigned sigh, she moves to stand but freezes when the purring abruptly stops. Looking back to Dalt, she tilts her head questioningly.

"Everything fine over there?" she asks.

"I was about to ask you the same thing," Dalt responds. "You look like you're about to get out of your nest. I don't think that's wise. The healer said you shouldn't walk on your feet for at least one more rotation."

She's spent so much time with so many different species that the term rotation instead of Full Unit or day doesn't phase her. Almost every species maintains their words for measurements even if they use Common or Universal.

"It's fine. I walked on them when they were worse."

"You ran on them," Dalt argues, "and now you don't need to. If you permit me, I'll enter your enclosure and bring the tray to you. I won't touch you, and I won't stay."

She looks at the food, at him, and back at the food, debating his offer. Honestly, there isn't much to debate because the illusion of independence is important to her.

"Stubborn female," he mutters, reading the intent on her face.

"Overbearing male," she retorts.

Standing, she wobbles a little, hissing out a breath from the pain. Now that her shoulder doesn't hurt, her feet seem to hurt more than they did before. Strange how a body does that.

Survival mode meant she was only cognizant of what was too severely injured on her body to work. Things that hurt but worked, like her feet, were ignored. Now that she has no choice but to wait out her captors while she heals, the pain feels strangely more intense. It's probably just the lack of adrenaline and endorphins because she isn't in full fight or flight mode.

The distant-bass-drum rumble of worry sounds from Dalt as gets to his feet and strides to the door. She thinks he's going to come in, but instead he stands there, arms at his side and his hands in tight fists.

"Please, sit down. Let me bring you the food."

Ignoring him, she focuses on her goal instead of the pain and walks to the tray. Each step hurts, but it's nowhere near the agony she suffered the day she arrived in the box or while the damage was being inflicted.

She doesn't pick up the tray to carry it back to her bed. The walk over made her break out into a light sweat. Feeling just a little dizzy, she sinks to the ground in front of the tray, facing the gate. There's no reason she can't eat the food here, rest, and then make her way back to the nest.

Surprisingly graceful for a male his size, Dalt sinks to the ground on the other side of the gate. He's close enough that if the bars were wider, he could reach through the gate and touch her. As she shoves food into her face, he begins purring again. Unfortunately, the food's gone before her hunger is sated. It's not the first time her belly isn't full at the end of a meal and probably won't be the last.

"Eranan is worried you are undernourished and might react badly if given too much food too quickly."

"Well, that's going to affect his tip," Lakin murmurs and then licks her fingers clean. Dalt doesn't react to her little joke.

Putting off walking back to her pallet, she rests her hands behind her on the soft, lush ground cover and leans back while she studies Dalt. "You can come in here at any time. Right? You can unlock the gate?"

"Yes."

"Why didn't you?"

"I gave my word I wouldn't. I can only come in if you requested my presence. Otherwise you would need to be dying before I'm allowed."

"Or I'm attacking some poor defenseless guy."

"I've seen Nol defend himself effectively against a bigger human male. He's not defenseless. He could've hurt you. He chose not to."

Guilt washes through her. "Do you think Nol will let me get close enough to apologize?"

"Perhaps, in time. Nol's a good-natured and calm male. That's why Eranan put him in here. He thought waking up with another human in the enclosure would make you feel more secure, but none of the females were willing to do it. Except for Henni, but Ianino forbid it. He was worried you'd hurt her. Nol was the best choice of all the male humans." He pauses for a moment as if weighing his words and then speaks again. "I told Eranan it was a bad idea. You're a warrior, ready to fight. Not a simple female to be soothed."

"You think I'm a warrior? All you've seen me do is run and hide," she says with a small self-deprecating laugh. "I did blindly attack Nol, I guess. But that doesn't count as being a warrior."

Damn, she feels guilty about that. She needs to apologize. He didn't deserve a punch to the face.

"Despite severe injuries, you escaped, evaded superior numbers, and successfully hid within enemy territory. You did all of that while in great pain. Those are signs of a warrior."

His words of admiration fill her with pride and pleasure.

"Or someone desperate to escape," she feels obliged to point out. "In the end, all my efforts didn't get me anywhere but right back in a cage." She looks around, reminding herself that at least it's a nice cage. Her current owners saw to her injuries and fed her. This is the nicest captivity she's endured so far.

Still, as far as she's concerned, cages are meant to be broken out of.

"You were caught, but that was inevitable. You attempted to escape with no proper plan or resources while you were not at optimum physical fitness."

"Yeah," she says with a little sigh. "But the opportunity was too good to pass up."

"It's an indication of your intrepid nature that you didn't sit and wait for rescue or resign yourself to a new role. Some simply give up and let others decide their fate," Dalt continues. "Even unto death. You fought with everything you had. You're safe here and don't need to escape, but until you realize that, I understand why you'll keep fighting and trying to escape. It's part of your nature, little warrior. Capitulation isn't in you."

Eyeing him with interest, she moves the tray out of her way and scoots a little closer to the gate. The soothing smell of cedar fills her nose. "Who took your quills?"

The rusty purring falters and she regrets the question. He told her earlier it was torture, and asking about it feels petty and unnecessary. She's not even sure what drove her to voice the inquiry.

"I'm sorry. You don't need to tell me. I–"

He begins to talk, interrupting her. "We were at war with the Braxin over a planet we both wanted to colonize. The Braxin didn't have our tech or numbers, but they had the money to hire mercenaries. I was in charge of twenty soldiers assigned to guard a civilian outpost. We had control of the planet at the time and were already drilling for minerals. We thought the Braxin had given up. We didn't know they'd hired others to fight for them. Because of this, the outpost was taken easily. I told my men to wait. To accept capture. To bide their time and attack when we had the chance. I didn't want them pointlessly dying in combat against overwhelming numbers. I thought waiting was the better option. I was wrong." He stops talking, and his eyes become unfocused. He's staring into the past instead of at her.

"Did they start executing everyone?" Her question causes him to refocus his eyes on her.

The purring starts up, falters, and stops again. It's a clear message to Lakin that Dalt's struggling to tell his story.

"Execution would've been too merciful. They tortured each of them to death. Pulled them apart, piece by piece."

Horrified, Lakin instinctively reaches through the bars and touches Dalt's pant-covered leg. The bars are too narrow for Dalt to even fit a hand, but she can get her arm through almost to the shoulder. It's a bit of a squeeze, but nothing too uncomfortable.

Dalt drops his gaze to her hand. Feeling foolish, she starts to withdraw. He swiftly brings one of his big four-fingered hands down on top of hers, gently trapping her against his warm thigh. He's not hurting her so she doesn't struggle to get free.

"I listened to them shriek and wail, unable to do anything to help. Some of my men begged for death. Some of them screamed that all of it was my fault. I ordered them to stand down instead of letting them die honorably in battle."

"You couldn't have known, Dalt. You thought you were giving them a chance at survival. I would've done the same thing."

"Perhaps," he answers. "It was a relief when they ripped into me. They took my claws and quills first, just like the others. Then my back plates. Most of us passed out at that point, so I pretended to be unconscious. When they couldn't rouse me, they called for the medic to give me drugs to wake me and keep me alert, the same thing they did with the others. Torturing unconscious prisoners is no fun. The only place on our body where they can administer that kind of medication is right here."

Leaning forward, he lifts her hand to place her fingers at a slip of skin where the natural armor plating of his neck meets his shoulders. His hold is gentle so she knows she can pull away from him if she wants to.

"It's the only place where a vein can be easily accessed."

Feeling bold, she runs her fingertips along the soft bit of skin, taking in the smooth texture and steady pulse underneath. Dalt's eyes close, and his hand falls away from hers. His purring starts up again, strong and steady, although still with the familiar rusty signature.

"Is this a sensitive place?" she asks.

"One of several," he admits as she plays her fingers across that strip of skin. He tilts his head away from her hand, making the gap in his armor slightly larger and encouraging her to continue to touch him.

Feeling strangely empowered, she lays her whole hand along the length of skin and starts stroking. Dalt jolts under her touch, but he doesn't pull away or try to stop her. She continues the petting until her arm fatigues, and her hand shakes. Opening his eyes, Dalt puts his large hand over hers. He draws it away from his neck and back to where she originally touched his leg.

"Thank you," he whispers. "Your touch is a gift like no other."

A few times in her past a mission led to her being captured, and she spent time in captivity before being rescued. None of those experiences were pleasant, but they were always temporary.

Unfortunately, no matter how brief, each time she was held against her will, it left her damaged in some way—sometimes physically and sometimes mentally.

She spent almost a month kept naked in a cage as a local attraction at a small shop on an out-of-the-way space station. Individuals would bang on the cage bars, demand she dance, sing, talk, or move on command. Some species had arms long enough to reach her through the bars, and they would delight in poking and prodding a reaction out of her.

When her captain finally found her, she was an aggressive mess. She even bit one of her crewmates before she recognized him. The crewmate didn't hold the bite against her. The entire crew felt guilty for taking so long to get to her that they moved her to the only room with a single bunk on the entire ship outside the captain's quarters.

Even with a room to herself, it took a while before she stopped waking up in a cold sweat.

Memories like those make her sensitive to unwanted contact and cause her to shy away from relationships, even casual ones.

Conversely, experiences like those make her even more determined to fight. Far from making her give up, they inject her spine with steel because she'll be damned if she's going to let others live like that when she can help them.

Despite her aversion to touch, however, this Talin doesn't make her defensiveness flare. It's probably because he invites her to touch but doesn't demand it. He encourages but doesn't force. It's a novel experience for Lakin, and it's causing her to have conflicting feelings toward the scarred male. She wants to use him to achieve her ends, but she wants to pet him and make him feel better too.

Akk, this is uncomfortable! Stupid emotions!

"I'd like to know how the story ends. If you're willing to share." She tells herself she's learning how to manipulate him. Wanting to know about his pain has nothing to do with her growing sympathy for him. Nothing.

His only reaction to her request is a brief tightening of his hand on hers, and then he talks again.

"They wanted to dose me, but to get access to my vein they had to release the manacles holding my wrists. They were secured together over my head, effectively protecting my neck. When they released me, several of the mercenaries were standing close by, and I made sure my body fell into them. None of them were expecting any resistance. I was able to grab a weapon and kill the three of them and the medic before anyone realized what was going on. By the time they were firing their weapons at me, I had the mercenaries' bodies piled up around me and their weapons in hand."

"You used their bodies as a shield," Lakin says with admiration. She probably wouldn't have thought of doing that under those extreme circumstances.

"I didn't expect my gambit to work. I thought perhaps I'd kill a few before they killed me. But I was fortunate because after taking the outpost they left only a handful of men behind. They were supposed to hold us for ransom, but these mercenaries cared more about hurting us than a little extra money. I freed the everyone still alive, and we hunted down the few mercenaries who were out on patrol."

"How many survived?"

"Six civilians and five soldiers, including me. One of us, Palforma, took a round to the head. He hasn't been the same since. The rest died in agony. And it was my fault."

Shaking her head, Lakin tugs at her hand. Dalt releases her, but she doesn't draw her hand away from him. Instead, she grabs his wrist and tugs him closer to the bars. Going onto his knees, he presses himself against the bars, allowing Lakin to twine her smaller arms through the bars and around his waist.

Her aversion to touch has disappeared in the face of his pain.

His cedar scent is strong now, and the sides of his face in front of his ear holes look a little swollen. Maybe that happens to Talins when they feel powerful emotions, like humans with tears.

"You're looking at this the wrong way," she tells him, squeezing her arms around him as tightly as she's able. It's uncomfortable to press her face against the bars, but it's worth it to soothe Dalt. He might be a Talin and she might be human, but she understands torment.

Like recognizes like.

"How else can I possibly look at it?" he asks. Because he can't slip his arms through the bars to hug her back, he rests his hands on her arms, encouraging her to keep embracing him.

"Six civilians and five soldiers makes eleven. Eleven lived," she points out simply. "They hurt a lot of people and many died anyway, but eleven survived. If you hadn't put down arms, that number would have been zero. Eleven is more than zero, Dalt. Any child knows that."

"Your math is correct," he murmurs. His tone indicates he doesn't agree with her, but at least he's listening. "The soldiers who survived are here on this planet with me. We were discharged after that. No longer allowed to serve. Those men blame me. They don't say it, but I know they blame me. How can they not?"

"Or they blame themselves for not being braver, or stronger, or faster." She thinks about the nature of guilt and images of those she couldn't save float through her mind.

"They're blameless. I was in charge."

"Guilt doesn't need to follow logic." Hazarding a guess, Lakin asks a pointed question. "Do you blame Holian? Wasn't he in charge of you?"

"Of course he was in charge of our group, but I don't blame the commandant. How could I? He got us off the planet despite the mercenary blockage."

"But he put you there. He ordered you and your men there. If he hadn't done that, none of this would've happened. And what about your government? They decided the planet was worth the lives of their people. Decided that minerals were more important than preserving life. They share the blame too. Why should you bear this guilt, Dalt, when so many others are equally at fault?"

"That's not something I've considered," Dalt answers, his purr starting up again. "I'll contemplate this further."

Withdrawing from the hug, Lakin sits back down and rubs her cheek where it was pressed hard against the bar.

Dalt's purring stops. "You hurt yourself?"

"Not really," she assures him. "Only a minor discomfort."

"You should rest. Try to sleep more," Dalt comments, worry back in his voice. Lakin looks over to the nest and then back to Dalt. She's not sure if it's because he's stayed with her but kept his distance, if it's because he could have used his greater strength several times and didn't, or the stories they just shared. But for whatever reason, she feels a connection. She doesn't want to admit it, but there's more between them than her wish to manipulate him. She trusts Dalt, and that's huge to her because she trusts very few.

"Are you going to stay here? Stay while I sleep?"

"I'll guard you, little warrior," he promises. "I won't leave you vulnerable."

"Thank you," she whispers. Slowly, painfully, she gets to her feet and totters back to the nest. Dropping down with a relieved sigh, she sees that Dalt's moved to sit on his bed, his back leaning against the bars so he can keep a lookout for intruders or danger. The sun hangs low in the sky, casting long shadows down the aisle between the rows of enclosures. Its light shines through a nearby bush, casting a strange pattern of shadow over Dalt and giving him a stone-like appearance.

Her very own gargoyle, keeping her safe.

"Good night, Dalt," she calls out.

"Rest well, Lakin."

Despite the pain in her feet, his loud and rusty purring starts up and makes her smile. She falls asleep with that smile on her face.

CHAPTER 7

Lakin

Blinking awake, Lakin sits up and looks around her dark enclosure, unsure of what disturbed her sleep. Stifling a yawn, she notes the soft lights illumining the aisle between rows of enclosures and then looks for Dalt. He's sitting in almost the exact same place he was when she fell asleep, except now he's facing into her enclosure instead of away.

But something is wrong. She can't quite put her finger on it, but it's almost as if his body is too still. This isn't her gargoyle of earlier, her silent sentry. This version of Dalt doesn't look right.

"Dalt?"

No response. He doesn't even tilt his head. It's too dark for her to see his face. Easing onto her feet, she gingerly walks over.

"Dalt?"

His eyes are open and staring straight ahead, unfocused and not tracking. Something's wrong with him. She kneels in front of him and tries to touch him through the bars. Unlike the gate, these bars are set closer together and she can only reach her arm to the elbow. Her fingers fall short of touching him. Making a frustrated sound, she pulls her arm back.

"Dalt!" she shouts his name, not caring who she disturbs. Still he doesn't respond.

The way he's acting reminds her of a Hoquin they rescued several years earlier. He would have flashbacks and end up going perfectly still as he relived the most horrible parts of his experience as a slave. Now that she thinks about it, the physical way the Talins are built reminds her a little of that guy although he didn't have the armor or quills like they do. And he definitely wasn't as big. But his general shape, color, the way he would rumble out sounds could mean he was a related species.

He explained his flashbacks were like waking nightmares. He wouldn't be able to move or make a sound while he was trapped. All he could do was wait for the memories to play out.

Touch was the only thing that would "wake" him up. If Dalt is suffering from something similar, Lakin needs to get her hands on him somehow, which is hard to do considering he's sitting too far from the bars for her to reach.

All the Talins wear belts with a pouch and Ident Cubes hanging off them. Dalt's belt is off and lying on the ground between him and her cage. She gets the very tip of her fingers around it and nudges. After several minutes of agonizing effort, she gets it close enough to grab. She drags it and the attached pouch through the bars.

Inside the pouch are a few odds and ends, but one item makes her almost crow with triumph—a narrow, needle-like tool that's as long as her hand. She doesn't know what its original purpose is, but she knows exactly what she can do with it. Hurrying as fast as her painful feet will allow, she carries the belt, pouch, and her new tool to the enclosure gate and starts pulling apart the display pad mounted on the bars next to the gate.

Once she has the cover off, she uses the needle to manipulate the optic system until she figures out how to make the it unlock. It's tedious work and because there's no way for her to mark connectors, she just has to keep track of the combinations she's already used in her head. When her gate finally clicks open, she carefully puts the display back together and tucks the needle away in her wrap.

Free of the cage, she steps into the aisle and freezes, realizing the larger implication of what she just did. The impulse to run for freedom is as strong as her need to comfort Dalt and makes her mind whirl with indecision.

Running is problematic. Her feet are still healing, and she doesn't have enough intel on the planet to know the good places to hide yet. Even knowing that running isn't a safe choice, the nearby forest beckons her. The dense trees offer hiding places and the opportunity to be free from the cages.

And she hates being locked in a cage.

But the other half of her demands she go to Dalt. He's done nothing to hurt her and everything to see to her comfort. He even shared his pain with her, admitting to the torture and his feeling of guilt, so much like her own. She glances down at the pallet he's sitting on. He must have a home of his own, yet here he is, bedding down outside her cage. He faced outward earlier as she slept, watching for threats to her. Somehow she knows that if anyone threatened her, even another Talin, Dalt would come to her aid with deadly force if necessary.

No, she can't run off and leave him.

With only a few quick steps she's at his side. She drops his belt and pouch on the ground where it was before and runs critical eyes over him.

He sits frozen, unmoving and barely breathing. She's taking three breaths to his one. Not a good sign. Deciding to try touch first, she eases down to a crouch, ready to jump away if he confuses his nightmare with her and becomes violent.

Using only her fingertips, she runs a path down his upper arm, but he doesn't respond. Assuming a light touch won't do it, she wraps her small hand around his arm. Her grip doesn't even make it halfway around his massive bicep, but she squeezes anyway, tense and ready to leap to safety. But there's no response. Going for broke, she smacks his arm with her open hand.

Nothing. Touch isn't working.

What about his other senses? His eyes are unfocused and not tracking, so visuals are out. What to try next? Sound didn't work when she called to him from inside the enclosure. Smell seems to be the next step. She knows Talins have an excellent sense of smell from the way Eranan could track her, but what scent can she use?

Using her own weaker sense of smell, she tries to pick out the strongest scent floating in the night air around her. The blooms at the end of the aisle are closed, but still filling the air with perfume despite the late hour. Ignoring her protesting feet, she runs over and gathers several handfuls of the small flowers and takes them back to Dalt.

Crushing them in her hands, she holds her open palm full of mangled flowers up to his face, wrinkling her nose at the potent smell. These things are so pungent, she's amazed Dalt isn't at least trying to draw away from their overpowering perfume.

He remains stubbornly still.

Dropping her hands and dumping the flowers on the ground, she slumps down to sit next to him, at a loss as to what to do next. Everything around them is quiet except for the rustle of plants and the chittering of some night animal in the distance.

She's tempted to run to the house and get someone, but if this was her having a flashback, the last thing she'd want is more people to witness her at a moment of weakness. She suspects Dalt will feel the same way.

Suddenly, she feels very alone, which isn't something that normally bothers her. She's spent her adult life with few people to count on day to day, and even fewer she could call in case of emergency. But every once in a while she feels so alone it's like the weight of the universe is sitting on her chest.

Right now, unable to figure out how to help Dalt, an intense feeling of desolation invades her.

Deciding to comfort herself for a moment before going to get help, she crawls onto Dalt's lap and twines her arms around his neck. She rests her cheek on his shoulder, the strip of exposed skin on his neck right in front of her nose. Maybe, deep down, he's aware she's there trying to help. Like a coma patient dreaming of a relative who in real life is sitting at their bedside trying to talk them into waking up.

Frustrated and sad, she huffs out a lung full of air.

His body twitches around her, and suddenly his arms come up and encircle her. She remains still as he hugs her tightly to his chest. She squeaks at the sudden movement and pressure but doesn't protest otherwise. His breathing increases to a familiar rate and his rusty purr starts up. The relief she feels is so profound it makes her a little shaky.

"Dalt?"

"I'm here."

They sit like that for a long time, holding each other and comforting each other because make no mistake, she needs comfort as much as he does now.

"You scared me," she finally whispers.

"I'm sorry, little warrior. Our conversation put my mind down a dark path I couldn't pull myself out of."

"Was it like a flashback?" she nuzzles his neck, running her lips over the strip of skin. She feels him shudder, but he doesn't pull her away. He must like it.

"Flashback?"

"Where you relive something from the past, almost like it's happening again."

Dalt considers that for a moment. "Yes," he finally says. "That's what it was. A flashback. I was there. Tied and helpless as they took pieces from my body." When she shivers at his words, he draws her away so he can look down at her.

"Are you cold? I can wrap you in one of my blankets." She's about to assure him that she isn't cold, but then he seems to realize she's sitting there with him, outside of her enclosure. "Your gate's open," he murmurs. "You're out here, but I didn't open the gate. Did Eranan let you out?"

"Uh…" she tries to think of what answer might cause the least amount of trouble for her. The marbles-clinking-together-in-a-bag rumble of amusement interrupts his purring.

He shifts her weight and then stands up while cradling her to his chest with no apparent effort. Holding her, he strides over to the gate and nudges it closed. He jostles her a little so he can hold her to him with one arm and then tries to activate the locking mechanism. The display beeps but the gate's lock doesn't engage.

Groaning, Lakin hides her face in his neck. She thought she left the gate undamaged, but her prodding must have broken one of the delicate circuits. If she'd had more light and more time, she would have left the gate working perfectly, but she was in a hurry and laboring in suboptimal conditions. At least she still has the needle-like tool. With that, she should be able to get out of any of these enclosures.

Still holding her close, Dalt turns and makes his way to the next cage. It appears they've moved all the occupants out of this area because all the other enclosure gates stand open. When he walks into one of them, Lakin stiffens and Dalt freezes, one foot past the threshold.

"You don't like the enclosures," Dalt comments.

"I don't like being locked in," Lakin corrects. "I like the way the cages are mostly open, so I can see the sky, but I don't like the way I'm trapped inside."

"You don't seem to remain trapped for very long," Dalt grunts with another rumble of amusement.

Lakin tries to school her features into a scowl, but a grin forces its way out. "What can I say? We all have our talents."

"I'll make a bargain," Dalt offers. "I'll put you back into the other enclosure if you let me place my mat inside. I'll lay it in front of the door, far from your nest."

"Going to act as an alarm system?" Lakin teases.

"It seems the only way to keep you corralled," Dalt comments. "Is that an acceptable compromise? I'm afraid to put you in another enclosure and have you break out of a third one. Eranan might not handle that well."

"I didn't run," Lakin points out. "I stayed with you."

"You didn't run this time," Dalt counters. "I know you, human. You didn't run because you lack information. You're the type to bide your time and develop an escape plan instead of just running off blindly. The pain you were in when you first got here made you act precipitously. Now that you're healing, you're more likely to plan before acting."

Blinking in surprise, Lakin can't think of any retort or comeback to his accurate assessment. Her silence is answer enough for Dalt because he rumbles out another laugh. "You're like me, little warrior. We are prepared to act at a moment's notice. But, if possible, we'd much rather gather data before taking action."

"Fine," she says. "You can sleep in my enclosure."

She's willing to agree to a lot of things at the moment just to change the topic. Dalt's known her for all of two days, with most of that time made up of her sleeping. Yet he understands her better than crewmates she worked with for years.

"Very well." Backing up, he turns and carries her into the familiar enclosure. He carefully sets her down in her nest and then leaves to put his belt back on and gather his bed. Carrying it in, he shuts the gate and then arranges his bed against it.

When he moves to settle down on his pallet, she gets up and starts tugging at her bedding. With a displeased rumble, Dalt jumps up and hurries over to her.

"What are you trying to do? You need to stay off your feet," he insists as he scoops her up. "You've already walked around too much."

"I want to move my bed," she explains. He sits her down on a stone bench near the top part of his bed and picks up her nest. It's an unwieldy bundle of bedding but he manages to keep it all together.

"Where?"

"Parallel to yours, with about half my body length separating the two beds." A strange jolting sound rumbles out of Dalt, and it takes Lakin a moment to figure out it's a sound of surprise.

"You want to be that close to me?"

She's worried that he might drop off into another flashback but doesn't want him to feel judged or vulnerable. Practicing her rusty skills, she goes for tact.

"You're safe. If I'm next to you, I'll be safe too."

The familiar rusty purr erupts from Dalt's chest, loud enough to make her jump. He moves fast and just about flings the nest across the enclosure. It lands almost on top of his own and with a few tugs, he has the two beds separated. They're a little closer than Lakin likes but not so close that she's going to object.

Turning back to her, he lifts her up and deposits her on her bed. "No more walking," he orders as he plops ungracefully down on his pallet, still purring ferociously.

Snuggling down into her bed, she looks up to find Dalt still sitting. "Aren't you going to sleep too?"

"Not yet. I'm going to watch over you for now. Unlike your species, we don't need to spend so much time sleeping."

"Some species need more time than humans," Lakin says defensively. "The Massoc sleep for days on end!"

"They sleep for several rotations once a solar," Dalt corrects in a dry voice.

"They do? No wonder that Massoc tech got so much done. Well, we humans have our strengths too."

"Of that, little warrior, I have no doubt."

CHAPTER 8

Lakin

"What is going on here?" Eranan's outraged voice wakes Lakin, and by the sound of Dalt's grumpy rumble, he's not happy about it.

Sitting up, she rubs the sleep out of her eyes. When she's finally able to focus, she sees Eranan standing just outside the open gate of her enclosure, sounding the buzzing rattle of irritation. Dalt stands on his pallet, blocking the other man's entry, his intense eyes focused on the keeper.

"Dalt, what do you think you're doing? The commandant gave very explicit instructions!" When Dalt doesn't answer right away, Lakin realizes he doesn't want to admit to the flashbacks. Waving an arm, she gets Eranan's attention.

"The gate stopped working." It's not entirely a lie. The gate stopped working—because she broke it. "And Dalt wanted to make sure I didn't sneak out."

Holding the tray with one hand, Eranan steps back so he can push the gate closed. When he taps the display, nothing happens. He tries a few more times and then sounds his frustrated rattle and turns his attention back to Dalt.

"Still, you shouldn't be in here," he insists.

"I asked him to be in here." When both of them turn to her, she does her best to look hurt and helpless. "I'm not used to nighttime planetside. Ships don't have forests or wildlife. What if an animal gets in here and attacks me? If Dalt's on the inside, he could close the gate, hold it shut, and keep us both safe."

The agitated rattling stops, and Eranan starts up a smooth, melodious purr, a sharp contrast to Dalt's version. It's strange, but Lakin finds she prefers Dalt's erratic rusty purr more.

"Poor human, it seems we keep failing you," Eranan murmurs as he smoothly steps around Dalt. "I'll have your gate fixed by the end of the day. If it can't be fixed, we'll just move you to another enclosure. Several can still be made viable with minimum fuss."

Leaning over, he sets the tray on the ground between the beds. "I've brought you food and medication." Straightening up, he steps out of the enclosure. "If Dalt makes you feel safe, he can stay. But don't be afraid to tell us if you feel alarmed by his presence. He's only allowed in here as long as you agree to it."

That's right, he can't come in unless she allows it. These are the most considered jailers she's ever had. Looking up, she meets Eranan's gaze, keeping her own eyes wide and needy.

"I'm not scared if Dalt is here."

That makes Dalt rumble out a laugh. Looking over at him with a raised eyebrow, she waits.

"I think very little makes you fearful," he explains, and she feels herself flush from the compliment. His statement is far from true. Plenty of things terrify her, but it's nice to be thought of as fearless.

"Very well, I'll leave Dalt to comfort you. Don't forget to take your medications." Eranan points to the vials on her tray. "They won't make you drowsy. I know that's a concern for you. They'll just help with the discomfort and the last of the healing. By tonight your feet should be fine to walk on for limited distances."

The smile that curls Lakin's lips is genuine this time. "It'd be nice to walk without pain." With a last nod and a purring rumble, Eranan hurries off. Lakin looks down at her tray and then at Dalt who sits back down on his bed.

Frowning, she doesn't reach for her food. "You don't have anything to eat. Do you want some of mine?"

"No. Eat," Dalt commands, making Lakin sigh and then laugh.

"So, we're back to single-word sentences? You were so chatty last night. It was nice."

A quick laugh rumbles out of Dalt. "You worry so much about your captivity because of your previous treatment that you keep trying to escape. You pretend to be helpless and scared with Eranan. Yet you think nothing of challenging me."

"You're not one of my captors," she retorts, but it's not until the words are out of her mouth that she realizes it's the truth. She doesn't see him as an owner or jailer. Thoughtful, she picks up a bowl full of thick soup and sips at it cautiously. It's only mildly warm, but the flavor is rich and enticing.

"How do you see me, little warrior?"

When she doesn't answer right away, he doesn't push. In silence, she finishes her stew and thinks about who Dalt is. Or, more importantly, how does she feel about him?

"You're a compatriot," she finally answers with a firm nod of her head. "If I had a ship, I'd want you to be on my crew."

His rusty irregular purr starts up, showing his pleasure at her words.

"That's a high compliment." He points down at the tray. "Don't forget the vials."

Wrinkling her nose, she picks one up to look closely at the label. "If you guys are lying about any of these, I'm never swallowing any of them again," she mutters as she watches information scroll across the label. Finally, the label reads in one of the common languages, informing her that it's a *standard, low-level, long acting pain reliever fit for*, and then lists the species. Nodding her head when she sees *human* on the list, she downs the contents and then does the same thing to the next two vials.

Within moments of finishing the last vial, her feet stop throbbing.

"Oh, that feels nice," she murmurs, running her hand over one of the bandages on her feet.

"Would you like to leave the enclosure for a little while?" Dalt asks her. "You'll need to let me carry you. I could take you to the Goj bird clearing. They're in the midst of their mating season so they're very entertaining to watch."

"Yes, please," she answers without hesitation. She starts to get to her feet, but he stops her with a gentle hand on her shoulder and a negative rumble.

"Be still," he commands and then unhooks his Ident Cube off his belt. After tapping a few times, Eranan's face appears over it in a holo display.

"Dalt?" Eranan asks. "Is Lakin well?"

"She's feeling the effects of being caged," Dalt explains. "I'm going to take her out."

"Fine, but don't leave the compound," Eranan says dismissively, and the holo link disconnects. Dalt hooks the Ident Cube back on his belt and rumbles out a pleased sound as he stands up. With the easy strength of his species, he leans over and plucks her off the ground to cradle her high on his chest. She gives out a little squeak of surprise and grabs him around the neck.

"You may clutch at me," he tells her. "But only if you want to. You don't need to do it to hold yourself up. I'd never drop you."

"It's still weird to be carried around. Are the Goj far?" she asks as he pushes the gate open and walks out. He turns to cross an expanse of lush green ground cover, heading toward the edge of the nearby woods. She isn't that interested in watching a bunch of birds, but being outside the cage is nice, and it's been a long time since she's been in a green zone, let alone planetside surrounded by forest.

And, of course, any time she can spend outside the cage gets her information.

"Not far," Dalt tells her as he walks them down a dirt path. High above them, the tree canopy shields most of the sun. Lakin thinks the woods should feel sinister, but they don't. With Dalt carrying her, she thinks about the fairytales her mother would tell her and her sister at night before bed. Those stories always included handsome princes and happy endings.

Hmmm. She's not one to believe in happy endings, but Dalt could qualify as a prince. Especially if he ends up helping her get off-world, even inadvertently.

When sounds like a baby crying hit her ears, she tenses.

"It's the Goj," Dalt whispers as he leaves the path and maneuvers the two of them carefully through the dense forest. He sets her down on a bare patch of dirt. They're surrounded by greenery, blocking their view in all directions, but he reaches out and pulls a branch back to secure it with a convenient hook she didn't see before. This must be a place set up for viewing because now she can see that the spot she's sitting in has been deliberately cleared.

With the branch pulled back she has a clear view of a small valley filled with hundreds of enormous birds. The closest ones to her are probably only about twenty feet away, giving her a front-row seat to the show.

The gray birds are massive by human standards, probably just a little bigger than she is. They have wickedly sharp curved beaks and long claws, not only on their feet but also at the middle joint of their wings. They fold the wing in half and use that middle joint to walk on land with the same kind of stride a four-footed animal would use.

While she watches, one Goj lands almost right in front of her and, with a high-pitched cry, drops the carcass of an animal right in front of another Goj. The two Gojs look very similar except one has a higher crest on its head.

"The one that brought the meal is the female," Dalt explains as he sits down behind her. He draws her back between his legs so she's surrounded by his warmth. "The one with the larger crest is the male. Gojs spend the first few days of their reproduction season deciding on mates. The females bring a kill and invite a male to join the meal."

"That's nice of them," Lakin says and watches as the female attacks the male who tries to take a chunk of meat out of the dead animal. "Oh, shit!" she breathes, but Dalt rumbles out a warning.

"You need to keep your voice down. We aren't considered a threat to them, but during the mating part of their season, the Goj are easily upset."

"But why did she attack the guy if she wants to share a meal with him?" Lakin whispers back.

"It's a test," Dalt explains. "The male needs to prove he's worthy."

"By getting beaten up?" Lakin asks and flinches as the female pulls a beak full of feathers out of the male, just missing getting a chuck of his flesh with them.

"Exactly," Dalt says. "The first male that can get a bite of the food she killed is the one she'll pick to have young with. The females are usually bigger than the males because they bear the eggs, but the males need to prove they're tough and can defend the nest when the female needs to leave to hunt."

"The male doesn't just bring her back food while she watches the eggs?" Lakin asks.

"No, they'll both take turns watching the eggs and hunting. This isn't actually what I wanted you to see," he tells her, his eyes searching the area closest to them. "There." He points at a far corner of the clearing. "This is what I want you to see."

Lakin focuses her eyes on a pair of Goj working industriously to construct their nest. No, nest is the wrong term. The thing they're building looks more like…

"That looks like they're building a mud version of an old C78 A-frame cargo hauler!" Lakin says, her volume rising a little before she remembers to quiet down. "It even has the round bay top!"

"It does look remarkably like that kind of ship," Dalt agrees with an amused rumble. "I thought you might find it interesting."

"I'm assuming it's a coincidence," Lakin says as she watches the birds meticulously place balls of mud alongside small stones and pebbles to create their home.

"It is, yes," Dalt agrees. "But an amusing one."

"It sure is," Lakin says and wishes she had an image capture device so she could record the Goj. Transfixed, she loses track of time. It's easy to forget everything else as she watches the birds fight, gather materials, and build nests that look eerily like a ship.

"They'll have babies within twelve rotations." He points to a bird standing vigilantly on top of its house. "The structures hold in the heat of the day, so the Goj sits on top, guarding. If the temperature drops too low, both birds will stay, one on top and one squeezed into the shelter to keep the eggs or young warm. Once the eggs hatch the young will spend several days in the shelter until they're steady enough to walk. Then they'll venture out. The young are fascinating. Unlike the adults, they're bright pink and very round. Their beaks are just tiny nubs, barley visitable past the fluffy feathers."

"That sounds adorable," Lakin admits with a grin, wondering if she'll still be around when the babies emerge.

"They're amusing to watch because they're very playful with each other and the adults," Dalt tells her. "We can come back each day to observe their progress. Many Talins go out after reproduction season is over to collect the discarded pink fathers. They make excellent bedding and insulation."

"I bet some species would pay good money for those feathers," Lakin tells him with a muted chuckle. "A lot of folks out there like that color pink."

They both lapse into silence and watch.

All too soon Dalt is unhooking the branch so it can swing back into place and then lifting her up and carrying her away. Instead of taking her back to her cage, he carries her through the woods, skirting the main area of the compound until they get to what looks like steaming hot springs.

"Holian had these built," he explains as he sets her down on the stone edge of one. "The water is heated by the same system that heats the water in the mansion. But this water is imbued with healing and cleansing microbes."

"I don't want—" she starts to explain she doesn't want to strip down to get in when he reaches for her foot and almost upends her into the water. Grabbing his quill-less forearm, she scoots away a little from the edge of the hot spring.

"I don't want to get dunked," she teases as he unwraps the bandages on one of her feet.

"If you did, it would only be good for you," he tells her. "But I thought we could start with just letting your feet soak in the water."

Lakin looks at her feet with interest once he's finished removing the bandages. They still have a lot of bruising, but the lacerations look like the flesh knitter did its job and is helping them to heal well. She's going to have a lot of scars, and it looks like one of her little toes is going to permanently poke out at an odd angle. That'll make fitting shoes on that foot problematic.

Oh well, better a crooked toe than no foot at all. Or dead. Yeah, one crooked toe is better than dead.

"You've endured so much for one so little," Dalt says softly. He's unwrapped both her feet now and guides her to lower them into the water. It's hot, and she hisses as she gets used to it. But her feet quickly go from uncomfortable to painless as the microbes in the water do their job.

"Some out there have suffered worse," she says dismissively. "Aren't you going to join me?" She pats the stone next to her. Dalt sits down and lowers his bare four-toed feet into the water.

"That others have suffered more doesn't negate the pain you endured," he responds.

Lakin eyes him thoughtfully. "You know what, Dalt? You're a smart guy."

"Thank you," he says with a gratified rumble.

Then she gives him a broad, smug grin. "Do you abide by the advice you give out?"

Lakin decides the next rumble that comes out of him is what irked sounds like.

CHAPTER 9

Lakin

Over the next few days, the two of them develop a pattern. Dalt fetches them both a first meal in the morning from the kitchens in the manor. First meal is the only meal he eats for the entire day, even though it makes Lakin uncomfortable to eat while he watches her during second and third meal. Talins have an incredibly efficient metabolism so at most they eat once a day, and if not engaged in much physical activity, they might go several days between meals. Just another thing for Lakin to envy about the species.

After first meal, he carries her out to the nearby hiding spot in the woods where they watch the Goj birds. After spending a few marks doing that, he carries her to the hot spring on the far end of the property, and they dangle their feet into the water. The soak is more about doing something enjoyable because her feet were completely healed by the third day they went. But it's still pleasurable to soak and enjoy the canisters of chilled, mildly sweet beverages always waiting for them at the hot spring when they get there.

The quiet time at the hot spring is her favorite of the day. Although Dalt's cedar smell is always present, when he relaxes it gets stronger. Now she associates the smell of cedar with contented happiness. She knows it's not intentional, but Dalt is coming to represent joy in her life more than anything else.

During these relaxed times, it's easy to get him to share stories from his time in the military before the war with the Braxin. She even finds herself eager to share memories from her life in space. But she's careful about what stories she shares because he gets upset when she talks about any of her more dangerous adventures.

When the drink is gone and he's decided her feet are sufficiently soaked, they go back to her enclosure for second meal and a nap. No matter how much she objects, Dalt stands firm. She naps or doesn't get out of the enclosure in the afternoon.

After a nap, he carries her some place new. They never stray too far from the compound, but that doesn't matter. Dalt finds all kinds of interesting things for her to see. A little army of water ants building an island fortress. An extensive field with only one corner full of plants. She was flummoxed why they were watching plants grow, but he just kept telling her to be patient. Then she was floored when the plants migrated from one section of the field to another, chasing the moving sunshine. Another time he perched her high in a tree where they watched a migration of tree-hopping animals. To Lakin, the things looked vaguely like many-tailed dogs with stubby wings.

Then it's back in the enclosure for third meal. After that Dalt spends the rest of the evening entertaining Lakin with stories Talins tell their young or answering some of her questions. She can tell he won't answer many of them because he's uncomfortable giving her too much information, but she'll take what she can get.

She can't blame him. He knows she's not content to stay as a piece of property among the Talins.

If she was honest with herself, she'd admit she could be working a lot harder on plotting and planning. She should be stealing tools, finding out about the colony's port, and figuring out how best to utilize Dalt as a resource for escaping.

Instead she spends each day telling herself that tomorrow she'll do all of those things. Then tomorrow is over and she curses herself as a sentimental fool as the sky gets dark and they settle down to sleep in separate beds. The bottom line is that she wants to spend time with Dalt enjoying Kalor. She's not motivated to escape.

Hell, she's worked nonstop her entire adult life. Maybe she should look at this interlude as a well-deserved vacation. Dalt wasn't lying to her when he explained that her job was to get well and be a companion to Talins. Or at least one Talin because everyone else seems to give the two of them a wide berth. Even Eranan, who she's come to learn is in charge of all the humans living in the outside enclosures, only approaches her occasionally to inquire about her health and well-being.

No matter what he says or asks, she always insists that Dalt stay with her. To her utter shock, he accepts her demands and leaves the two of them in peace. She's only seen other Talins at a distance, except for a few visits from the healer. And barring Henni and Nol, she hasn't encountered another human. She's made a few inquiries, but Dalt explains the other Talins were told to keep their distance for now, and most of the humans are kept inside compound housing. He offers to take her over to meet the studs kept in the outside enclosures and she declines. Maybe later.

Under Dalt's care, she's gained a little weight, her skin has turned a soft brown from exposure to actual sunlight, and her facial muscles hurt from smiling and laughing so much. She hasn't gained any muscle because Dalt insists on carrying her everywhere, even though her feet are healed.

She'll never admit this to anyone, but she likes it. She can't remember a time in her life after childhood when she's been this happy.

The problem is that good feelings also make her feel guilty. While she's here, being pampered, fed, and housed, her crew is probably out looking for her. Without her to help plan, they probably haven't even attempted any jobs recently. At least not any jobs that would save lives. They're probably just doing bread-and-butter cargo hauls for good money but no thrill. No refugees saved. No slaves smuggled to freedom. No food or supplies carried illegally into border zones or past blockades.

She's here having fun while others out in the universe are suffering.

Frustration at her own mixed emotions makes her toss her empty bowl down on the tray with too much force, cracking the red material of the bowl and denting the tray. Dalt sounds an inquisitive rumble.

"Is this first meal not to your liking?"

"It's nothing like that," she says with a wave of her hand. "Sorry, I'm not used to being idle."

"I can request permission to take you further from the compound," he offers. "This planet is sparsely colonized. Most of it is wild with a large diversity of plants and animals you haven't viewed yet."

"That's not the kind of activity I'm used to, Dalt," she says carefully. Now's a good time to see if she can get him talking about colony security. "You know I've spent most of my life on board a ship."

"That life is over," he says, quashing her attempt to engage him in a conversation about space travel. "You're Talin-owned now. You'll come to accept it, eventually."

"Yeah, right," she mutters, touching the collar she's wearing. She's gotten so used to it that some days she forgets it is even there. That can't possibly be a good sign. "Look, don't you ever miss traveling? Visiting new space stations or planets? Getting to know other species?"

"I enjoyed that during my career," he admits. "But that's over. Kalor is my home now."

"Does your family live here?" she asks, genuinely curious.

"No."

She waits for a beat, expecting him to elaborate. When he doesn't, she huffs out a laugh. "Don't flood me with details," she teases.

"I know you jest," he says with a rumble of discomfort, "but my family is a difficult topic."

"Did they die?" she asks, feeling bad for bringing up a painful topic.

"No, as far as I know, they're all alive and well. My parents live on Talarian, which is our homeworld. My sister lives on her ship. She hires herself out as protection for transports and cargo ships."

"Sounds like you guys aren't close," Lakin says carefully. Dalt doesn't make a sound. She tilts her head. "Was it always like that?"

"We were as affectionate as any Talin family," he says reluctantly. "They were pleased when I was elevated to ground commander. They attended my ceremony and told me I brought honor to the family. But I haven't seen them since…" He rumbles a frustrated sound, and suddenly Lakin understands.

"You haven't seen them since you got captured and hurt," she finishes for him, getting angry on his behalf. "Did they cast you aside? Because if they did…" she snarls. "Get me close to them, and I'll—"

"No need to issue threats, little warrior," Dalt says with a rumble of humor. "The choice to remain separated is mine. They requested my presence on Talarian after Holian rescued us, but I didn't respond. I cut off communications and came here to live under Holian's authority."

"They don't even know where you are?" she asks, confused. "Why would you do that?"

"I couldn't bring myself to face them," he admits. "Not after my shameful actions during the war. Not after I lost so many."

Reaching over, she smacks her palm down on his thigh. "Shut up about that shame and blame thing. We've covered this already. You did what you had to do."

For a moment he silently regards her. "You're a forgiving soul, little warrior."

"I'm really not," she counters. "I just know nonsense when I hear it. We've already gone over that. You might as well blame your whole damn species."

"What are we blaming the entire Talin species for?" a voice asks. They were both so distracted by the conversation neither of them notices a small group of Talins walking up to the far side of the enclosure. Three of them are standing there now, crowded into the small, plant-free space and staring at her through the bars.

"What has Dalt done now to bring criticism to all of us from a little human?" another of the men asks.

"What are all of you doing here?" Dalt growls out. He remains sitting, but his body is tense, ready to jump into action.

His unfriendly reaction makes Lakin wary. "Everyone was told to keep their distance from this human."

"Holian decided she's been given enough time to become accustomed to Kalor," the first man says.

"We heard he's planning to meet with her soon," the second man says with a rumble of excitement. "That means we can meet with her too."

The third man remains silent, but Lakin finds her gaze resting on him more than the others. Despite his silence, he strikes Lakin as the one to pay attention to. Something about him feels deadly.

"Hello, little one," the first man addresses Lakin, sounding a very low purr that seems halfway salacious to her ears. "We heard you were damaged when you arrived. Are you better now?"

Unwilling to play this game, Lakin raises her chin and meets his gaze dead on. "Who are you? You said Holian is coming to talk to me, but that doesn't mean you have the right to be here."

Instead of bristling at her questions, all three of the men rumble with laughter.

"High-spirited," the second man murmurs. "Let me give you our names and titles. I'm Tisuran, second officer and winner of three Mattil medals." He points to the first man. "This is Iansif."

"I also have three Mattil medals," Iansif says proudly. They both look at the third man, who remains silent. With an impatient rattle, Iansif gives the silent man a little shove. "This is Palforma. He rarely talks. He has four Mattil medals."

"Five," the man mumbles so quietly she can barely hear him. That one word, spoken so quietly, softens him a little as Lakin realizes he's uncomfortable. For all his intense staring, this male is unsure about talking. These must be Dalt's fellow soldiers. She's still wary, but doesn't feel so threatened any longer, even if Dalt is still tense and ready to fight. This is probably more about him being overprotective than any real threat.

"I'm Lakin," she answers.

"Hello, Lakin. Is it true that one of ours hurt you?" Tisuran asks. Palforma must not have known about that because his enraged rattle is so loud, she feels it in her chest. With a little gasp of surprise, she jumps onto Dalt's pallet and crouches next to him, ready to run or fight depending on what the three males do next.

Unlike her, Dalt isn't startled by Palforma's intense rattle. He remains stiff and motionless except for a comforting hand he places on her thigh.

"Be at ease," he tells her, even while he eyes the men fiercely.

Iansif and Tisuran are already in motion, pushing Palforma with harsh shoves.

"Cursed idiot," Iansif swears at Palforma. "What are you thinking? If one of ours abused her, sounding your war rattle isn't going to help her trust us."

"Fool," Tisuran mutters.

Stopping his rattle, Palforma hangs his head, silently accepting their admonishments.

"Apologies," he mutters.

When Lakin realizes her mouth is hanging open, she shuts it with an audible click. What is going on here? She feels so confused about everything to do with this species.

"It's fine," she assures the men. "I was given to a couple of Talin and they hurt me. Then I was brought here, and a healer here fixed me. I guess that evens everything out."

"You seem to trust Dalt. Do you think you can come to trust others as well?" Tisuran asks.

Again, she doesn't understand. "Why would that be important?" All four Talins sound rumbles of concern at Lakin's question.

"It's very important. If you don't trust us, you won't let us hold you," Tisuran explains, and his voice sounds like he's talking to a child or a very slow adult.

Lakin sighs. "What are all of you even talking about? Why do you want to hold me? Is that a euphemism for sex? Is that why I'm here?" She lets out an agitated breath. Is the honeymoon period with Dalt over? Is she going to be forced to service the men on Kalor? Feeling a little dramatic, she throws up her hands and lets her voice get a little hysterical. This is a rude awaking after spending so many blissful days with Dalt.

"I don't understand any of this! First, some of you hurt me, then you heal me and treat me almost like a guest, except you keep me locked up and put a collar on me. And now you're talking about trust and 'holding.' What's going on?"

Dalt leans forward, puts his arms around her, and pulls her onto his lap. She doesn't resist, but she doesn't relax either. She's used to dealing with a universe that's doing its best to hurt or kill her. If these Talins end up sexually abusing her, that just fits in with familiar patterns she's witnessed so far. She'd be disappointed but not surprised.

"Be at ease, little warrior," Dalt murmurs, his rusty purr vibrating against her back. "Try not to upset yourself."

"Dalt, you lucky, clawless mongrel," Tisuran says without any heat in his voice. "First Sora and now this one."

"Don't touch her," Dalt responds. The high level of aggression in his voice makes Lakin startle.

"Don't worry. Commandant Holian gave us very strict instructions," Iansif tells them. "That's why we're all the way over here instead of at the gate. Remember what he decreed? We aren't allowed to be within three body lengths of any new humans until he gives permission. But we thought we should at least introduce ourselves so she can meet those here to guard and protect."

It doesn't escape Lakin's notice that no one explained "holding" to her yet, or why the Talins would collect humans specifically. None of this makes sense. Why would a slave owner invest in property that doesn't earn any profit? Why are they spending so much time getting her well and letting Dalt see to her when she could have started working days ago? And if her job is to see to the men's "needs," why hasn't anyone taken advantage of her yet?

"Answers," she demands. "I want answers."

"Later." Tisuran dismisses her demands and leans his body into the fencing, resting his fingers on a crossbar and then putting his chin on his hands. "Tell us about what happened to you."

Stubbornly, she crosses her arms over her chest and glares. "Answers for answers," she counters.

Palforma rumbles out a laugh, making them all look at him. "Tenacious," is all he says.

"Very well," Tisuran looks from Palforma back to Lakin. "Ask a question."

"Why do you guys collect humans?"

"Humans are soft and helpless," Tisuran says. "You don't even have a homeworld any longer. Bringing you here gives you a home."

"It's there," Lakin protests, not sure why he's bringing this up. "Earth is still there. It's not blown up or missing."

"But it can't sustain life any longer," Tisuran points out. "It's a barren, toxic wasteland."

"It's being cleansed," she counters.

"By engineered bacteria that will take several millennia to undo what your species did," Tisuran says, effectively winning that argument. "Because of the loss of your homeworld, not many of your kind are left. Humans are forced to live on the charity of other species or carve out little communities on neutral planets or space stations. I commend your species' determination to survive, but there's no denying your kind are atrocious keepers of resources."

Lakin can't think of a single thing to refute his assessment. It's all true and paints a very unflattering picture of humans. Individually or in small communities, humans might do the right thing for each other and their environment. But as a whole, they tend toward selfishness and blind refusal to acknowledge long-term consequences.

"Fine, we fucked up our planet, and we don't have political power in the universe," she agrees grudgingly. "But what does that have to do with you guys?"

"We're prepared to take care of you," Iansif states simply. "That's why we collect humans. Your species is going extinct, but if we collect you, your kind can be kept alive among the Talin."

"But why? In exchange for what?"

"Oh no, it's your turn to answer one of our questions," Iansif responds. "How did you end up with the Traditionalists?" Accurately reading her confused expression, Iansif elaborates. "The two Talins who hurt you are part of the Traditionalist political movement. They were insurgents, extremists. They believe any change will be the death of our species. Change includes allowing humans any kind of autonomy in our society. They hurt you because they resent the laws the Prime Son is trying to change regarding humans."

"That explains some things," she mutters, remembering many of the comments the two made as they tortured her. Memories of that torture make her shudder after so many calm, perfect days. Dalt's powerful arms come around her in a warm hug.

"Please elaborate," Iansif requests.

"Right, answers for answers," she mutters. "Too bad your answers don't seem to explain much."

"Lakin?" Dalt's quiet voice breaks into her thoughts. "I can make them go away."

"No, it's fine," she responds. She needs to know about this species, and these guys will talk. She could try to get more answers from Dalt, but he's got a habit of shutting down, so she'll probably have more luck with these three. Or two, because Palforma is so damn silent she can't imagine getting anything out of him.

"Our ship accidentally caught the attention of a Leemron patrol," she explains. "We were trying to outrun them, but our ship started having some issues."

"Your ship? You weren't a slave?" Iansif questions. "Most humans come to us as slaves, not free-born."

"No, I've never been a slave, only a prisoner several times. I was crewing on the Release. We mostly ran cargo in the Larox system, but we got a call to pick up some refugees from Galous. Long story short, the refuges turned out to be escaped slaves, but we picked them up anyway."

"Why do I get the feeling you knew, or suspected, they were runaways when you first responded to the request for pickup?" Dalt asks, making the other men tilt their heads with interest.

"Maybe," she hedges but then blows out a breath and gives a small shrug. "Look, as far as me and my crew are concerned, no one deserves to be a possession. Those refuges were owned by the Anvat and they have a strong political relationship with the Leemrons. That means they always return runaways to the Anvat. Anyway, when we realized we couldn't outrun the Leemron ship, my captain sent me over to negotiate with them. Mostly I was supposed to buy some time so Captain Makie could figure something out. But there wasn't much she could do, so once I was on board the Leemron ship, I sabotaged it and told the Release to run. That's how the Leemrons ended up with me."

"Why would you do something like that?" Iansif asks. "The Leemrons would've been well within their right to execute you right there."

"Well, they definitely talked about it," Lakin tries to joke, but it falls flat as the three Talins standing outside her cage make upset rattling noises and Dalt hugs her to his chest a little too tightly.

"You are a danger to yourself," Tisuran breathes. "We'll all be monitoring you. You can't be trusted to make safe decisions."

Great, just what she needs, more Talins paying close attention to her. This little impromptu meet-and-greet isn't turning out how she hoped.

"As I've stated," Dalt comments with a rumbled agreement, "she's a danger to herself."

"Safe doesn't get people their freedom," she huffs out. "Anyway, the Leemron held me in their brig for a few days, trying to decide what to do with me. They finally decided to give me as a gift to a couple of your guys as part of a trade deal. You all know the rest. Now it's my turn."

"I believe it's my turn," Commandant Holian states as he strides up behind the men. They three men move away from the enclosure fence and smack fists loudly to their breast plates as they formally greet their commandant.

He returns the gestures. "You're all dismissed. You can talk to Lakin at a later date." Without protest, the men move away, quickly disappearing out of sight.

Holian turns his piercing gaze to Lakin. "Human, you and I have things to discuss."

CHAPTER 10

Dalt

"Did the men holding you ever mention any names? Or say anything about servant citizens or assembly citizens?"

Dalt watches Lakin closely for signs of distress as Holian interviews her. The commandant is now seated on one of the stone benches in the enclosure, and Dalt is sitting across from him on the other bench with Lakin secured on his lap. She didn't protest when he moved the two of them to the bench instead of setting her down and leaving to let her be interviewed alone. She might not be resigned to life as a pet yet, but she trusts him. That's an important step.

It also helps that she doesn't appear to be intimidated by Holian at all, despite his high status among the Talin.

Then again, Lakin isn't intimidated by much, which isn't necessarily a good thing.

"They mentioned a servant citizen," she murmurs, rolling her eyes up as she thinks. "I think the name started with an 'n' sound."

"Try hard to remember," Holian encourages. "This is very important. Your information could save a lot of lives."

"What is a servant citizen anyway?" she asks as she snuggles back against Dalt. He lets loose with a loud comforting rumble so abruptly that she startles. Annoyed with himself, he focuses on his rumble and tries to make it as smooth as he can, despite the damage to his sound box.

"You're fine, Dalt," she whispers to him with a little pat on his chest. "I like your special purr." It takes him a moment to realize what she means, but then he stops trying to smooth out his rumble and lets it come out in the irregular way all his rumbles sound since he was tortured. She gives him a smile and turns her attention back to Holian.

"Servant citizens serve on the Apogee Assembly," Holian explains. "Every area has a Clan Assembly, and they send one representative to serve on the Apogee Assembly."

"And that's your government?" she asks thoughtfully. He can see the wheels turning in her head. Information is the bread and butter of independent haulers. Otherwise they are apt to run into trouble. Or, with Lakin and her ship, get into even more trouble than normal.

"Those assemblies and the monarch work together to rule the Talin people," Holian clarifies. "If one of the men who hurt you works for a servant citizen, then we need to know."

"Uh, why?" she asks. "I mean, I didn't like the whole torture bit, but at that point I was a slave. It's not illegal to do what you want with your property. Don't get me wrong. I wasn't happy about it, but I don't understand why who these guys worked for is such a big deal."

He hates this. He hates that she was hurt and put herself in danger to save others. He hates her blasé attitude about it. His human shouldn't have suffered so much pain.

One thing's for sure. She'll never experience anything like it again.

"We have strict laws about the treatment of human pets," Holian tells her. "If those men hadn't died trying to resist capture, they would've been prosecuted for several crimes, including their treatment of you. You're a pet here, Lakin. Not a slave. That's an important difference. Talins don't keep slaves. We don't believe in the institution of slavery."

Her nose winkles at Holian's words, and Dalt knows she doesn't believe him. In her mind there's no difference between being a pet and a slave. In time she'll understand, but for now there's no point in trying to convince her.

"What I need you to appreciate," Holian continues, "is that our people are facing great political and cultural change right now. It's been going on for a while, but it's accelerated since Prime Son Searin started advocating for change. Over the last few hundred solars two political factions emerged, Traditionalist and Reformist. Traditionalists want everything to stay the same and refuse to acknowledge the Fading. They even refuse to acknowledge how many of our kind seem to die by suicide, blatant or hidden, through the simple act of accepting deadly tasks. It's an epidemic, and we can't open new creshes fast enough. The numbers are there. Our population is declining at a rapid pace."

"Fading?" Lakin asks, interrupting Holian. "That's the second time I've heard that term. What's it mean?"

Holian sounds an impatient rattle but cuts it off almost immediately when Lakin flinches from the sound. Shifting in his seat, the commandant sounds a brief calming rumble before he speaks again.

"My apologies. I know you have questions, but I need to do many things today, and some of them hinge on what kind of information I can get from you. I don't have time to give you explanations, but Dalt can do that later."

"Right, sure," Lakin agrees. By her tone Dalt can tell she's annoyed. As much as he doesn't want to, it looks like he's going to need to explain the Fading to her soon. "From what you're saying, the guys who had me must have been Traditionalist. They said something about Reformists ruining everything."

"We know they're Traditionalist, Lakin," Holian reminds her. "We need to know what servant citizen they worked for. What they did to you wasn't the only law they broke. We also have laws about what weapons can be imported to our homeworld, and the punishment for breaking those laws is harsh. It was a fluke those two were discovered smuggling the weapons in. Someone powerful was helping them, and we need to find out who."

Comprehension dawns on Lakin's face. "I get it. You need to figure out who's manipulating everything at the top." She taps her fingers absently on his forearm as she thinks. "Honestly, I can't remember the name. But if you can get me a list of all the names on the Apogee Assembly, I might recognize it."

"That's an excellent idea," Holian says with obvious relief. "Come with me."

Dalt ignores Lakin's startled squeak when he stands up and cradles her to his chest.

"It'd probably be good for me to walk occasionally," she mumbles even as she snuggles into his hold.

"I know." He doesn't set her down.

Matching his gate to Holian's long strides, they're soon across the green and entering the main house. The place is massive and built like a maze. When Holian walks them toward the back, Dalt hesitates at the first set of heavy double doors. Holian taps the biolock on the door and it beeps open, but Dalt doesn't step through it to follow. Stopping and looking back, Holian sounds an inquisitive rumble.

"Are you sure?" Dalt asks.

Some of the secrets at the center of the house could cause a great deal of trouble for the commandant and all those he protects. He knows Lakin's trustworthy, but she's also naïve about their politics and the significance beyond those doors. If she inadvertently says something to the wrong Talin, it could ruin all of them.

Kalor Colony was started by Holian's mother. She began the rule breaking by giving live birth to and raising her son instead of having him created in an artificial womb and raised in a cresh. She bought the entire colony of Kalor to keep her secret safe, and soon she was welcoming like-minded Talins to the colony and sometimes even into her own home.

Holian continued his mother's legacy by allowing what Lakin will see beyond those protective doors. Dalt doesn't think she'd deliberately hurt any of them, but a careless word to the wrong earhole and the military will be there, raiding the compound and destroying everything Holian has built.

The Traditionalists aren't the only ones breaking laws. But the big difference is that Reformists like Holian are trying to protect instead of destroy by disobeying Talin law.

"I'm sure she'll be discreet," Holian announces and then focuses his intense gaze on Lakin. "What you're about to see could have us all put to death," he explains to her. "If you're the kind of female who would sacrifice her life to save a bunch of slaves, I'm sure you'll also keep this secret safe."

Feeling mildly ashamed for not having more faith in Lakin, Dalt follows Holian again.

"Are you guys doing some kind of secret experiments back here?" Lakin asks in a teasing whisper. "What's so important and illegal that it's locked behind grade three barrier doors? Weapons stores? Precious metals? I'm so curious now!" Dalt rumbles out a small sound of humor at her banter.

"You're correct, Lakin, something very precious is housed here," Holian tells her as they step through the third and last set of barrier doors, entering a large room full of noise and bustle.

Children and adults are clustered in small groups. Some are sitting with information squares, learning. Others are playing some kind of group game. A few are engaged in mock battles, and others are playing a skipping game that sends them into fits of laughter every few skips. Dalt can tell she's so overwhelmed by what she's seeing that she's struck dumb.

"This is where we keep our hearts safe," Holian states simply.

Dalt watches Lakin take in the scene around them as Holian calls out a name. An adult human among a group of children separates to join them.

"Some of these children are hybrids," Lakin breathes out. Then her eyes focus, and her brows furrow. "Humans and Talins are breeding compatible. That isn't a big deal. Humans are breeding compatible with a bunch of species. Why the secrecy?"

"True," Holian says without looking over at her. His eyes are focused on the human woman hurrying to them, an overly large information square held to her chest. "But in our culture, affection and what you call love are illegal. This room with its children, born naturally and raised by loving parents, is about as illegal as murder."

"Murder is more acceptable," the woman scoffs as she reaches them. "The Apogee Assembly sanctions political murders all the time when they approve a Contest of Strength request. But if they found out about this, it'd all be dismantled in a day. Holian would be put to death and these perfect children would be sent to live out their lives in isolation, never shown love or affection again."

Paling, Lakin looks at her with wide eyes. "But that's barbaric."

The woman shrugs. "Welcome to Talin culture where love is more illegal than murder. And raising your children is about as well-received as openly declaring insurrection."

"This is Madel," Holian introduces the woman to Lakin. "She's our expert on the Apogee Assembly, so I want you two to go over the names to see if you recognize any of them."

Casting her a sympathetic look, Madel gives a little wave. "Call me Maddy. I heard about what happened to you. I promise that's not common, even among the Traditionalists."

"I fear you might not be correct any longer. Their rhetoric is becoming quite violent," Holian says with a small sigh. "I worry that Lakin's treatment will become more common."

"Holian!" Maddy looks aghast. "What about pets held by Traditionalist families?"

"We are trying to get them out, but it's difficult because they're seen as a mark of status. We have keepers infiltrating the worst places, trying to keep them safe and comfortable. But we can't do much for them right now."

Lips quivering, a tear slides out of Maddy's eye. "Tonel?"

"Calm yourself," Holian says gruffly. "One of our keepers is there taking care of him and the other pets communally owned by the Havir Clan." Dalt can hear the anxiety in Holian's voice, even though he tries to hide it. "Tonel and the others are safe, but only for now. In the current political climate, there's no telling what a clan might do to prove loyalty to the Traditionalist faction."

"I understand," Maddy says and rubs one of her dainty fists over her eyes, brushing away her tears. "You'll always be the first to put yourself in danger for us and the last to shelter."

The traditionally Talin compliment coming from a human makes Holian sound a soothing rumble "You're a kind human, Maddy."

Holian always makes it difficult for assembly officials to keep tabs on the Kalor Colony. Part of it is the need for privacy. The Apogee Assembly might not approve of so many ex-soldiers living in the same place, especially broken ones like him and Palforma. But Holian also does it to keep his humans safe. If no one knows exactly how many are living in the colony, it's easier for everyone to disappear into the dense forests and jungles that cover most of the planet.

Most of the retired soldiers have two homes—one they live in day to day and another one carefully hidden and outfitted for survival as taught by their military.

The second homes are in case the hybrids here on Kalor are ever discovered. It's a testament to the worsening tension among the factions that Holian encourages all his soldiers to keep up their combat training despite their civilian status.

Maddy calling his name brings him back to the present. They've been talking while he was lost in thought, and now all of them are staring at him. The two humans have expectant expressions, as if waiting for an answer from him.

"That would be nice. Right, Dalt?" Lakin says to him. "To sit outside with Maddy and go over names?" She's still held securely to his chest, and now one of her hands is petting down the scar tissue on the back of his neck. The touch is comforting and soothing, so he lets out a rumble of pleasure.

"Dalt?" With a grunt, he looks over at Maddy's concerned face. Her expression makes him realize they probably think he was in the middle of a memory episode. Ashamed of his weakness, he's half tempted to set Lakin down and disappear back into the forest.

"You with me?" Lakin asks gently. "Because I'm a little tired and I don't want to talk about this stuff without you holding me."

"The east garden will be the best place for this discussion," Holian tells Maddy and then looks to Lakin. "The three of you go sit at the fountain benches and talk outside the hearing of little earholes." He glances meaningfully down at a child who runs past him, laughing as a few others give chase. "Maddy can answer any questions you have." Holian looks up to Dalt. "You're responsible for both of them while they're outside. Don't leave the compound. You know the rules about escorts."

Grunting again, Dalt dips his head, feeling better now that he has a purpose. Lakin needs him, and Holian gave him orders. He doesn't have time to wallow in his weaknesses.

"This way, you two," Maddy calls out as she turns to walk back through the barrier doors. The biolocks unlatch at her touch, and Dalt easily caries Lakin's slight weight.

It's a brief trip back down the hall through the sets of hallway barrier doors to finally reach an outside barrier door that leads into the east garden. Breathing in full lungs of air, Dalt realizes only now how tense he was inside.

"I'm impressed," Lakin murmurs after they exit the last set of doors. "Those barrier doors alone must have cost as much as the entire building. Those things are heavy duty."

"So is the rest of the building," he informs her. "The entire place was built to withstand ship-grade weapons fire."

Lakin makes one of her human sounds through her lips, and it takes a moment for Dalt to remember it's called a whistle. "I take it back. This whole mansion probably costs more than every ship I've ever served on all put together."

"I wouldn't be surprised," Dalt responds dryly. "I have a suspicion my pants are worth more than some ships you crewed on."

She glances down at his old and faded pants and chuckles. "Probably!"

As they talk, he follows Maddy to a set of benches and sits down opposite her. No sooner are they seated than a few canisters of drinking water and sopa are brought out for the three of them to share.

Before he can even uncork one of the canisters, a hulking shadow suddenly breaks away from the nearby forest and sprints toward them.

CHAPTER

11

Dalt

Dalt recognizes the shape before it's even a full stride into the sunlight. He doesn't move. His body tries to move the muscles that would've made an annoyed rattle if he still had back plates.

Maddy and Lakin are so busy chatting that they don't see the rapidly approaching individual until he's right on top of them.

Sweeping Maddy off the bench, the hulking figure swings her around several times, making her squeal in surprise, and then casually sits back down on the bench with her in his lap. She's gasping, laughing, and clutching the information square so tightly to her chest that it's beeping angrily.

"Bastard," she gripes as she laughs, loosening her hold on the information square and looking down to make sure it isn't damaged.

Tisuran is unrepentant. "You never come out anymore." He's rumbling loudly now and nuzzles his nose into her hair. "I miss you."

"I've had a lot of work to do," she tells him primly and smacks his chest, making him sound a rumble of humor.

"Too busy to visit your favorite fini cub? She's grown and almost full size. Her teeth are even descending and you're missing it."

A look of regret and longing takes over Maddy's face. "I've been so busy," she mutters. "Everything's so tense right now. The attacks on the Prime Son, the plots. I have to organize and process a constant barrage of information."

Maddy's shoulders slump a little, and that's when Dalt notices her weight loss and the fatigue on her face. This little human is working herself much too hard. It's useless to point any of this out to Holian. The man's well aware of the state of all his humans. He must be ignoring Maddy's condition because her research and analysis are so important.

By the way Tisuran is holding Maddy, Dalt can tell that his fellow soldier is aware of the human's exhaustion too. That's probably why he lurked outside the mansion, hoping she'd step outdoors. The soldiers are rarely allowed inside the mansion, but Holian wouldn't bar him from seeking Maddy out once she stepped outside.

"Let's just go over these names first and then visit the cubs," Maddy counters. "I won't have much to do for at least two or three more marks because I'm waiting for the next wave of intel to come in. The interstellar coms have been slow for the last few rotations."

Dalt looks down at Lakin. His little human has a thoughtful expression on her face. "Sure, I'll go over names, but I still want answers for answers. I help you figure out who's ordering those mercenary assholes around, and you guys explain to me what the hell Fading is."

That catches them all by surprise. Dalt and Tisuran go rigid while Maddy draws back a little and blinks.

"I can answer that," she agrees after a moment's hesitation. "Where did you hear the term?"

Lakin just points to him and gives a little shrug. "Everyone acts like I should just know what it means. And the way these guys react, I feel like I'm saying a terrible cuss word." Glancing over her shoulder at Dalt, her mouth forms a familiar half grin that tells him she's about to misbehave.

She brings her face close to his, makes her eyes go wide, then says, "Fading!" At the same time, she pokes him in the chest with her finger. He doesn't jerk, jump, or rumble with displeasure, but Tisuran rattles unhappily.

"You shouldn't make light of it," he scolds her. "It's a serious disease taking a toll on our species."

"Well, if someone had just told me that I wouldn't be so flippant," Lakin retorts, her expression equal parts annoyed and guilty.

"Ease up, Tisuran," Maddy tells him with a frown of her own. "Lakin's new to Talin culture. You can't expect her to just know things. She's used to having easy access to knowledge, and now she can't even look it up. And with the Talin tendency to be tightlipped, it's got to be frustrating."

She gives Lakin an apologetic smile. "I forgot that you're wild-caught. It's always fascinating to see the reaction of those not raised among the Talin. Names first and then an explanation about Fading, and whatever other questions you have. I'll tell you everything I know."

"I'm holding you to that," Lakin warns. It appears Maddy's assessment is correct. His refusal to answer all of Lakin's questions has been bothering her more than he realized. His little human doesn't like not knowing things.

His human.

He keeps thinking of her as his, but he probably shouldn't. He's restrained himself from rubbing his scent glands against the top of her head, but only barely. Each day it gets harder to fight his instincts. Even now, the glands on the sides of his face are swollen and painful, urging him to mark her. He's forced to unobtrusively rub at them to relieve some of the pressure and worries they might even start leaking. That would be embarrassing. His scent glands haven't leaked since he was very young.

They didn't fill when Sora lived with him. His scent glands remained mostly empty for the entire time she was on Kalor. Maybe he subconsciously knew her heart belonged to another and he was only a way station for her. With Lakin everything is different.

Sora experienced pain in her life, but she also had this strange serenity that never felt right to him. She might have been willing to fight for her life and the life of her unborn child, but other than that she was passive and agreeable. She never argued. She never objected. She never tried to negotiate or wheel and deal with Holian or him. She had a gentle soul, content to live her life as it unfolded.

He's glad that she ended up back with Searin. By all accounts they're both healthy and happy, with the monarch doing everything in her power to keep the parentage of the child growing in Sora's belly a secret. All of them take significant risks, but Searin and Sora get to experience something most Talins never will.

Scent-bonding and a child they'll both raise.

But because of it, Sora must remain hidden, only coming out of the Prime Family's compound under heavy guard. Searin leaves his human rarely and never for long. From the few missives Sora has sent him, she's more than satisfied with her life now.

He's not sure he could ever be content hiding behind castle walls, surrounded by guards, attendants, and rules. Here on Kalor Colony, he and the other soldiers have the freedom of the forest and Holian's lenient command.

That's why he likes Lakin so much and why he keeps thinking of her as *his human*. Like him, she could never stay shut in. She could never give up her life just to remain "safe." The drive to help is too strong in her.

"That name sounds right." Lakin's loud pronouncement brings Dalt back to the conversation going on around him. They'd been going over names with Maddy pronouncing the Talin sounds in a perfect accent to help Lakin recognize the right one. Apparently it worked.

"Nonaceum?" Maddy repeats.

"That one, but there was more to the name," Lakin says.

"Hmmm," Maddy taps her information square a few times. "Assembly Citizen Nonaceum of Family Urm with in the Uroka Clan?"

"Yeah!" Lakin says with excitement. "Urm! That's it. They kept saying Urm, not just Nonaceum. Something about meeting the Urm for transfer."

"That's even better information than I hoped for," Maddy says, tapping at her information square with quick nimble fingers. "Uroka Clan are most closely allied with the monarch, but rumors say one of the families in the clan, the Urm, are starting to disagree with the clan. They might be pushed to rash actions because without the clan they have no wealth at all. The Uroka Clan pools all their resources."

"Rash action such as dealing with an illegal arms trade?" Tisuran asks.

"Potentially. I'm thinking the Urm family aren't Traditionalists or Reformists. I think they're opportunists," Maddy declares grimly as she taps away. "I'm sending all this new data to Holian. I'm not sure if we can act on it, but he can pass it on to Searin and the monarch."

Standing up, Tisuran holds Maddy tightly to his chest. "That means you're free to go home with me to see the cubs," he declares. Maddy wiggles in his arms.

"Just for a little while," she warns him. "I need to get back before fifth mark. Holian is attending a holo meeting, and I want to be there to observe."

"That's several marks away, plenty of time," Tisuran declares and starts striding off. Dalt stands with Lakin in his arms to follow.

He loves the idea of taking Lakin into the forest, past the boundaries of Holian's compound. Ultimately, he wants to show her both his homes—the one he lives in and the one he built for emergencies.

He's only gone a few strides before she pushes against his chest and protests.

"Put me down, Dalt," she demands.

Stopping, he wonders what's wrong. His intrepid human can't possibly be afraid of the forest. He's been careful not to wander too far before now, but he planned to take her deeper into the forest today anyway. He was just waiting for the right opportunity. With another human to accompany them, any fears Lakin might have should be allayed.

"Do you want to go back to your enclosure?"

"Hell no," Lakin says with a grin, "but I want to walk. My feet are all healed and moving around sounds nice."

Ahead of them, Tisuran and Maddy are having a similar discussion. When Tisuran places Maddy on her feet next to him, Dalt reluctantly does the same thing for Lakin.

"Tisuran in front, you two between us, and me at the back," Dalt orders, glad when Tisuran nudges Maddy into position.

"Are all Talin like this or just the soldiers?" Lakin asks Maddy.

"I don't know because I've always been surrounded by soldiers," Maddy says with a resigned shrug. "If you're not careful, you don't get to walk anywhere once you're outside the mansion."

Neither Dalt nor Tisuran comment as Maddy chats with Lakin about Kalor, Holian, and Talin culture in general. About halfway to Tisuran's home, Lakin asks about Fading again.

Dalt tenses at the question, and he can see Tisuran's back go stiff. Neither wants to discuss such a horrible weakness, but the tenacious human won't let it go.

A sad expression settles on Maddy's face. "Fading isn't a pretty topic. I can give you the longer explanation later, but to put it simply, Talins made it illegal to fall in love with each other."

"Right, you guys mentioned that back in the mansion. No love, no live-birth kids." Lakin comes to a stop and looks over her shoulder at Dalt. "But—"

"Hold on to your questions for now," Maddy says, reaching back and drawing Lakin next to her. The path is wide enough in this section for the two humans to walk side by side. "Let me explain everything. First, Talin biology is a little on the odd side. For a female to get pregnant, she must be in a scent-bonded relationship. That means—"

"Scent-bonded?"

Maddy takes a deep breath. "Right, this might get complicated. Talins have these glands on either side of their face that secrete a scented oil. Partners can get addicted to each other's smell, and that's called scent-bonding. If the couple ends up separated for too long, they could both get sick. Kind of like a drug addict going through withdrawal but much worse. Talins often die from scent withdrawal."

"Fading is scent withdrawal?" Lakin asks.

"Oh no, not at all. Talins who suffer from Fading never scent-bonded," Maddy says. "The withdrawal is why scent-bonding was made illegal." Lakin makes a small sound of frustration. This must be confusing to someone who's never been exposed to Talin customs, laws, and society before.

"But it doesn't make sense to make scent-bonding illegal if women can't get pregnant without it," Lakin points out, annoyed.

"If you'd stop interrupting, I'd explain it all," Maddy says with a small laugh. "You're impatient."

"You have no idea," Lakin mutters and then adds, "please, go on. I'll try to keep my interrupting to a minimum."

"Right. Anyway, about the time they started passing laws making scent-bonding illegal, they already developed artificial womb technology, so they didn't need women to carry babies anymore. They still have marriage contracts and stuff like that, but now Mom and Dad hand over genetic data to a facility and that facility creates the kid."

"I still don't see why they bothered doing all that when they could just scent-bond and be a happy family," Lakin objects.

"This was thousands of solars ago," Maddy tells her. "They were just coming into their power as a space-going species and ended up engaged in some pretty nasty conflicts. This was also before way points were discovered and jump drives were developed, so space travel took a lot longer. Bonded pairs would end up separated for too long and often die. They call it Collapsed Scent Disease, but most just call it the Ending. It was becoming a big problem, so that's when they started making it socially unacceptable to bond and eventually the social taboo got written into law."

"Got it," Lakin says with disgust. "Sounds stupid but fine. What does this have to do with Fading and why are humans mixed up in it?"

"Now here's where it gets interesting for us," Maddy says with a tinkling laugh. "Some Talins end up suffering from a disease called Fading when they don't scent-bond with someone. They lose their appetite. They stop wanting to work. They stop interacting. They basically stare off into space and die."

"Sounds like depression," Lakin says with confidence. "I saw a lot of that when I was growing up. Especially when our area of the space station lost a legal battle and then we didn't have access to a communal green space anymore. It was almost like a bunch of people just willed themselves to die."

"It's not depression," Tisuran growls.

"Yeah," Maddy says, and Dalt sees her give Lakin a conspiratorial look. "It's not depression because it's physical, not mental. The Talin would never be mentally weak enough to suffer from something like depression."

Dalt's not sure, but he thinks Maddy's tone might be mocking.

"Anyway," Maddy continues. "The official story is that no one knows why the Fading happens, and the best thing is to let those who suffer from it die because they must be weak links in society. Healer's aren't supposed to give add to a Fading patient. It's not even studied!"

"I'd say that's dumb, but I remember some human history back on Old Earth where they treated some diseases differently simply because they were sexually transmitted. As if that made the disease worse or something."

"Kind of similar here," Maddy agrees. When he and Tisuran made sounds of objection over being compared to human history, Maddy shakes her head at them. "Hush you two, the humans are speaking."

Her admonishment makes Lakin laugh, then she urges Maddy to continue speaking. "You said *officially*, so there must be an *unofficially* too."

"Unofficially everyone knows that the Fading happens because Talins aren't allowed to scent-bond. It doesn't happen to all of them, mind you. But it can hit anyone at any time. The percentages get worse every year. Without love they're more likely to die."

"Don't use your human terms on us," Dalt announces grumpily, and that makes Maddy laugh again. "Scent-bonding is biological. Love is some kind of emotion."

"Sorry, Dalt," she demurs. She gives Lakin another conspiratorial look. "Maybe we should have had this conversation outside the hearing of these guys."

"Too late now," Lakin says. "You might as well finish explaining. Don't worry. I think I'm starting to understand. Let me guess. If Talins can't scent-bond with each other, they turn to humans for comfort."

"We *give* comfort to the humans," Tisuran objects. "You humans need us to hold you and touch you, or you get depressed and die. That's how fragile you are."

"According to Talin literature, we humans need to be held and cuddled a lot or we get sick. Luckily for us frail humans the Talins keep us as pets and take good care of us," Maddy says playfully. "And the Talins don't get any enjoyment when they cuddle us or rub their scent glands in our hair. They certainly don't get satisfaction when the oil from their glands gets to our scalps and changes slightly so it's almost like a new scent that they can rub onto themselves. No, that's not like scent-bonding at all."

"I feel vaguely insulted," Tisuran commented. Both women ignore him.

"Their culture, laws, and taboos mean it's really hard for even the more enlightened of them, like those who live here on Kalor Colony, to engage in scent-bonding with each other, so we fill that void. As the laws and customs change, I'm sure Talins will start scent-bonding with each other again, and maybe we humans will someday get full status among them. But for now, it's all a big secret. Well, the worst-kept secret among the Talins because a lot of them know that we're breeding compatible and they can scent-bond to us just like another Talin."

Tisuran makes a discontented rattling sound and is about to say something when Dalt watches Lakin's face light up as she makes a connection.

"Cedar!" she almost shouts out, coming to an abrupt halt and almost causing Maddy to stumble. Turning to face Dalt, she steps close and stands on her toes. She sniffs a few times and then grins. "Is that why you smell like cedar? Because of your scent glands?"

"I don't know what cedar is," Dalt admits. He leans over a little and taps the side of his face. "This is where my scent gland is."

Lakin puts her nose right on the spot and a bolt of pleasure goes through him. It's a simple touch, but the soft skin of her nose and mouth are in contact with part of him that's aching with need. Suddenly his scent glands are so full they're painful, and to his horror a small trickle of oil starts down his face. Before he can pull away, Lakin reaches up with a finger and swipes the oil off his skin.

Stepping back, she rubs it between her fingers, her face full of concentration and curiosity. Dalt's too stunned to move. First of all, he hasn't leaked oil since he was very young. And then there's the effect of her touch on him. Her soft fingers gliding over his scent glands have sensation rioting through him.

"It smells just like cedar," she exclaims. "I love this smell."

More oil trickles down his face from her words. The scent glands on both sides are leaking, filling the air with his bonding scent. Tisuran is staring at him, making a horrified rattling sound at Dalt's loss of control.

He shouldn't be at the mercy of his biology. He's Talin and an elite warrior. Before they were captured, his group was considered one of the best.

Is this inability to control his glands some new aspect of his torture-damaged body?

Shame roars through him, making it impossible to understand what Lakin is saying. She's still rubbing her fingers together, staring at her hand, saying something about smells.

All he can focus on is the evidence of his weakness glistening on her fingers. She looks up at him, smiling. But the smile dies, probably because he's not responding to her. He's gone still, torn by two diametrically opposed impulses.

One tells him to grab Lakin, hold her tightly, and rub his aching scent glands in her hair, covering her in his scent.

The other says to run and hide, withdraw from everyone until he's back in control.

Oddly enough, the changing scent of his oil on her skin pushes him to turn and flee. If he stayed, he'd scent mark Lakin, whether she wanted it or not. That's not acceptable and it's the one thing he has control over at the moment. Leaving the path, he disappears into a dense section of forest.

He can hear them calling to him, but he ignores their voices. His mind is too filled with his disgrace to turn back. Tisuran can keep them safe. Without Dalt, he'll turn around and walk them back to the compound. They'll miss out on the cubs, but that's of little consequence. It's far more important that no one's forced to be near him.

No one should have to share space with a shameful male who can't regulate himself.

CHAPTER

12

Dalt

Unable to stomach the idea of returning home, Dalt runs the forest for the rest of the day. He checks all his gathering pods, the traps he and the other soldiers set out to capture the tiny insects that are used to flavor foods when dried and ground up. He also spends many marks climbing trees to gather flowers on the highest branches. He falls several times because the smaller branches don't like to take the weight of a full-grown male Talin. He brushes off all the falls, telling himself he's not injured and any pain he feels needs to be ignored.

Pain without serious injury is just a state of mind. Talins have control of their minds. Succumbing to his pain is nothing but mental weakness.

As if to prove to himself that he's stronger than his leaking scent glands, he pushes himself hard the entire rotation. He only heads home when darkness descends and stars start twinkling in the sky.

He's carrying several quickly woven bags full of flowers and gathering pods. The day's harvest is more than he normally gathers in twenty or thirty rotations, and his body is exhausted. His legs feel like they want to collapse under him, and his torso hurts from the last fall he took. But he ignores all of that, pushing hard to finish his journey home.

His stone hut is dark and cold. Dropping the fruits of his day's labor just outside the front door, he shuffles inside. If not for the fatigue, he'd slam the door shut, but he doesn't even have the energy for that. Leaving the heavy door open, he focuses on making it to his pallet. His feet don't seem to want to take full strides, and he stumbles as he walks.

At least his thoughts are blissfully silent after he spent his time not just laboring, but spewing vitriol at himself in a non-ending internal monologue.

His body might be screaming with discomfort, but his mind is wonderfully numb. Falling into bed, he doesn't even bother turning on any of the lights in the hut or stripping off his filthy pants. He just curls up on his side and closes his eyes, thankful that tomorrow he'll have more strenuous work to do. The last thing he wants is to spend a moment unoccupied by tasks.

When a strange noise wakes Dalt up from sleep several strikes later, he lies perfectly still, trying to parse out what he's hearing. The tread is too soft to be one of the bigger animals in the forest and too heavy to be any of the smaller ones. It also sounds bipedal, which eliminates all but a couple of creatures on Kalor— Talin and human.

Silently, he gets out of bed just as a figure appears in the open doorway of his hut. He vaguely remembers being too tired to even close let alone latch it. The nightly mist has moved in, so there's almost no moon or starlight to outline the intruder.

If his body wasn't still recovering from his earlier exertions, he would've recognized the scent sooner. Unfortunately, nothing but the fact that someone has invaded his homestead makes it into his fatigued mind. He charges the intruder without hesitation. By the time Lakin's scent registers in his brain and his fingers touch her warm, soft body, he's already barreled into her, sending them both tumbling out the door.

She gives a startled cry as Dalt's bulk hits her. He maneuvers their fall so he's on the bottom and takes the brunt of it, but he hears her gasp with pain anyway.

A renewed sense of shame fills him as he realizes he just brutalized a helpless human. And not just any human, but Lakin. He promised Sora he'd take care of her and then, not only did he abandon her in the woods, now he's physically attacked her.

Humiliation washes over him.

Wait… what is Lakin doing at his cabin?

He comes fully awake, and the humiliation is replaced by bewilderment.

"Dalt?" Lakin wheezes as he sits up with her in his lap. He grunts at her and runs his hands down her limbs, looking for anything broken. She's only got her breath back and begins protesting as he's feeling up her left leg.

"I'm fine," she tells him as she pulls his hands away from her knee. "Nothing's broken. You just knocked the wind out of me."

Humans don't have wind in them, so she must mean he pushed the air out of her lungs. He puts his ear to her chest and hears a steady heartbeat and working lungs. It's a crude but effective measurement. Assured that she's not seriously damaged, he turns his attention to other matters.

"You couldn't have run away from Tisuran," he states.

"Of course I didn't run away from Tisuran," Lakin agrees, her tone grumpy. "After you left, he turned us around and we had to march right back to Holian's compound. I guess there's some rule about one Talin per human or something. He put me back in my enclosure and took Maddy out to see the pups. Thanks for that. I totally missed out."

Nothing she's telling him is surprising, but it doesn't explain how she ended up at his cabin either.

"The gate to your enclosure has long since been fixed," he says, thinking out loud. His eyes have fully adjusted to the dark and his brain is finally awake, so when Lakin swings her gaze away from him and looks pensive, he knows. "Did the gate conveniently malfunctioned again?"

"I guess you guys just buy poor quality biolocks," she says with forced casualness. He's not sure how she did it, but she's broken out of her enclosure. How many times has she done that? Is this the third or fourth time?

No sooner does he stop sleeping across her gate and she's loose again.

This human is extraordinary, and he'd admire her abilities if not for the fact that she wandered into the forest at night by herself.

"It took a long time to find you," Lakin tells him. "First, I had to wait until it got dark, and then I had to skip around a lot to keep the patrols from finding me—"

That's when the overwhelming smell of Barbo bush flowers hit his nose. She's covered in the smell of them. Like she rolled around in the bushes or…

"You used Barbo flowers to hide your smell," he murmurs. "No wonder I didn't catch your scent right away."

"Do you mean those little purple flowers outside my enclosure? Those things are potent. I figured there's no way to get rid of my smell so I just covered it with something more pungent."

His human is clever.

No, not his human. She isn't his.

"How did you find my home?" he asks.

"That was the easiest part. I just asked Tisuran where it was when he was walking us back. He pointed to the path that leads to your place."

The amount of danger she put herself in stuns him. Several paths intersect with the one that leads to his home. She could've gotten lost, not to mention the danger of walking in the forest at night with no weapon and no escort.

Did he think her clever? No, he's mistaken. She's the stupidest human he's ever met.

"You could've been killed," he rages, giving her a little shake. Sounding a surprised squeak, she grabs his hands where they're gripping her shoulders.

"It's your fault," she blurts. Her words cause him enough confusion that his grip slackens and she's able to tug his hands off her shoulders. Holding both his hands in hers, she drops their joined hands into her lap.

"My fault?"

"If you hadn't run off, I wouldn't have gotten worried and wouldn't have needed to come looking for you," she explains. "I had Eranan message your Ident Cube, but you never responded, and he wouldn't send anyone out to check on you. No one was concerned, so I didn't have a choice. I had to make sure you weren't hurt or anything like that."

His Ident pinged several times over the course of the rotation, but he'd ignored it. It never occurred to him that it might be Lakin trying to contact him.

"Your logic is convoluted and inaccurate," he says as an unfamiliar warm sensation spreads through him. This human cares so much that she risked her life just to check on him. Then his resolve hardens as he thinks again of all the ways she could've died tonight.

"You shouldn't have worried." His tone is harsh, but he needs her to understand. "You should never leave the compound without an escort."

"Good luck giving me orders," she says flippantly. "You're not my captain and—" she taps the collar around her neck. "I'm pretty sure this means Holian is officially my owner, so you're out of luck there too."

He wants to shake her until her teeth rattle. He wants to pick her up, carry her into his home and barricade the door. He wants to roar at her for being so cavalier with her life. He wants to clutch her to his chest and beg her never to do something so dangerous again.

As if to add even more distress, his scent glands are swelling up and aching fiercely. It took a day of extreme physical labor to make them calm, and in just a short time in Lakin's presence they're ready to overflow again.

As if sensing his discomfort, Lakin reaches up and strokes the side of his face with her small, soft hand.

"Maddy told me about Talin scent glands as we walked back. She said it's, uh, unusual for you guys to leak. I hope you know I don't care about that."

How can she not care? How can she be so accepting in the face of his obvious deficiency? Not only does he lack quills, claws, and backplates, but now he can't even master his own body. It's humiliating. He should disgust her. She should shun him.

Except she isn't. She's here, snuggling closer to him. She's wiggling her body in his lap until her head is resting on his shoulder, her lips against the sliver of exposed skin at his neck.

"The oil means you want to scent-bond to me. Doesn't it?" she asks idly as her fingers play back and forth along the skin over the gland in his right cheek. Her touch is making it hard to think. "I don't think I'd mind that, being scent-bonded to you, I mean."

She hesitates for a moment, her fingers tracing a path around his painfully engorged scent gland. Each stroke of her fingers makes pleasure radiate from his gland.

"Maddy told me a lot of you guys think we humans scent-bond to you, but you can't scent-bond back because we don't have our scent gland to mark you with. She also explained that many Talins think we get sick if we bond with a Talin and then get separated. I don't want you to worry about that. I love your smell. I do."

She leans close and pulls a deep breath as if to emphasize her point. "It took me a while to figure it out, but your scent was missing all day today. That meant nothing was right. The food didn't taste right. The colors weren't right. I felt restless, and couldn't focus on anything. I think it's because you left and took your scent away with you."

She gives a little self-deprecating chuckle. "That probably means I'm already a little addicted to your scent."

As she talks, she continues to touch him, rubbing his scent glands with her gentle fingers and nuzzling her nose against his skin. Every brush of her fingers is sending too much sensation rioting through his body.

It's taking all his willpower not to cock his head to the side and disgorge his scent all over her. She can't possibly comprehend what a lowly Talin she'd be binding herself to.

"I had a lot of time to think today," she continues talking, unaware of the internal battle he's waging. "Except for Eranan, no one came near me all day, and he only brought me food. You know, I've worked on seven different ships since I left the human colony on Develia station—seven in the last ten Universal standard years, or I guess solars to you. Anyway, I've never been fired. On one ship the captain retired and sold the ship to a shipping fleet that wasn't interested in hiring any of us as crew. All the other times I left."

She pauses to give him an arrogant grin. "I'm always looking for the next important assignment. I'm a pretty skilled electrical systems tech, so I'm in high demand, even if I'm human.

Despite being offered some lucrative positions, I've always picked my jobs based on what the ship did. Never on how much they could pay me. I didn't care if they did legal or illegal trade as long as they were fighting the good fight. Supporting colonies that needed help. Smuggling supplies to a war-torn area. Sneaking past political quarantines to get people to safety. Eventually, every captain would get spooked and we'd stop taking those jobs, so I'd quit and go look for work on another ship."

It's an interesting feeling to realize that Lakin deliberately put herself in the path of danger her entire adult life. Compared to what she's done in the past, taking a night stroll through the Kalor forest is nothing to her. This human doesn't know the meaning of security or safety.

"For me, it's always been about making a difference," she continues. "I don't care who I'm helping as long as they need the help. And I'm thinking you guys could use my help here. What I saw this morning in the mansion shook me up. All those kids—happy, healthy, and adored. When I first got here, all I saw were the collars and cages. But now I'm seeing the nuances of everything going on."

She stops for a second, her human face twisting into a thoughtful expression. "Develia station has almost no humans left on it. It had a thriving human colony while I was growing up, but only about a dozen people there now. I get missives from my mom or siblings occasionally, and it's gotten worse for humans there. But they don't move because it's getting worse everywhere. One of the things I've been looking for is a safe place to resettle them."

"You could…" Dalt begins, but she stops him with a finger over his lips.

"I know what you're going to say, big guy, but I'm not ready to make that call yet." She taps her collar. "I'm not sure this is acceptable for them. But either way, I can see you guys here on Kalor are trying to make a difference too, trying to take care of the vulnerable. This place makes me think of what's happening at Develia, only in reverse. You're carving out a safe space instead of giving up. That means I'm in."

"You're in?" he asks. His translation program isn't giving him anything more than the term means agreement.

"Yeah, I'm in. Here to assist. I'm good at strategy and planning. I'll stay for a while and help out."

Grunting, Dalt refrains from pointing out she doesn't have much choice but to stay. She has no ship, no money, and she's on a colony planet almost entirely owned by Holian, and well inside Talin-controlled space.

Then again, Lakin's proved immensely resourceful. Who's to say she wouldn't figure out a way off Kalor given enough time?

"That means, if I'm staying for a bit, I need to pick a Talin to own me." She snorts, rolls her eyes, and murmurs, "Own, ha!" Then she continues in her regular voice. "Anyway, if I need an owner, I pick you."

"You pick…" he croaks, going stiff as he tries to understand what she's saying. He's so stunned a strong breeze could blow him over.

The zings of pleasure he's getting from the press of her fingers on his scent glands and her face against his neck aren't helping him think either!

If he compares his brain to an engine, right now it's full of grease, misfiring, and belching black smoke. Despite the poor state of his mental acuity at the moment, he manages one sentence.

"You pick *me*?"

CHAPTER 13

Dalt

Lakin can hear the incredulity in Dalt's voice. This Talin can't imagine anyone would deliberately pick him over other candidates. She'll need to work on making him realize how special he is. He's not broken. His tortured body only means one thing to her–he's a survivor.

Sometimes remaining alive when others have been lost is the hardest kind of surviving.

The way he cared for Sora, and now her, tells her that his torture didn't kill the part of him that wants to love. She only needs to teach him that it's safe.

"Yes, you," she replies.

She reclines on Dalt's lap and breathes in his cedar smell. She wasn't even exaggerating when she told him she spent the entire day thinking about him, or more accurately trying not to think about him and failing.

Even as she tried to come up with basic strategies to suggest to Holian, she kept bringing her finger to her nose to smell

Dalt's cedar scent. She's not even going to mention her relief when she realized the oil had soaked into her skin and continued to smell strongly of Dalt's cedar even after she had to wash her hands.

"I pick you because when I have nightmares, you'll understand," she explains. "When I need quiet and gentleness you gave it to me. You've treated me with more care and respect than I've experienced since becoming an adult. Most importantly, I know that if I have to be bold, you'll be at my side. What more can a girl ask for?"

"I'm not whole," he points out.

She makes a *harumph* sound. "I like you more because of your trauma. Would you like me less if I was missing an eye, ear, or some fingers?"

"Of course not!" he answers.

"Then why would I think less of you? Besides, why would I want someone who doesn't understand. You're the most appealing male I've ever met and I want to keep you."

"The feeling is mutual," he whispers, as if worried that saying it too loud will cause Holian to appear and take her away.

She gives him a half grin. "I'm counting on it. It's been a long time since I allowed myself the luxury of getting close to someone. Knowing that Talins are sex compatible with humans is the golden nugget on the Tavorian pie."

"That's an odd saying," Dalt comments. "Why–"

She cuts off his words by leaning forward and putting her lips on his scent gland, gently kissing him there.

His body jolts like she's shocked him. His oil coats her lips and fills her nose. It's strong and perfect. She turns her face to rub her cheek against his. That last move seems to be his undoing.

Grabbing her head, he holds her still as he rubs first one cheek and then the other in her hair. The rich scent of cedar fills the air as the oil penetrates to her scalp. Even with her much poorer sense of smell, she can tell the scent changes slightly as his bonding oil hits her skin. The cedar smell becomes fuller, richer somehow.

That change makes him groan and clutch at her.

"You're so perfect," he murmurs.

"Not really, but we can pretend," she responds, feeling a little breathless. Her heart is beating hard. Tentatively, she runs her fingers over his chest. "How much can you feel?" she asks as she explores the texture of his chest plates. "Where can I touch you? I want to give you pleasure."

"Pleasure?" he asks with a small moan. "You don't need—"

"Here?" she asks, cutting off his words as she kisses the strip of skin at his neck. Kissing his scent gland was nice because of the oil, but kissing here feels good. That little strip of skin is soft and experimentally she runs her tongue along it. He shivers.

"You make me feel like a youth with no control," he mutters and tries to gently push her away from him. She resists, and he doesn't force the issue.

"An awful lot of little Talin-human babies were running around inside Holian's mansion," she points out. "And considering how you guys have treated me, I guess those babies happened between willing partners. I'd like to know what it was like for those mixed-species couples." She sits back and gives him a wide grin. "For research purposes."

"I want you more than is safe," he warns her, his tone gruff. She's gotten to know him well in a short time and recognizes fear when she sees it. Cupping his face in her hands, she brings her lips to his.

"Good, because I like you too," she whispers and then kisses him.

He doesn't open his lips to her, so she licks across the seam. He gives a little gasp and opens to her, letting her pull his thin lower lip into her mouth and suck on it. His hands tighten, convulsing on her, and a deep rumble of lust bubbles out of him.

She could get addicted to those rumbles! His whole chest vibrates slightly and that, along with the taste of him on her mouth and the smell of cedar in her nose, has her more turned on than ever before.

"I want to see you naked," she demands boldly. Without missing a beat, he stands up, holding her to his chest. With just a few strides, they're inside the cabin and at his bed. With his familiar gentleness, he's laying her down on his pallet. It's not as soft as the one in her enclosure, but that doesn't matter right now. What matters is that he's standing over her and practically ripping off his ornamental belt and pants, but she can't see anything inside the dark cabin.

"Lights?" she asks. As if responding to her question, the whole cabin lights up, making her squeeze her eyes shut at the sudden brilliance.

"Light dim to ten percent," Dalt barks out and Lakin slits one eye open. The lower setting fills the cabin with soft amber illumination, allowing her to see all of Dalt without disrupting her romantic mood.

"Perfect," she breathes and opens both eyes wide to take him in.

He stands tall and proud, letting her scrutinize him. He has no scars or bits missing below the waist. His muscled body tapers to narrow hips and, below them, powerful legs. When her gaze finally rests on what's between his legs, she sits up on her knees and reaches out.

Unlike humans, he doesn't have a penis dangling down. Instead, he seems to have some kind of pouch, and as she watches it, the tip of his sex emerges.

"Our mating shafts stay tucked away unless needed," Dalt explains, remaining still as she skims her fingers along the tip of his "mating shaft." The skin there is silky and soft, just like the strip of exposed skin on his neck. But it's also hard and rapidly emerging from the pouch to point at her with fierce need, just like a human male's would.

Along with his engorged mating shaft, something else emerges from the sack as that bit of skin retreats around the base of his sex. Bringing one hand down, she cups it, rolling it gently in her hand. He makes a strangled sound and then starts a deep rumble that makes her grin. By the sound of it, he likes it when she touches him.

"That's my seed sack," he tells her.

"No further explanation needed," she assures him quickly as she explores him with her fingers. "I think I get the idea."

When his legs quiver, she glances up at his face. He rumbles with need. "Your touch is sweet torture," he tells her.

Sitting back on her heels, she undoes the tie to her wrap and pulls it off her body. "Come over here," she orders. Eagerly, he drops to his knees and crawls onto the pallet. "Are you familiar with human anatomy?"

"Very familiar," he grunts as he urges her onto her back. She lets him push her down, expecting him to settle between her legs and spear into her. She's turned on enough that even with his large size, it shouldn't be too uncomfortable, and then she can demand her satisfaction after.

But he doesn't do that. He parts her legs but then explores her sex with his fingers, keeping up his deep rumble of desire the entire time.

"You're so soft everywhere," he comments, his voice full of awe. "When I first moved here, I read everything published about human care. I watched many vids on human grooming, social interaction, and facial expressions. I even watched mating vids just in case a human picked me to be more than a caregiver."

"Did you get to practice on Sora?" Lakin asks, feeling a spike of jealousy go through her. Dalt's passionate rumble turns soothing as his rusty purr starts up.

"She was never interested in me in the way you are, little warrior. And even if she was, she would never be so bold as you. Your body might be human and soft to the touch, but your will is made of something we might use to construct ships."

"I've never been compared to a ship before," she says with a little chuckle. "How romantic."

"Romantic?" he repeats, testing the human word. It sounds guttural and strange when pronounced with a Talin accent. "There's no translation for this word."

"Romantic is when couples do things for each other to show love and affection. Or sometimes just trying to put the other person in the mood to mate," she explains.

"I can do that," he responds and runs one blunt finger along her sex, parting the folds there and sinking into the warm, pink skin underneath. She gives a little gasp as his fingers explore, finally settling on her clit. "I also watched vids of humans mating with each other. They were very informative," he explains, rubbing a broad fingertip repeatedly over that sensitive nub of flesh.

"We call that porn," she mutters and then gasps. "But I'm not complaining." Her hips jerk as he touches her. He leans over and flicks his tongue over her right nipple. His tongue has a bit of a rough texture that sends sensations bolting through her. "More!" she demands, and he does it again. Then he alternates, lavishing attention to both her nipples.

Between his tongue and his fingers, she rapidly approaches her climax. Her breathing turns ragged as her hips buck. Then he pulls her nipple and a good deal of her breast into the warm cavern of his mouth. He bites down gently while his tongue strokes her. He slips a finger inside of her with one hand and keeps the insistent pressure on her clit with the other.

She cries out as she orgasms, twitching and jerking under him. His rumbling gets louder, and suddenly he pulls his mouth and hands away. Grabbing her thighs, he wedges his hips between them and eases the tip of his engorged shaft into her. Still feeling the effects of her powerful climax, she wraps her legs around his waist and urges him down, eager to feel his hard length inside of her.

"No rushing," he grunts out, his breath sawing harshly in and out of his lungs.

"Now!" she demands and pulls herself onto him because there's no way she can pull him down to her. She gets him half buried inside of her, and although he's big, he feels good. "Oh! Like that."

His rumbles turn frantic, and he jerks a little. She realizes he's trying to keep the pace slow to be gentle. He's afraid of hurting her. "More," she pleads and reaches up with a hand to run her palm over the scent gland on his right cheek. Oil covers her fingers and she rubs it on her chest, covering more of her body in his scent.

That's his undoing. With a loud rumble that vibrates so strongly she feels it in her chest, he plunges into her, making both of them gasp.

"This feels like nothing I've known," he says and starts a pumping rhythm that Lakin fully approves of.

The sound he makes deep in his chest has an added benefit she never considered. As he rumbles loudly, it vibrates through her body, but she feels it the most between her legs. That little bundle of nerves that sits just north of her stretched opening is eager and ready to perform again. Before long she's moving too, trying to meet his thrusts to get more of that delicious sensation from the rumbling.

"So close," she says, eyes half closed and body tense. "Keep doing all of it."

He doesn't answer but does as she asked, and soon she's cresting again as she cries out and convulses under him. No sooner is her orgasm sweeping through her than he shouts a hoarse exclamation of pleasure and thrusts one last time. Then he goes stock still, emptying himself into her.

They stay like that, quivering with the aftereffects of their pleasure until the sweat dries on Lakin's skin, causing her to shiver. Dalt withdraws from her body and lies next to her, drawing her tightly against him and covering them both with a thick blanket.

With a happy sigh, she snuggles into him. She never thought she'd feel so content in the arms of a male, stuck planetside with limited agency. Yet here she is, not even trying to get access to an interstellar comms anymore.

Life is a curious path.

CHAPTER 14

Lakin

Lakin wakes to find Dalt gone. Blearily, she sits up looks around. Predawn light shines through one of the small windows of the house making her think it must be close to first mark.

Now that she understands Talin timekeeping, it's easy to figure out what everyone's talking about when they refer to marks and strikes. A day is made up of marks and a night is made up of strikes. Days stretch from first mark at sunrise until thirteenth mark, and nighttime starts with first strike at sunset until the end of the thirteenth strike when the sun rises and first mark starts.

 Marks and strikes are composed of submarks and micromarks. Because each colony might have longer or shorter days than the Talin homeworld, the amount of submarks that make up a mark or strike change to accommodate the individual colonies.

It took her a little while, but she finally figured out that strikes and marks are roughly forty-five Earth minutes here on Kalor. The marks and strikes are probably longer on the Talin homeworld because it's bigger with a longer daily rotation than Kalor, according to Maddy.

Humans like Lakin might not have grown up on Earth—heck no human has been on Earth for many generations—but they still use the same timekeeping equivalents among themselves. Consequently, Lakin always compares other species' timekeeping with old Earth.

She should tell Maddy about that. It'll make the woman laugh. She might not have ever heard the words days, hours, or minutes. It would be interesting to learn more about human culture among the Talin, where humans are so separated from their history.

But first things first, she needs to get up and start her day.

There's still no sign of Dalt in the one-room cabin, so she throws aside the covers and looks around the pallet for her wrap. It's nowhere to be seen, but she finds a brand-new wrap folded and waiting for her next to the bed. It's a cheerful, red color instead of the deep eggplant purple ones that most of the humans in Holian's compound wear. She wonders if Dalt bought it for Sora.

It doesn't matter. Lakin's never been one to waste time on things so petty as jealousy. Sora's not here; Lakin is. That's the end of it.

She slips into the wrap and ties it at each hip before running her fingers through her tangled hair. The scent of cedar fills her nose, making her smile. Her hair is almost dripping in Dalt's marking oil, and the rest of her body isn't much cleaner. She could use a shower.

Braiding her hair to keep it out of her way, she meanders to the door and pulls the heavy mass of wood and metal open with a grunt. Outside, she finds Dalt crouched over a small fire, roasting something on a short pole.

He looks up at her, and his rusty, rumbling purr fills the quiet space between them.

"Whatcha doing?" she asks, making her way to where he's crouched. He's placed several cushions around the small fire, and she plops down on the one closest to him. He snakes out an arm and pulls her against his side, rubbing his cheek on the top of her head briefly before turning his attention to whatever he's roasting.

"Cooking diemas for you," he grunts. "It's a fruit you humans like. But it needs to be cooked just right or the flavor is ruined. This is the best way to do it."

"How long have you been up?" she asks, absently stroking his face. His purr stutters a bit but resumes a little louder.

"Since twelfth strike," he tells her. "You need double the sleep I do, so after I was rested, I decided to make you a fine meal." He nods to a nearby plate. "There's flatbread to begin with if you're ready to eat."

Her stomach rumbling, Lakin reaches for several slices of the black flatbread Talins eat with every meal. The stuff isn't her favorite, but it's hearty and filling so she can't complain. Tearing a slice in half, she shoves one piece into her mouth and holds the other half up to Dalt's lips. He takes the food by sucking her fingertips into his mouth before releasing her digits with a little popping sound that makes her giggle.

They sit there in silence for a while, him carefully roasting the diemas and her feeding him bread. Lakin has rarely experienced such quiet, tranquil moments. She's not sure she's ever spent time with a male doing something so mundane as feeding each other.

"What's on the agenda today?" she asks, breaking the silence after the flatbread is all eaten.

"We need to be at the compound before everyone panics because you're missing," he tells her.

Thoughtfully, she taps at her collar. "I don't suppose we could take this thing off for now? I mean, it's not like I'm going to run away or anything."

"No," Dalt tells her firmly. "The collar has trackers so if you're stolen or get lost, we can more easily find you."

"They'll always be able to find me," Lakin mutters. "As long as this thing's locked around my neck, I can't really escape."

"Truth," he agreed. "If I don't get you back, they'd eventually track you down here. But they'd panic until they had eyes on you again." He goes silent for a moment, then grunts. "You like to wander too much. The collar needs to stay on."

"I just don't like the fact that I can't take it off," Lakin confesses, tugging at it a little. Dalt's purr stops, and a rumble of confusion sounds from his chest.

"You can't?" he questions. "You should be able to. After Sora hurt herself to get her collar off, Holian made sure all the humans can take their collars off themselves. It's a good idea because they can get caught on something and hurt your fragile necks. Only Holian, Eranan, and the human wearing the collar can unlock it."

"What?" Lakin yelps out, the shock making her go rigid.

"Put your thumbs on either side of the locking mechanism," Dalt instructs her. "Make sure they're both flush to the metal."

It's a little awkward, but she gets her thumbs in the right place and after pressing down for several moments, a chime sounds and the collar clicks open.

"I'm an idiot," she mutters to herself as she stares down at the collar in her hands. It never occurred to her that she could unlock her own damn collar. Then again, no one bothered to explain to her that she could unlock it either.

"You're a pet but not a slave," Dalt comments. "And your status as a pet here on Kalor gives you more freedom than humans have just about anywhere else in the Talin Empire. But don't let anyone who's not from here know you can take it off yourself. It could cause problems."

The warning is unnecessary. After seeing what was hidden inside the mansion, she's well aware of how easily she could put everyone, including herself, in danger by saying something to the wrong Talins.

No one here has mistreated her, but the simple act of being able to take her collar off is monumentally important to her.

Without hesitation she snaps the collar back on and grins up at Dalt. And just like that, it's no longer a symbol of oppression. Now it's a prop and a tool.

"Are those diemas ready yet? It looks like we're getting close to second mark, and Eranan will check the enclosures soon."

She's not looking forward to the repercussions of their discovering she's missing, but she's confident she can be persuasive enough to convince Holian to let her stay with Dalt from now on. After all, Talins tortured her, and that's got to be good for at least one guilt trip with the commandant.

They're near the edge of the forest, almost to Holian's compound, when the first loud boom sounds. Lakin's still processing what she heard when Dalt snatches her up off the ground and runs full tilt down a side path, parallel to the compound.

Clutching at him, she watches a plume of smoke rise over the tree line in the direction of the mansion. Then another boom goes off, making the trees around them shake as the sounds of discharging weapons fill the air.

The compound is under attack, but instead of running to help, Dalt is dragging her off into the forest. Images of all the noncombatants in the house makes her beat her fist against his chest.

"Dalt, we can't—"

The sound of something big and mechanical fills her ears and Dalt dives to the side. He pulls the two of them deep into a thick bush and puts a cautionary hand against her mouth. She doesn't need his warning; she knows better than to make a sound as an all-terrain armored transport rips a path through the forest right in front of them.

Its massive treads gouge out the Earth as large guns mounted to the top of the huge vehicle continuously fire toward the mansion. The compound is returning fire, but none of it seems to affect the transport.

Who's attacking Holian? It can't be the Talin military. No way would they just attack the highly decorated and respected Commandant Holian. This has to be a group of Traditionalists attacking what they see as a vulnerable seat of Reformist power.

Neither of them has any weapons, but Lakin knows if she can just get on board the transport, she can sabotage it. She's got a gift for breaking things. Before she can suggest that Dalt help her onto the war machine, a group of Talins appear. They're all dressed in mismatching outfits and a hodgepodge of gear. The way they're outfitted would be evidence enough that they're not military, but their movements confirm it.

Instead of being organized and in tune with each other as a well-trained group of soldiers would be, these guys almost bump into one another in their haste to get to the transport. It would be laughable if several of them weren't dragging an unconscious Holian between them. Blood is running down his chest and soaking into his pants, but Lakin can't see where the wound is.

The men hurry to the transport as a hatch opens. More men on the inside grab Holian and haul him in. The rest of the Talins file in until everyone's inside, and then it makes a wide, ungainly turn, and starts back the way it came.

Everyone at the mansion must realize Holian's been captured because all return fire ceases and no one tries to stop the transport. The Traditionalists must have come to kidnap Holian.

"We can't let them leave with him," Lakin whispers to Dalt.

"There must be a ship waiting for them," Dalt tells her. "The only place a ship could land outside the port is in the dry lakebed near here. I'll follow and see if I can get on board. You need to go to the mansion and tell everyone what you saw."

"Nope," Lakin says evenly. "Not going to happen. They already know what's going on. That's why they aren't firing on the transport. My intel won't help, and my place is in the thick of things. You're stuck with me, Dalt."

His rumble turns to a growl, and he gives her his full attention. "This is too dangerous," he insists.

She grins despite the dire circumstances. "I know. It's perfect."

She slides out of his grip and sprints off before he realizes what she's doing.

There's no way she can stay ahead of him, so she doesn't even try. When he snatches her up and keeps running after the transport, she giggles. He's grumbling about stupid females and delicate humans, but he's not trying to make her leave.

Under it all, she knows he's desperately worried about the commandant. Otherwise he'd be carrying her away instead of toward danger.

They catch up to the slow-moving transport in no time, and Dalt puts her down so they can watch it behind the cover of convenient greenery.

"What's that hatch right there?" Lakin asks, pointing to the belly of the transport just behind the tread on the left side.

"It's to load ammunition into the reservoir chamber," Dalt tells her.

"Is the reservoir chamber sealed? If I climb up the shaft, will I be able to get out the other side?"

Dalt's angry rumble tells her he doesn't like that plan at all. "No."

"No, I wouldn't be able to get out? Or no, you're not going to let me try?" she asks.

"The reservoir chamber has an access door to the gun room," Dalt tells her grudgingly as they move to another spot to follow the transport's progress. "But you're not climbing up that thing. You wouldn't fit anyway."

"You wouldn't fit," she counters. "But I'll fit perfectly. Trust me. Humans are some of the smallest sentient species in the universe. That means I've been the one crawling through the tightest areas of ships since I started working. I'm a good judge of where I can fit. As long as it doesn't get any tighter than that opening, I know I can squeeze through."

"Lakin," Dalt starts, but she cuts him off.

"You need to let me do this," she tells him. "Would you listen to me if I told you going after the transport was too dangerous and you should go back to the manor and hide?"

Dalt's angry rumble is a clear indication of what he thinks regarding that idea. "But you're a fragile human."

"And you're a useless soldier with no claws or quills," Lakin fires back, regretting the words the moment they're out of her mouth. Dalt pulls away from her slightly, as if her words were a physical blow.

"I didn't mean that like it sounds," she tells him quickly, grabbing his arm and pulling him back toward her. "I only meant that appearances are deceiving. I might be small and fragile compared to you, but it doesn't take much strength to damage delicate electronics. Think about voldi bugs. Those things are the size of my pinky nail, but once they're on a ship, you might as well scuttle the whole thing because they're destructive and impossible to get rid of."

"Did you just compare humans to an invasive insect?" Dalt asks with an amused rumble.

"Maybe," Lakin says with a grin. "But you know I'm right. You know my enclosure gate doesn't just stop working. I'm making that happen and none of you superior Talins can seem to figure out how I'm doing it."

"Larger and stronger, not superior," Dalt corrects her.

"Thanks, big guy," she says, realizing she might be winning this argument. "If you don't let me try to help here, I'll just figure out a way off this planet and get myself into trouble trying to help in some other way. At least this way you can keep an eye on me."

"You'd do it," Dalt mutters. "Somehow you'd leave Kalor despite all the protocols in place." He eyes the transport. "What do you plan to do once you get on board?"

"They must be heading to a ship," she says, and Dalt makes a sound of agreement. "If I can't stop the transport, I'll just sabotage the ship. They're easy to break. It only takes a few disruptions to ground a ship. I might not know military transports like that one, but I know ships."

Dalt makes a discontent rumble. "I still don't like it."

Lakin knows she's won. "That means I'm probably going to have fun," she counters.

CHAPTER 15

Dalt

Dalt doesn't like this idea at all. He should say no. He should grab her and carry her to his secret hidden second home buried in the base of a nearby mountain. He should bar the door, chain her to him, and shelter in place until everyone else figures out how to clear this up.

But they have Holian.

He goes still as Lakin grabs his face with both her hands, pressing her fingers against his scent glands and rubbing them gently. He wishes he never told her how good that feels. It's as if she has a magic button to press on him that makes thinking difficult.

"I need to get on that transport, and you need to help me," she tells him, her large earnest eyes demanding he understand. "On old Earth, there was a piece of text from an ancient religion that always bounces around in my head at times like this. *If not now, then when? If not me, then who?* Do you understand Dalt?"

Reluctantly, he sounds an affirmative rumble. He understands, but he wars with himself. Protect Lakin or let her fulfill her basic nature as a warrior?

He regards his clever, resourceful human and lets her words sink in. The Talin have ancestral writings with a saying that strikes a similar chord as Lakin's saying: *Refusing to act is a form of action.*

Not helping Holian is the equivalent of aiding the enemy.

"What if you die and I don't?" There it is. Everything Dalt fears most. Surviving when others are lost. She's silent for a moment, as if weighing her words. He trusts she won't say something simply to placate him. That's not Lakin's way. Not now that she knows and trusts him.

"Well, I'll try hard not to get killed," Lakin says with a soft smile. "But there are no guarantees, Dalt. You're a soldier. You know this. It's not in me to stand off to the side when I know I'm capable of helping. Get me on board that transport, and I'll promise you two things. I promise to do my best to stay hidden. I'm a sneak and saboteur, not a fighter. I know my strengths, and I try hard not to step outside of them."

That makes Dalt grunt in acknowledgment. She is very good at hiding. If he hadn't watched her climb onto the cabinet, he never would've thought to look there for her. Even with her smell in the room, it just wasn't a place he thought a human could fit.

"What's the other promise?" he asks as he picks her up and trails after the transport. They're getting close to the dry lakebed, and he can just see a ship sitting there, engines on and hot enough to make the air around them shimmer.

"The second promise I can make is that no matter what happens, if I get out of this alive, I'll find you. I've spent my life looking for a partner like you. I'm not giving you up if I can help it."

It's a strange feeling for Dalt to have another want him above all others. Lakin is well-traveled and experienced. She must've interacted with males of many species, including other humans. Yet here she is, practically pledging herself to him.

He knows humans are emotional creatures, quick to fall into a dependent, impassioned state they refer to as "love." But Lakin doesn't act anything like most of the humans he's interacted with. She's calm, calculating, and shrewd, unlikely to give in to emotions in a time of stress.

She thinks like a Talin.

If she's saying she'll come back to him, that can only mean one thing.

"You've scent-bonded with me." Hope and desperation make his voice almost inaudible.

"Sure," she agrees with a careless grin, her eyes never leaving the transport. "If scent-bonded means I love you, that is. Now, can we focus, Dalt? We can get all gushy and heartfelt later. First, we need to get me on that transport."

Transport. Traditionalist. Holian.

He shakes his head a little to clear out all the feelings welling up in him. If his Lakin wants on that transport so she can join the Talins in what's rapidly turning into a civil war, he's going to make that happen. He sets her down and points a finger at the ground. "Stay," he orders and sprints off.

Many small guns are mounted to the underside and lower sections of the transport, but he can tell they aren't active at the moment. Either the operators don't have the ammunition for them or, more likely, none of the Talins inside know how to use them. He's not worried about being seen. Even if they've figured out how to use the image captures mounted next to the guns, they'll assume he can't do anything to hurt them.

Under normal circumstances that would be true, but there's no way they'll see his brilliant human coming.

It takes three tries before he gets a good hold on the moving treads and launches himself up high enough to grab onto the munitions loading door. The door is reinforced, but this is an old transport, and he can see worn spots all over it where it hasn't been properly maintained. He tugs at the door and finds one side of it is weakened. With sheer brute strength, he bends one corner.

Fishing his harvesting tool out of his belt pouch, he wedges it in the corner and starts sawing. The tool isn't meant for this kind of use, and he ends up breaking it off but not before he's able to saw around two sides. The hatch sags. He grabs it with both hands and lunges, bringing his weight and momentum against it.

The door rips off, throwing him to the ground. Now an open hatch is staring down at him. No sooner is he back on his feet than Lakin comes running.

She doesn't waste time with words, just shimmies up his body and reaches up as he keeps pace with the moving vehicle. She's still not high enough, so he takes a running step, launching her at the open hatch so she catches the inside lip with her fingers. He lands on the ground and walks under her, watching as she struggles for a moment and then gets purchase. Faster than he ever expected, she wiggles herself up and disappears into the hatch.

Is that it?

Before he can figure out what to do next, her head reappears. How did she turn herself around in such a tight space?

"Throw that to me," she orders and points to the broken tip of the harvesting tool lying discarded in a track behind the ground transport. Running back, he snatches it up and sprints back to the transport. Tossing it to her, he watches with relief as she manages to catch it without cutting her delicate little fingers.

"Great!" she calls out. "Time to break this thing." And then she disappears.

The transport doesn't stop moving. Dalt follows it to the dry lake bed, keeping himself hidden from the men he hears tramping through the forest. He catches a glimpse of them here and there, but they're much too skilled to get caught out in the open. All these men are his fellow ex-soldiers, loyal to Holian but unable to do anything for fear of hurting their commandant.

Unlike the males operating the transport, the ones on the ship know what they're doing. A few soldiers overtake the slow transport and attack the ship, but it lays down suppressing fire. Large bombardments fire from the mansion, but the ship is too well-shielded for any of them to do damage.

When the transport hits the tree line at the edge of the dry lake, Dalt starts to panic. He expected Lakin to disable it by now, but it's apparent that's not going to happen in time. He's not letting her get on that ship without him.

He's calculating the best way to approach the ship when someone drops down to crouch next to him. He looks over to find Palforma looking at him expectantly, holding out a bag full of weapons. Wordlessly, he takes the bag and opens it. He dons the weapons vest and shoves the pockets and holsters full of extra munitions and weapons.

Nudging him, Palforma points to the transport and sounds a questioning rumble.

"They'll have to turn off all the ship's automated fire to allow loading," Dalt says, and Palforma nods because with that one sentence they have a plan.

It takes the transport an eternity to crawl its way under the ship. Massive doors open and an automated system reaches down to latch on to the top of the transport. Palforma and Dalt exchange one quick look and then sprint for the ship.

No sooner do they break cover than men hidden along the tree line open fire on the ship. The automated system can't be used, but several smaller guns come online. The way they're firing tells Dalt they're being operated by men who are about as skilled as the men on the transport–poorly!

The other soldiers in the woods draw the attention of gunners on the ship away, so the two of them can make it under the transport without being noticed.

Both men grab onto the treads of the rapidly rising transport and haul themselves up. It takes some maneuvering, but they squeeze their bulk between tread wheels. They're effectively hidden but dead if the transport moves even a handsbreadth forward.

For the first time, Dalt's lack of backplates is a boon because he can hear Palforma panting in pain as his backplates get caught on the gears around them and are twisted uncomfortably. They stay like that, motionless and silent as the transport is pulled into the ship. The weapons fire cuts off the moment the doors start to close. He hears a loud shout from the forest but can't make out the words. Then the voices of the ex-soldiers start shouting together.

They're chanting.

They're chanting the warriors' code. Their ancestors sang it before battle or after the fighting's over when they gathered to mourn dead comrades.

The men in the forest are telling him and Palforma they know the two men are on the ship and wishing them good fortune in battle.

It makes Dalt proud. If they knew Lakin was on board, they'd sing it for her as well.

All sounds from the outside cut off as the door hisses closed. The ship rumbles around them, and he can hear an automated system warning everyone about imminent launch. They can hear men on the ship calling out as the rear door to the transport drops open.

He can't see much from where he's hidden, but he can hear Holian. The commandant's awake and calmly addressing his captors. He doesn't even get a full sentence out before Dalt hears a blow and then stumbling. Holian goes silent, and the men rattle mockingly.

Something creaks, and he wiggles his head until he can see Palforma. The man's eyes are closed, and he's holding a bit of metal so tightly it's bending slightly under his grip. He watches Palforma fight to keep a hold on his rage and is proud when the soldier finally opens his eyes and lets go of the bit of twisted metal.

They wait as everyone clears the bay. Even after the bay is silent, they continue to wait, both of them knowing the danger of revealing themselves too soon. The ship shakes around them as it launches. Holian doesn't have any space support for his colony. He invested in a strong ground defense but never considered he'd be attacked by something as massive as an orbiting ship equipped with armored ground transport.

The men who attacked are all amateurs, but someone fed them information on Holian and the Kalor Colony. Otherwise they would have had no chance of succeeding. These men are also well-funded and connected because, while the equipment might be old, it's high military grade. It should never have found its way into civilian hands. When he gets back, he's going to hunt down the traitors and personally execute them.

After it's apparent no one is in the room and no one's coming back right away, both Dalt and Palforma begin the arduous task of freeing themselves from the treads. Dalt does it without injury, but Palforma's bleeding from several partially ripped backplates. Dalt tries to turn Palforma so he can assess the damage, but the other man waves him off and silently indicates the door. Dalt shakes his head. He needs to find Lakin first.

He hurries onto the transport, finding the reservoir room easily enough. It's empty, and he panics a little until he spies a second hole in the room and pulls the flimsy grate off. He can see fresh scratch marks where the grate was loosened, probably with the end of his broken harvesting tool. He looks up the narrow conduit but doesn't see Lakin.

Hurrying through the rest of the transport and trying to figure out where the conduit leads, he finds himself on top of the vehicle staring up into the ceiling of the bay at yet another narrow hatch. Dalt knows Lakin's already inside it, making her way through the ascending ship.

He doesn't know how many men are on board the ship or where they are, and he doesn't know where they're keeping Holian. Without that information, searching the ship blindly has the potential of getting the two of them killed quickly.

Sniffing the surrounding air, Palforma points to the tiny opening in the ceiling. "Lakin?"

"Yes," Dalt says with a sigh. There's no help for it. He and Palforma need to stay put so Lakin can carry out her sabotage plans. When things start failing on the ship, he and Palforma can begin taking men down. With the crew's poor discipline, he knows chaos will ensue the moment the ship malfunctions, giving the two experienced soldiers an immense advantage.

"Lakin's going to do something to the ship," he explains to Palforma as he searches the transport for anything useful. "When she does, we'll go look for her and the commandant."

"Backup?"

"I don't know," Dalt says. "Potentially Prime Son Searin could command the military to come to our aid, but that hinges on Kalor getting in contact with the homeworld. I'm guessing the Traditionalists disabled Kalor's interstellar comms before landing. It's going to be a while before anyone even finds out we've been attacked."

"We take ship," Palforma says with confidence. Dalt can't help the sharp laugh that rumbles out of him. Palforma says it casually, as if proposing they walk the forest together. But then again, Palforma hasn't been quite right since he took that round to the head.

"We take ship," Palforma repeats stubbornly. He points to Dalt and then himself. "Soldiers. Skilled. Honorable." He gestures to the walls around them. "Stupid craven civilians." Then he rumbles a pleased sound and points up. "Lakin, little human with bold plans. And nimble fingers." He's silent for a moment but then continues. "I saw her. I watched her. Break the lock and go to you. Pry open the biolock pad. Poke, poke. Beep, beep and the door opens. No smell of burning circuits. No sound of ripping. Just beep, beep and she's free. Put cover back on and nothing shows. But gate doesn't lock anymore."

It doesn't surprise Dalt that Palforma witnessed Lakin breaking out. The little human has done it so many times now that at some point, someone was going to see her. But why didn't he snatch her up himself? Take her home and try to make her his human? Or at least steal her away for a few marks.

"And you didn't stop her?"

"Not mine," Palforma says with a dismissive rumble. "Like Sora, she picked. Sora picked twice but didn't pick you second time. Lakin only picks once. Picks you." He points up to the ceiling again and gives a soft, satisfied rumble. "She's like us. Like soldiers."

"Yes," Dalt agrees. He knows Palforma doesn't mean that she's big and strong. He means that she's got the spirit of a warrior. "Just like us."

They fall into silence for a few moments, but then Palforma talks. He's absently loading and unloading the weapon in his hand as he speaks, refusing to meet Dalt's eyes.

"No blame. Never any blame. All choices bad. All die or some die. All die or some hurt and some live." It takes a moment for Dalt to realize Palforma's talking about their last assignment, where he surrendered and ended up getting most of the company and civilians tortured and killed. How can this man not blame him? But before he can object, Palforma starts talking again.

"Not all right." He taps his head. "Never going to be right. Not too bad. But not right. Not your fault. Battle. Orders. Choices. Never easy. But we're alive. Breathing. Eating. Fucking. I take that. Take that over death. You made it so I live." A slight rattle of frustration. Palforma might be annoyed at his halting speech, but Dalt's impressed. This is the most he'd heard Palforma say since he was shot in the head.

"Words hard. But should've tried earlier. No blame. No shame. Iansif, Tisuran, Narmolo, no blame. No shame either. You made choices. We lived. Others died. Someone had to make the choices."

"What if I could've made a better choice?" Dalt asks. A rude sound issues from Palforma's chest.

"Stupid question. Leave it. Bury it." He points up to where Lakin might even now be causing some kind of damage. "She picked you. You pick her back. Can't dig up old and think to start new. Time for new steps. New beginnings."

Before Dalt can ask what he means by that, a warning klaxon sounds and the lights around them flicker.

That's their cue. Time to find Lakin and Holian.

CHAPTER 16

Lakin

Lakin watches with intense satisfaction as men scramble to figure out why the engine started an emergency shutdown. It took her a lot longer than she'd like to figure out where the engine room was. Several conduits were much too small for even her lithe body to get through, so she was forced to find crawl spaces between walls and floors. It was much dirtier and tighter work, full of piping, optic cables, and life-support tubes to wiggle around.

Once she finally got to the starboard engine, she almost giggled with delight. The control room relays were right there in the wall she dropped into. She didn't even need to get out of her hiding space.

Pulling out the long, thin metal needle tool she stole from Dalt's pouch when he was having his flashback, she pokes around. She's used the tool enough times now to mess with the enclosure gates that it's a familiar weight in her hand. Figuring out what cable, wire, switch, and transponder doesn't take long. Once she's confident in her knowledge, she triggers the one that tells the engine it's overheating and needs to shut down. The entire ship goes down for a moment but then emergency lighting comes back on.

Alarms sound through the ship, and she hears men run into the room, all shouting at each other and sounding panicked rattles. She can't make out much of what they're saying over the sound of the noise their backplates are making.

Then they start arguing with each other. Even better!

Any noise she might make is covered by the men in the next room deciding it's a better idea to be aggressive with each other than figure out what's wrong with their ship.

The next thing she needs to do is find Holian and figure out a place where they can hole up until the cavalry arrives. She wishes Dalt made it onto the ship with her. With him there she could come up with a plan to take the ship. But she knows better than to wish for things that aren't available. She has to work with what's on hand, and for right now, that's just her.

She catches a break when she clearly hears the men argue about moving Holian. One man wants to take him to the bridge.

"Having him on the bridge will only complicate things," the other man says. "Leave him in the storage locker. It's secured from the outside, and we can flush the entire room if we have to get rid of him."

That makes her blood run cold. She needs to get to Holian before any of these aspiring anarchists decide he's too dangerous to keep alive. She listens carefully but doesn't get any more clues from the two men.

When they move off, she makes her way back to an empty room so she can climb out of the wall. She taps on a small display near a closed door. After a little while, she pulls up a rough map of the ship. It's meant to show paths for emergency evacuation, but she's able to use it to figure out where various storage lockers are. She has no way of knowing which one has Holian in it, so she'll start with the closest one and move out from there.

She's able to use the crawl space between the walls to access the first room, but it's empty of everything except food dispenser refill packets. She's not surprised. Finding Holian on the first attempt would go against all the trouble the universe likes to throw in her path.

She makes it halfway to the next storage locker before she's forced out of her wall. Thankfully, this section of the ship is relatively quiet, so she ducks from room to room until she gets to the locker.

She takes it as a good sign when the door is locked and the biolock doesn't want to let her in. Using the tip of the broken sawing tool Dalt threw her, she gets the faceplate off and then starts manipulating with her needle tool. Because she's had so much practice recently, she gets it open in record time.

Inside are two Talins, but neither of them is Holian, and both are shocked to see her.

"Human?" one almost shouts out before she can shush them. One is female, and she's been in a fight. Her pants are ripped, she has a little blood on her face, and she's cradling her right arm with her left. The male looks a little dirty on one side, like he fell on the floor, but other than that, he doesn't have a mark on him. Both are wearing the same color and style of pants and have matching emblems dangling from their belts.

Sounds from down the hall spur her into action. She grabs the female and pulls her forward a little, pointing to a room two doors down. "Get in that room and keep quiet," she whispers.

The female sounds a rumble of confusion and tries to grab her back, but she's moving slowly, probably from pain. It's easy for Lakin to avoid her reach.

"We need to get you to safety," she insists, reaching for Lakin again. "They'll kill you if they find you."

"Don't I know it," Lakin replies cheerfully, making the female Talin rumble in shock. "Trust me. I know what I'm doing. Go. I'll be right there once I put the faceplate back on the biolock. I don't want anyone walking by to notice it's been tampered with," Lakin explains, giving the woman a little push. Lakin's words makes the male look at the biolock and rumble in confusion.

"How…" he begins, but the female grabs him. The sight of the biolock so expertly broken into must convince the female that Lakin knows what she's doing.

"Let the human work," she says. "We need to move."

The male grumbles but lets himself be pulled down the hall.

Lakin turns her attention to the biolock. She closes the door to the storage locker and then shorts it so the door can't be reopened without replacing the whole biolock pad. Or forcing the door with a hydraulic tool. Either way, once the pad's back in place, it'll just look like it's malfunctioning, not tampered with. Perfect.

She hurries down the hall and ducks into the room just as several men rush around a corner. For a moment she's worried she tripped an alarm, but they keep rushing past the storage locker and down another hall.

Breathing a sigh of relief, she turns to face the two Talins. Judging by the empty tool belt around the woman's waist, Lakin makes an educated guess.

"Is this your ship?"

"Yes," the woman says adamantly.

"No," the man says at the same time.

"Right, well, that clears everything up," Lakin says with sarcasm.

"Human, what are you doing here?" the male asks. "We didn't have any pets on board before those men took over the ship. Are you a prisoner also?"

"I'm the rescue," Lakin states confidently, knowing that probably won't go over well with either of her new buddies.

"Impossible," the male hisses.

"We're going to die," the woman says with no inflection to her voice. Lakin can appreciate her candor if not the sentiment.

"Answer for answers," Lakin says. "What's this ship, and who are you guys?"

"This is an obsolete Class Sigma warship," the woman answers promptly. "We're the skeleton crew assigned to get it to Rekam station for resale as part of a contract we have with that station. This is the first and only ship I've ever served on." A sad little rumble comes out of her chest, and now Lakin understands why the woman said the ship was hers.

"We were almost there when we got a distress call from a Talin ship," the male explains. "When we pulled them into a bay, they had weapons and took over this ship."

"We aren't soldiers," the woman explains. "He's a pilot, and I'm a status three technician. We didn't even have anything to load into the guns on board, and neither of us are cleared to carry personal weapons."

"Huh, they must have brought their own munitions specifically for this ship and the transport. From what I've seen so far, these guys aren't the best tacticians or soldiers, so someone else planned this whole thing, and from the way they're acting, I don't think the planner is here with them. That'll make it easier."

"Make what easier?" the woman asks.

Lakin chuckles evilly. "To mess everything up!"

Jaliean, the grade three ship technician who's served on the ship her entire career, knows every nook and cranny of the ship, unlike Belbian the pilot.

She knows the ship so well that getting to Holian ends up being anticlimactic. Instead of sneaking between walls or ducking from door to door, Jaliean walks them to what looks like an access hatch. It opens to reveal a panel of display screens. She taps on the one in the middle, waits, taps it again, and then a hole in the floor opens behind them.

"Huh," Lakin murmurs. "You're useful."

"Usually," Jaliean agrees, eyeing the pilot crowding in next to her. "Unlike others."

"Oh, that was snarky," Lakin says. "I didn't know Talins could be snarky. I think you're my new best friend."

Belbian rumbles unhappily but only asks, "Where does this go?"

Jaliean closes the access hatch to the displays and leads them down a short flight of steps. "This is an auxiliary systems maintenance shaft," she explains as she taps a display at the bottom of the stairs to close the hole in the floor panels above their heads. "If Holian is being held in one of the storage lockers, like us, this will take us right to him."

Eagerly, Lakin follows Jaliean. "Can you get me access to the electrical network control system?"

"Certainly," Jaliean confirms.

"What about navigation systems? Is there any way we can bypass the bridge and remote pilot the ship?"

"That's much harder to do," Jaliean says with a worried rumble.

"That's fine," Lakin says with a wave of her hand. "First, we get the commandant; then we go from there."

"You're very self-possessed for a human," Jaliean murmurs as they hurry down the tight corridor. Both Talins have to crouch to fit, but Lakin only needs to keep an eye out for any protrusions, otherwise she can walk upright. "You haven't needed to clutch me at all. I met a human once, and she constantly had to clutch to her owner."

"Clutch?"

Jaliean holds out her arms and pretends to wrap them around something. "Clutch. You humans need a lot of reassurance and like to cling to us for it."

"Oh!" Lakin says, understanding the Talin now. "You mean hugging! Right, yeah, I like hugging, but now doesn't seem like a good time to be, uh, clutching anyone."

"That's why I said you're very self-possessed. Much stronger than other humans. You should be very proud of your confidence."

Even though the Talin is trying to compliment her, it's a fight for Lakin to keep from voicing a sarcastic retort.

"I don't think humans are as weak as you guys seem to think," she says diplomatically.

"Have you been bred yet?" Jaliean asks.

Lakin chokes on her next breath. "Bred?" she squeaks.

"You look to be breeding age. Are you bonded to a male or have you visited any studs? My clan has several very nice, handsome males," Jaliean offers. "I'm sure I can arrange with your owner to let you visit us. I'd take excellent care of you. Maybe we could even arrange a sale or a long-term contract. Your offspring would be very strong. My clan isn't as rich as others, but we're well-known for being excellent human keepers."

"Uh, no," Lakin says, deciding to nip this in the bud. "I'm not for sale. I'm not being bred." She wants to add that she's not owned but figures that's too much to get into in a cramped maintenance corridor. "How about we focus on the task at hand?"

"Very well," Jaliean agrees easily. "But tell me if you need to clutch. Or you can turn and cling to me if you can't speak."

"Sure, thanks, Jaliean. I'll keep that in mind," Lakin mumbles. She can hear a low, consistent angry buzz behind her and knows Belbian is irritated by their conversation. The sound he's making with his back plates is too low to draw attention, so she doesn't tell him to stop. But it cements the fact that she needs to monitor this guy. He has no clue how to be sneaky.

"Here," Jaliean announces, stopping and pointing up. "This opens right next to a storage locker. It's the closest locker to the control room."

"Perfect. Open it up and then you guys stay here," Lakin orders, but Belbian rattles in displeasure.

"Unacceptable," he says. "You should stay here, and I'll go up."

"Oh, so now you're ready to fight?" Jaliean asks, cradling her sore arm. Lakin finds it heartwarming that this Talin was ready to carry her despite painful injuries. She might not agree with the Talins about the whole being owned thing, but she likes how adoring many of them can be with humans. It's unique in a universe that cares very little about a powerless species.

"Both of you stay here. If I get caught, I can play dumb. If they get either of you, that'll be harder to explain," Lakin says. Belbian's rattling finally stops, but she can feel ill will pouring out of him. He might be a member of a species that doesn't have facial expressions, but he's sure doing a good job of conveying his dislike toward her.

"We're trusting a human," he mutters. "We're trusting our lives to a creature that destroyed her own homeworld."

Talk about a contrast. On one side is Jaliean who wants to buy her. And well, breed her, which doesn't sound all that great. But still, she seems nice. And then there's Belbian, who's acting as if she should be in the nearest cook pot.

"I didn't ruin Earth," Lakin mutters as she scampers up the steps to the hatch. "My great-great-great-great-great grandparents did it. But that should count in my favor if I'm setting out to ruin this ship."

She holds her two hands apart to show how far she wants Jaliean to open the hatch above them. She doesn't think she spoke loud enough for Jaliean to hear, but before Lakin can wiggle out the partially open hatch, the woman uses her uninjured hand to grab her by the wrist.

"Try not to hurt my ship too badly," she requests with a soft rumbling laugh.

"I'll keep it to a minimum," she promises. She pokes her head out and finds the corridor empty. Moving quickly, she pulls herself out of the floor hatch and starts prying open the biolock display. Now that she's done it a few times, it takes only a few seconds before the storage locker door unlocks.

It's not even fully open before a figure rushes at her. She doesn't have time to cry out before the world around her goes dark.

CHAPTER 17

Lakin

Angry voices fill her ears as Lakin comes to. Her head hurts, but muscular arms are holding and rocking her gently.

"Dalt?"

"She's coming around." It takes Lakin a moment, but then she recognizes that voice. Blinking open her eyes, she focuses on the face above her.

"Jaliean?"

"Yes," a relieved rumble sounds from the tech. "I was worried you wouldn't wake. Head injuries are often fatal for your kind."

"Not as often as you think," Lakin mutters as she pushes Jaliean away and tries to sit up on her own.

"Easy," Jaliean says with an anxious rumble. "Holian slammed you to the deck as if you were a full Talin."

"I told you I didn't realize it was her until too late," Holian snaps with an aggravated rattle.

"Shhh," Lakin pleads and closes her eyes again. Her head is pounding.

"I'd never hurt a human on purpose," Holian continues in a softer voice with no rattle. "Especially not a female."

"If you can't tell the difference between a tiny human female and a Talin, you shouldn't own one," Jaliean shoots back, clutching Lakin a little tighter.

Ignoring her throbbing head, Lakin opens her eyes and holds up a hand to get their attention.

"The human is fine." She's proud of how steady her voice is. "I've had my fair share of injuries, and I can tell you it's probably only a minor concussion. Nothing to worry about."

"You've been injured before?" Jaliean is incensed. Her rattling is deep and upset as she turns furious eyes on Holian. "I'm going to report you. I don't care if you are the great Commandant Holian! You'll pay for what you've done. If the Committee for Pet Welfare doesn't charge you, my clan will come after you!"

"Whoa," Lakin says, finally realizing this conversation has gotten away from her. "Holian's never hurt me. The corridor was an accident." She reaches out and grabs one of Jaliean's hands in both of hers. Long fingers wrap around her small hand in a gentle grip. The tech quiets her rattles as her gaze drops to meet Lakin's eyes. "I appreciate your concern, but until a little while ago I wasn't even in Talin-controlled territory." She taps the collar around her throat. "This is all new to me. I wasn't owned. I worked on ships."

"She smuggled ex-slaves and refugees," Holian informs Jaliean. A rumble of fear comes from the female's chest, and her hand tightens around Lakin. She rocks again as if Lakin's a child that needs to be soothed.

"That's not safe. No wonder you've been injured in the past. Poor human, you're safe now. I'll make sure no one hurts you again."

"I have a feeling Dalt might object to that," Holian murmurs, and Lakin shoots him a quick grin.

"Figured that out. Did you?" she asks saucily.

"Hard to miss it," Holian replies dryly. "You know I have trackers in the forest now. I watched you avoid the patrols and hike to Dalt's. I still don't know how you're getting out of the enclosures, but please don't teach the other humans. Henni is hard enough to keep corralled already. As far as I'm concerned, you can be Dalt's problem once we all get back home."

"Dalt?" Jaliean asks.

"One of my retired soldiers on Kalor," Holian explains. "But that's irrelevant right now. Tell me where we are, what we have, and," he focuses his intense eyes on Lakin, "how you ended up here."

Studying him, Lakin can see one wound on his head and several more on his torso, but none of them are actively bleeding any longer. His eyes are clear, and his voice is confident. Whatever damage he's suffered isn't compromising his thinking at the moment, making Lakin sigh with relief.

Jaliean quickly explains the stealing of the ship and ends with Lakin coming to her rescue. When all eyes turn to Lakin, she just shrugs and says, "I snuck on. It seemed like a good idea at the time."

That makes Jaliean rumble with shock. "How are you still alive?"

"Excellent question," Lakin replies. "Luck?"

"Did any of my soldiers make it on board?" Holian asks, bringing everyone's focus back to the task at hand.

"No idea," Lakin admits. "I know Dalt was going to try, but there's no way he could get in the same way I did. It's probably just the three of us."

"Four," Belbian reminds her with an angry rattle. He's been so silent, Lakin honestly forgot he was there.

"Right, four," Lakin corrects herself.

"Perhaps we should lock the human up for her own good," Belbian suggests as he eyes her. "She could get hurt if we need to engage with the men who took the ship."

Oh no, she's not going to let that idea gain traction.

"Are you talking about the same human who set you free?" Lakin asks aggressively. Holian gives a sharp rattle, telling both of them to be silent as he looks to Jaliean.

"What's the easiest way to take control of the ship?"

"Poison the biosystem," Jaliean says at the same time Lakin answers.

"Mess up the biosystem." Lakin feels Jaliean rumble with approval before the tech whispers in her ear.

"You're a clever one."

"And don't you forget it," Lakin whispers back.

"That's unwise," Belbian says. "Doing anything to the biosystem means we'll be hurt as well."

"Not if we put on breathers first," Lakin says and barely keeps herself from adding *you idiot* to the end of that sentence. "All we need to do is recalibrate. Make the system think the ship is empty. It'll mix for minimum organics, and they'll start dropping where they stand in no time. They won't even realize what's happening. They'll just feel a little woozy, then *bam*," she slaps her hands together for emphasis. "They're on the floor out cold."

All three Talins soundlessly eye her for a moment before Holian speaks. "Sounds like you've done this before."

"Maybe?" Her non-answer makes Holian rumble out a laugh.

"When I agreed to accept an abused female human found on a criminal ship, I never thought this could be a conceivable outcome. To be honest, I thought you might have been mentally, and perhaps physically, broken. I worried you might even be a danger to yourself."

"She is," Jaliean says quickly. "Brilliant, but an absolute danger to herself."

Crossing her arms over her chest, Lakin gives them her best steely eyed gaze. "That might be true, but for right now, let's see if I can be a danger to others.

Jaliean's superior knowledge of the ship gets them to the biosystem room in no time. At first, everyone lets Lakin walk, but the moment she stumbles, Holian picks her up and refuses to set her back down. To her disgust, she has to admit they make much better time with Holian carrying her. Although her headache is diminishing, it was bad enough for a little while to make it hard for her to see and avoid obstacles in the crowded maintenance corridor.

Stupid Talins and their big, stupid, powerful bodies and thick skulls.

Lakin rarely lets herself dwell on the hand fate dealt her by being born in a body considered weak by most species. And to be born to a civilization that doesn't even have a home planet anymore. The times she's been taken prisoner, there was no Earth government to come to her rescue. No Earth diplomats to bargain for her release, and no Earth trade goods to buy her freedom. Mostly, the fact that her species has no political or military strength never bothers her. She's encountered enough aliens to know she's clever and quick compared to many.

Often that's enough.

Besides, she's seldom truly alone. On all the ships where she served, crews looked out for each other, and most of the captains she served under took good care of those under their authority.

Despite all that, for a moment she wonders what it would be like to just let the Talins own her. No need to worry about helping others or righting wrongs. If she wanted, she's sure Holian would let her go back to Kalor and hide away from the evils of the universe. Even from the trouble the Talins themselves are having. She could have a life devoid of stress, danger, and potentially a premature death.

She could live a safe, secure life.

And be bored out of her skull.

"This is it," Jaliean says, pointing up and interrupting Lakin's philosophical musings. Holian sets Lakin down as the tech taps on a display.

"I'll go—" Lakin volunteers, but Belbian cuts her off.

"We'll all go," he declares. She turns to argue but freezes. Belbian is holding some kind of weapon, and it's pointed at Holian.

"I knew it!" Lakin says, not intimidated by the weapon at all. "There's no way you wouldn't fight the guys on the ship unless you were in on it."

"That explains why you ignored protocol," Jaliean mutters, rumbling with anger. "Foul, disgraceful, soiled male. How could you?"

"Shut up," he yells at her, rattling loudly in anger. "You've never treated me with the respect I deserve. Your clan are food producers. You shouldn't even be on this ship. The real disgrace is Talins like you, trying to rise above your station. Our society is on the brink of falling apart, and we'll be no better than this human. Something must be done to keep order and restore our glory!"

"Hey now," Lakin protests, observing his body language. It is obvious from the way he's holding the gun that Belbian isn't used to wielding a weapon. They need to be careful or he could kill someone by accident. "No need to get upset. You're the one with the power now."

"That's right," Belbian declares with a triumphant rattle, loud enough to echo off the walls. "When the Traditionalists are done, my family will sit on the Apogee Assembly. I will command my own fleet. The righteous will be in control. And you." He points the weapon at Lakin. "Your kind will learn obedience. I've seen how you're treated, as if you are as worthy as a Talin. You're nothing but pets. Nothing but lower lifeforms. Humans are one of the reasons we are failing. Humans are one reason the Prime Son has become so soft and complacent. We all know what his end goals are. He wants to let families breed naturally. He wants us to scent-bond again. He's trying to destroy us!"

It's easy to spot a zealot, and it's impossible to reason with one.

Lakin's scared to say anything that might set Belbian off. He hasn't shot any of them yet, but if they even put a foot wrong, he might open fire. Probably the only reason he hasn't so far is because he's not trained to fire on living targets. There's a difference between hitting drones in practice and actually ending a life, even if you consider it inferior to your own.

Holian steps forward, shielding Lakin from Belbian. "Stand down," he orders, his voice calm but authoritative. "You're acting against your monarch and your government."

"I might be acting against my government, but I'm acting for the best of the Talins," Belbian retorts. "Men like you, with no families or clan who think they can just change everything, need to be brought down."

"Don't," Lakin whispers urgently to Holian. "Don't agitate him. Just agree with him." A twitch of his back plates is the only way she knows he heard her words.

"Your words have merit," Holian says, a thoughtful rumble sounding from his chest. "Perhaps we have been letting ourselves be led astray."

As Holian talks to Belbian, Lakin looks around, trying to figure out what to do next. Belbian needs to be distracted somehow so the three of them might be able to tackle him and take the weapon away. And they need to do it before Belbian gets the attention of the other Traditionalists on the ship.

Looking up at the open hatch, she sees a familiar face peering down at her. Surprise makes her go still as the face disappears. It all happens so quickly that she's not sure it's real. Did she just see Dalt's face?

A loud bang comes from behind Belbian, making him turn and fire blindly down the maintenance corridor. At the same time, a large hand grabs Lakin by the back of her wrap and hauls her up and through the open hatch. Just as she's being pulled up, Holian lunges for the panicked pilot.

Belbian is turning back when Holian slams into him, sending both of them to the floor. The weapon goes off again, but Lakin can't see anything. Dalt has lifted her out of the corridor and is holding her tightly to his chest.

"He has a weapon," she gasps out and smacks Dalt a few times. "Get down there and help them!"

"It's fine," he grunts, grabbing her arms and trapping them in the hug. "Be still. It's finished."

He's busy rubbing his cheek against the top of her head, filling the air with the comforting smell of cedar. As much as she wants to relax into his embrace, Jaliean and Holian are still in danger.

"But," Lakin protests. Then Holian bounds up the steps into the hallway with Jaliean right behind him. Trailing after those two is Palforma, dragging an unconscious Belbian by one leg. He dumps the pilot at Dalt's feet with a satisfied rattle.

"Bad training," he says and gives the Talin a nudge with his foot. "Old man took him down."

"Don't call me old," Holian counters. "But you're right, his training was deplorable. Hopefully, none of the rest are any better trained."

"They weren't," Dalt confirms. "We've already secured the ship. We were just looking for Lakin and you."

"You're efficient," Lakin says. "How many were there?"

"Fourteen," Palforma says.

"Just the two of you defeated fourteen men?" Jaliean asks, rumbling with surprise.

Dalt and Palforma exchange a look, and then Dalt speaks. "We've had harder assignments."

"Dalt's team were the ones I often sent in when stealth needed to be employed," Holian explains. "If I hadn't been shorthanded, they never would have been guarding that civilian outpost. They would have never…" Holian doesn't finish. It's obvious to Lakin that Dalt isn't the only one burdened with guilt.

When Holian doesn't continue talking, Jaliean speaks up. "I'm Jaliean," she begins and then gives her family name, clan name, and finally job title.

Dalt and Palforma exchange introductions, but while Palforma gives his clan and family names in his halting way, Dalt just grunts and says, "Dalt of Kalor Colony."

"Quick question," Lakin says, getting everyone's attention. "Who's going to fly the ship now if all the rebels are neutralized and Belbian is lying here at our feet?"

"Automated piloting system," Dalt says.

"But can that land this thing?"

"I can pilot if we need," Jaliean volunteers. "I can't do anything that requires advanced skills, like formation docking, but I can do basic landings." She looks to Holian. "Are we going back to Kalor or to the nearest station?"

"Neither," Lakin pipes up. "I think we should take advantage of this opportunity."

"Opportunity?" Dalt asks with a puzzled rumble.

"Stealing this ship and kidnapping Holian doesn't do any good unless there's a larger plan at play. Do you have any idea what they were going to do with you, Commandant?" Lakin asks and all eyes turn to Holian.

"Torture for information," he says without a single rattle or rumble. The man's back to his soundless, inscrutable self. "They were hoping to find out who on the Assemblies are Reformists pretending to be Traditionalists. They also wanted detailed information on the monarch's guard and security protocols. I was the last one to design them."

"Logic says this ship is heading to a rendezvous with other members of their group," Lakin says as she thinks it through. "We could continue and meet with them. Maybe get some good information."

"Too dangerous," Jaliean says quickly.

"We can't know how many will be at the meeting or what kind of ship they'll be flying," Holian points out.

"It's got to be a civilian ship," Lakin argues. "Otherwise they wouldn't have needed to steal this thing."

"Her logic is sound," Dalt agrees, although his tone tells her he isn't happy about that fact. "In this ship, we'll outgun any civilian ship, even if only half the guns have munitions."

"This is too good to pass up," Lakin presses. "We meet with these other guys, figure out who they are, and then turn them in. We don't need to get off the ship or even dock. We just identify the ship and then turn around and leave."

"Won't that be suspicious?" Jaliean asks. "If we don't dock with them?"

"Of course it will," Lakin says. "But from what I'm hearing, the monarch or whoever you guys have ruling here, is a Reformist, right? We can contact him and have some trusted military sent to intercept whatever ship we identify. They do the capture, and we head back to Kalor."

"The monarch is a female," Holian tells her absently as he thinks about what she's said. "Your plan has merit, human. But it's still dangerous. We have no proof they're insurgents. It will be easy for them to claim innocence and suffer no consequences."

"They can pretend to be innocent all they want," Lakin responds. "But you guys will know who to keep an eye on and the Traditionalists lose a bunch of valuable members."

"Do you do this often, human?" Jaliean asks.

"Do what?" Lakin asks absently as she plans out the meeting in her head.

"Throw yourself into danger," Jaliean explains. "You shouldn't be here. At all. You put yourself on board the ground transport and then the ship, knowing it would be life-threatening."

"What fun is it to let everyone else go on adventures," Lakin responds with a little laugh.

"How have you survived this long?" Jaliean mutters with a concerned rumble.

"You're not the only one to voice that question," Dalt says.

Giving them an unrepentant grin, Lakin shrugs. "I told you guys. I'm lucky."

"Lakin's plan has merit," Holian finally says, interrupting the *Lakin's too clever for her own good* conversation. "The risk is minimal and potential information gain worthwhile."

"You know…" Lakin is interrupted when both Dalt and Jaliean make sounds of distress.

"No," Dalt says.

"Whatever you're going to say will be a bad idea," Jaliean continues for Dalt.

Lakin ignores both of them. "I think we should meet and greet the Traditionalists. I have a plan."

CHAPTER 18

Lakin

Lakin's heart is beating fast as they dock with the private space yacht, Uleman. She can see the craft from her perch. The thing looks expensive and luxurious.

And so very vulnerable.

Docking goes smoothly. As soon as she sees the seal is good, she scrambles from where she's clinging to the side of the military ship across the docking tunnel to the Uleman. It took her half the journey here to convince everyone to listen to her. Then it took the second half to convince them to let her be part of the plan.

Everyone finally agreed, albeit reluctantly, because she'll play a minor and relatively safe role. Her job is to make her way aboard the Uleman and break something. They don't want the ship to undock and leave before the monarch's military ships get there.

Contacting Searin, the Prime Son, potential heir to the throne, and an ally to both Holian and Kalor Colony, turned out to be easy.

It only took a brief conversation to convince Searin to send a few ships. Their only job now is to stall the Uleman. With just one or two carefully placed rounds, they could have disabled the Uleman's engines, but that would give those onboard plenty of time to destroy evidence. They need to take the Uleman before any of them know what's happening.

Lakin's not too familiar with this type of ship, but most of them are built along the same lines. She's confident she can find the engine room and do something similar to the Uleman as she did to Jaliean's ship. While she's doing that, Dalt and Palforma are pretending to hand Holian over.

Jaliean's in the control room, monitoring and keeping their comm lines hidden in galactic white noise. The tech is talented because what she's doing is almost impossible without the benefit of any expensive specialty equipment.

"I'm on the Uleman," Lakin tells them as she scampers over the smooth metal toward one of several dozen airlocks on the yacht. The suit she's wearing is a little large, but not so bad that it's inhibiting her movement.

Jaliean found her a child's suit to wear and then made cooing rumbling sounds as she helped Lakin into it. She might have appreciated the tech's help, but she wasn't fond of all the "adorable" and "cute" descriptors that went with it as Jaliean latched her into the diminutive version of a Talin space suit.

The electromagnetic grippers on the hands and feet make movement on the outside surface of the ships as easy as she promised Dalt it would be. That's when he found out this wasn't the first time that she'd done this maneuver.

He wasn't pleased with that information. Neither was Jaliean. Holian and Palforma didn't seem surprised in the least.

"Careful, Lakin," Jaliean says over the comms. "There might be a section of composite material around the airlocks. The grabbers won't work there."

"I'm on it," Lakin assures her, along with everyone else on the comm. "There's always metal frames, even if they use composite panels. I'm good. I promise."

"Don't make me hunt around in space for you," Dalt grumbles. The worry in his voice sounds clearly over the comms.

"Don't rumble yourself into a knot," Lakin teases. "I'm at the airlock now, so almost inside."

"That doesn't make me feel any better. You're moving from one danger to another," Dalt complains. He fought against Lakin's plan the hardest, but that isn't shocking. It took Holian pulling rank to silence Dalt, but then Holian turned to her and made her promise to hide, even if she couldn't make it to the engine room to initiate a shutdown of the ship's systems.

"Connecting doors are opening," Jaliean informs them. "No more comms talk from Dalt or Palforma. Passive receiving only."

"Good luck, guys," Lakin sings out and gets a few rumbles in response. Apparently Palforma isn't any happier with her part of the plan than Dalt is. Well, too damn bad! It's her plan and she's going to be a part of it.

She listens to Dalt talk to whoever they're meeting. Dalt and Palforma are dragging Holian, who's pretending to be unconscious.

"I see you were successful," the stranger comments.

"At a high price," Dalt tells him. "Only three of us got out alive. They were better armed than we were led to believe."

"I'm not surprised," the man says. "Commandant Holian isn't supposed to have armaments on Kalor, but considering all the laws he's broken, he would think nothing of breaking those as well." Lakin can hear some shuffling and then an exaggerated groan of pain. "Your time is over, Holian. A new power is on the rise." She hears a thud and then a painful gasp. Did this guy just hit Holian? What a bastard.

"Where would you like us to take him?" Dalt asks.

"My men can take him from here. You have your orders," the stranger says and she hears more feet.

"The military ship is still a quarter of a mark out," Jaliean tells them. Damn, this is all happening too fast. At this rate, they'll have to disengage the yacht before the backup arrives.

The small personal-use airlock hisses as it seals around Lakin. She jabs at the display with one hand and starts frantically unlatching the suit with the other. By the time the inside hatch swings open, she has the suit mostly off. She hops down a hall as she pulls off the last leg of the suit, leaving a trail of suit pieces behind her.

She entered through the closest airlock to the port engine. She promised to use the maintenance or crawlspaces to get to the engine room, but she doesn't have time for that. Fearful that the ship will leave and Holian will become a real prisoner, she sprints in the most likely direction.

"Tell them you need fuel," Lakin says over the comms. "Tell them the ship wasn't fully fueled when you took it and you don't have enough. Tell them you need to do a fuel transfer!"

Following her instruction, Dalt tells the stranger they need fuel because they only had enough to get them there. Lakin is so distracted by the conversation between Dalt and the stranger that she almost runs right past the engine room door. Skidding to a halt, she smacks the door display open and rushes inside, only to bounce off a male who's walking out.

With a startled gasp, Lakin ends up on her ass on the floor, looking up into the face of a Talin.

What a bad time for her luck to quit working.

Dalt

It doesn't take long for Dalt to convince these traitors that he needs fuel. He doesn't know what the original plan for this stolen military ship was, but he's sure a skilled navigations expert can tease out a route from data entered into the ship's system. The task right now is to stall until Lakin disables the engines.

Except she should have done it by now. The Uleman is almost done transferring fuel. Once they're finished, they're out of excuses.

Dalt looks over to Palforma. They're both standing just inside the Uleman, waiting for someone to come tell them the fuel transfer is complete. They claimed they wanted to stay on the Uleman because this kind of fuel exchange comes with a bit of risk. The Uleman and military ships don't have compatible systems, so the transfer must be done manually. If the person doing the transfer makes a mistake, the military ship will lose integrity.

"Something's gone wrong," Jaliean tells them over comms. "I just lost contact with Lakin."

Palforma's back plates rattle with stress at the news. They're alone in a hallway of the Uleman, but the crew might have devices watching. When Dalt turns to Palforma, he keeps his body language casual.

"Are you as hungry as I am?" Dalt asks in one of several prearranged code phrases. This one tells Palforma they'll be going on the offensive soon. Without moving his head, Dalt slides his eyes down the hall in the direction the men who greeted them took Holian. Palforma gives an almost imperceptible rattle to signal he understands.

Dalt isn't worried about the commandant. He has several weapons hidden on his person, and although the man doesn't physically fight in battles any longer, he trains right along with all the ex-soldiers on Kalor. Still, his first thought is to free Holian. Neutralizing the men holding him will be the first step to taking the ship.

"The last ping I got on her comm was right outside the engine room and then nothing," Jaliean tells them. "I'm sure she's in trouble. The little human's going to get hurt." All of them can hear Jaliean's rumble of distress.

"Starving," Palforma agrees, shifting his body slightly and readying himself for battle.

"Let's go hunting for our food," Dalt declares and starts sauntering down the corridor. He tries to be nonchalant as if he's simply looking for a galley, but Palforma isn't able to mimic him. His comrade moves with fluid grace, but there's no mistaking his intent. He's looking for a fight.

"The fuel's been transferred. You can go back over now," the man who greeted them says as he emerges from a nearby room. "Contact the message carrier when you're done, and he'll get word to us that your mission was successful."

Neither man answers. With brutal efficiency, Palforma reaches out and wrenches the man's head at the same time he lifts. A sharp cracking sound echoes in the hall as neck plates break under the retired-soldier's expert grip. The man doesn't even have time to sound a protest before his body falls in a paralyzed heap. He'll be able to live like that for several marks, but if he doesn't get medical intervention soon, he'll die.

"Scan," Dalt orders Jaliean. She's relied on passive scans to assess the Uleman up to this point. Active scans would've alerted the crew of the yacht that they weren't what they appeared, but they have no reason to be subtle any longer. He feels the ship vibrate slightly as Jaliean hits it with a full scanning array.

"Two men are coming to you," Jaliean informs them. "Two more are in the control room, and I've found Lakin. There's one more man and I think he's carrying her, but they're all the way at the fore of the ship. Hurry! I think he's taking her to a shuttle."

The two men Jaliean warned them about come around a corner at full tilt, weapons raised to fire. Dalt and Palforma jump away from each other as they pull their weapons. The fire fight is brief because their opponents aren't particularly skilled. Both men are dead before either gets off a second shot.

"Fore," Palforma orders, pointing toward the front of the ship. He taps his chest and points up. "Control room." Dalt gives a quick nod and sprints off after Lakin while Palforma hurries to take care of the men who are even now probably destroying valuable evidence.

Dalt covers the length of the ship quickly but not fast enough to stop the launch. He watches as the shuttle with an unknown Talin insurgent and his precious Lakin disappears.

CHAPTER 19

Lakin

Well, that didn't go according to plan, Lakin thinks sourly as she squirms, trying to find a more comfortable position. Her hands are bound behind her back, her legs are bound at the ankles, and her collar is secured to the base of the pilot's chair. At least she's conscious and only suffering from a few minor bumps and bruises.

The Talin who took her is talking to someone, but she can only hear his side of the conversation. Despite that, it becomes evident quickly that he was only hired help and not loyal to either side. For a moment, she wonders if she should try to talk him into joining the Reformists, but then she dismisses the thought. He won't believe a human has any authority to offer him a well-paying job, even among the lenient Reformists.

At least he isn't a zealot. That means she's not likely to be tortured while under his control, unlike the Traditionalists the Leemrons gave her to. That's good news because she doesn't think she could handle that again.

Death would be preferable.

"I don't know," the Talin tells someone over the comm. "This human just appeared out of nowhere. I grabbed her and left. We can make a lot more credit by selling her than working for Detrion and his group."

It sounds like this guy left before the others could resort to Plan B. If she couldn't get the engines offline to stall the Uleman, Palforma and Dalt were going to take the ship and she was supposed to hide until they had control.

"She looks healthy and of breeding age," her captor says, making her wince. She doesn't like the term "breeding age."

She'd tried to talk to the Talin who dragged her off, attempting to manipulate him into contacting Holian. But all he did was threaten to gag her, so she shut up. He wasn't interested in listening to a lowly human.

"I'll be there in three marks," the Talin says. "Be ready to transfer the credits when I arrive. I don't want to stay long."

Just over three marks later Lakin is unceremoniously carried off the shuttle at a small port and into a nearby building and dumped in a cage just big enough for her to stand up in or lie down diagonally. It has no bed, water source, or place for her to relieve herself. They don't even untie her, and she watches with horror as the low-tech cage door slams shut.

She still has Dalt's long needle tool tucked in her wrap, but that does her no good if she can't get to any of the locking mechanisms on the cage to manipulate them. Worse yet, this cage is set up so all the locks are on the outside and under manual control with no fancy biolocks or display pads. Just a big hunk of metal that slams across the door and latches.

Low tech but effective.

"Are you injured?"

Lakin turns her head to see a young man in the next cage regarding her with wide, anxious eyes. He looks to be younger than she is with eyes so dark they look black and long brown hair that swings over his shoulder as he edges closer to her. His dark skin gleams with sweat and he's got big patches of grim all over him. Despite the mess he's a handsome man and looks healthy, if very fearful.

"No injuries yet," Lakin tells him. "How about you?"

"I think I twisted my ankle," he tells her. "I tried to run, but I tripped, and they caught me. Now it hurts to walk. I'm Tani."

"I'm Lakin. You said you were caught. Tell me what happened."

"I was on Tomora station. I had a contract to work there while they retrofitted some old engines," he explains.

"Contract? Does that mean you're free? Not a slave?"

"Born free," Tani concurs. "I grew up in the Svelt Colony and started working on stations when I was seventeen Earth standard years. I'm twenty-three now. Tomora was supposed to be safe. I was just walking home from my shift when these big guys appeared out of nowhere. I tried to get away, but they were on me pretty fast. I'm an electrical systems tech, not a fighter. They stuck me in a box, and now I'm here."

"Any idea where here is?" Lakin asks, looking around the room as best she can while still tied. "If I wiggle over to your side of the cage, can you reach through the bars and untie me?"

"I can try," Tani agrees. It takes some effort, but Lakin gets her back pressed against the bars. Tani tugs and frets, sniffing past his tears as he works. The moment her hands are free, she starts in on the bindings around her ankles.

"You're wearing a collar," Tani comments. "Does that mean you're a slave? Am I going to be a slave now?"

"First thing, I was born free, like you," she says. "Second, those guys who grabbed you are Talins and this species collects humans." That doesn't have a comforting effect on Tani at all. He blanches and sucks in a sharp breath.

"Do they eat us?" he asks in a whisper, and it takes a moment for Lakin to figure out what he's asking. Laughing, she shakes her head.

"No, we aren't cattle. The best way to describe us would be as pets. I don't fully understand it myself. I've only been around them for about three weeks. But one thing I can tell you is they're a mixed bag. Some are evil, and some are pretty nice." An image of Dalt pops into her head. "And some of them are more than nice."

"So that's it. I'm going to be sold?" Tani sounds resigned.

"Maybe? I honestly don't know what's going to happen to either of us. I just know we're a prized possession among this species."

The door to the room opens, and several Talins Lakin doesn't recognize walk in. One of them is carrying some kind of blunt stick that he bangs on the cage.

"Stand up and put your foreheads against the bars," he orders. Lakin and Tani scramble to their feet and do as ordered. The second man leans over to look the two of them over.

"Have you ever bonded with anyone?" he asks Tani. He's rumbling out a soft purr and his voice is gentle.

"What?" Tani looks rightfully confused.

"He was free-born and newly acquired," the Talin with the stick explains to the second one. "But the tests we ran on him say he's young, fertile, and in good health. We've had him two rotations, and he hasn't displayed any behavior that would lead us to believe he's bonded to another human."

"Very good," the second man says thoughtfully. "And the female?"

"She just arrived. We haven't tested her yet," the guard admits. Both men eye her collar. "She was found wandering around, so either she ran away from her owner or her owner was negligent."

"Did you run away?" the man asks, and Lakin decides on the truth. Well, part of the truth.

"I was stolen," she says. "I belong to Commandant Holian."

"Unlikely," the man says with a scoffing rattle. "The commandant has a reputation. He's much too careful to allow a human to get stolen. The last ones who tried all died in the attempt. I can see you're a troublesome human." He looks at the guard. "I'll take the male. He's handsome and biddable. He'll be a pleasant companion for my other males."

"Excellent," the guard says. "I'll send him to be decontaminated. You can come back to collect him first thing tomorrow." The two walk out of the room, discussing Tani's paperwork and not sparing another glance at either of the humans.

"I guess that's it," Tani mourns. "I'm a slave."

"Come here," Lakin demands, stepping to the side of the cage closest to him. Tani moves to stand in front of her. The cross hatching of the bars is too tight to allow their hands to go very far, but with some wiggling and grunting, they manage a kind of hug.

"I don't know what's going to happen to either of us," she tells him. "But I've got friends coming for me. Talin friends. After they recover me, I'll have them find you. You're not alone. No matter what happens, I'm going to come for you. I promise."

Although there's no reason for him to believe her, he nods, looking mildly relieved. "I'm scared," he whispers.

"Being afraid is normal," Lakin assures him. "Just do what they tell you, and I'm sure you'll be fine until my friend and I can get to you. You've seen slaves. You know how to act." She thinks for a moment, assessing what little she knows about Tani. "Don't try to escape. Don't give them a reason to punish you. Even if you think you can make it, don't try."

Nodding his head, he takes a deep breath. "I know better," he says. They hear footsteps approach and pull away from each other.

Then the guard is there, striding to Tani's cage.

"You're a lucky little human," the guard tells him as he unlatches the door and pulls Tani out with more force than necessary. "Your new owner is part of a very wealthy clan. They already own two other humans." The guard sounds an annoyed rattle and gives Tani a little shake. "I don't know how he got on our list for another one. You should go to a family that doesn't have a human yet, but he managed to push himself to the top of the Acquired Human Redistribution queue." Clearly, the guard is angry at the other man, but unfortunately Tani is the one receiving his aggression.

With a little sound of fear, Tani hunches his shoulder and ducks his head. The guard makes a rumble of humor.

"Fearful little thing, aren't you?" he comments and gives Tani another shake. At this rate, Tani's upper arm will be black and blue.

"I bet that other guy doesn't even know how to treat a human correctly," Lakin says, forcing her tone to be simpering. She wants to shout and curse at the guard but knows that won't do her any good. Blatant fawning is more likely to be effective. "Not like you. I envy any human you own. Considering how delicate we are, I bet you're gentle with us."

At her words, the guard's grip relaxes, and he rumbles out a purr.

"I'm very good with humans," the guard agrees. "But I don't have any. I don't meet the minimum wealth requirements."

The guard lets go of Tani's arm and pulls the small man into a hug, making Tani squeak in surprise. With one arm around Tani, the guard holds him tightly against his chest and pets his head. "I know all the things humans need. The right kind of food. How they need to be held so they can clutch effectively, and of course all the different bathing and grooming needed."

Scared, Tani rolls panicked eyes toward her. Before she can say anything, the guard is rattling with displeasure. He pushes Tani away so he can look down at him.

"Why aren't you clutching at me?"

Lakin jumps in to keep Tani from saying something that might upset the guard.

"I've been talking to this human, and he's a little slow," she says. "I think he might have a mental deficit. It's good that he's going to a clan that already has humans because he's defective. I'd be sad if someone had him as their only human."

Ignoring the look Tani shoots her, Lakin watches the guard closely. Talins might not have facial expressions, but their body language still gives her a lot of clues. The guard's stiff posture relaxes slightly, and his rattling stops, replaced with a gentle, comforting rumble.

"That explains why he's here," the guard says. "Usually humans who end up here are bought from slave auctions or recovered from unpleasant situations. The report said this one was found wandering around on a station, starving and begging for scraps."

Wandering around? Nice code for kidnapping.

The guard pats Tani on the head. "Don't worry. I'm sure Citizen Wilian will be patient with you."

Lakin breathes a little sigh of relief as the guard handles Tani more gently and leads the young man out of the room, assuring the "mentally defective" human that he shouldn't be scared or alarmed. When he stumbles because of his injured ankle, the guard even picks him up and carries him while cooing out a gentle rumble.

"Score one for Lakin," she mutters to herself as she slumps back against the mesh wall of her cage. Her head hurts, and she's tired. Sliding down the wall until her butt hits the cold hard floor, she draws her knees up and sighs. Letting her head fall back, she closes her eyes and gives herself a moment to regroup. She's still wearing the tracking collar, so it shouldn't take them long to find her, assuming that no one got hurt when they took the ship.

If no one comes to get her, that can only mean one thing.

Dalt and Holian are dead.

If that turns out to be the case, she's getting herself free, and she's going to do her best to rain chaos down on these Talins. Revenge is something Lakin is very familiar with. She might be a small weak human, but these Talins don't know how dangerous it is to make her angry.

The last time she got pissed, half a space station ended up destroyed. No one wants to find out what she can do if she's enraged.

CHAPTER 20

Lakin

She's not sure how much time passes before another guard comes into the room. Without a word, he opens her cage, drags her forward, and pins her against a nearby wall. Then he slips a tool between her skin and the collar. She feels a little heat and then a cracking sound, and the collar drops to the floor.

"Now there won't be any confusion," the guard says as he shoves her back in the cage and secures the door. He picks up the broken pieces of her collar and carries them out of the room with him. She should've taken it off earlier and hidden it. The tracker inside would've helped lead Holian and Dalt to her. Now it's broken and being disposed of.

Cursing herself for being so stupid, she rubs her neck, surprised to find she misses the comforting weight of the collar.

Still, even without the collar she has a few tricks up her sleeve.

She has no way to keep track of time. The room doesn't even have any windows, so Lakin doesn't know how long it is before that same guard is back with another Talin. Standing up, she moves to the cage door as the guard opens it.

"She looks fit," the Talin comments as he examines her. "Human, remove your wrap."

"I'd rather not." The words are out before Lakin realizes it. *Docile*, she reminds herself. *I'm pretending to be docile.*

Before the guard can reach in and grab her, she steps back and hurries to undo the tie holding the dress together at her waist.

"I mean, I'm cold," she adds hastily, pretending to shiver. "I haven't eaten, and I'm so very thirsty."

"Do as you're told," the guard grumbles, not trying to reach for her again. Unlike the guard who took Tani away, this one isn't open to manipulation. With exaggerated shaky hands, she pulls her wrap off and lets it drop to the floor. The new Talin makes an unhappy rattling sound.

"She looks sickly," he comments, leaning in as he examines her.

"She's just a little thin. It's common for them to be underweight when they get here," the guard assures him. "Besides, she's only the second human we've had for quite some time. I would take her and not risk waiting for another one. And the other one was male. You know how much harder it is to find females."

"Very well," the new Talin says grudgingly. "I can see the merit in your advice. Thank you for setting my name at the head of the queue." He hands the guard something, and the guard makes a happy rumble as he drops the item in his belt pouch. Ah, that explains how Tani ended up with a Talin who already had humans. This guard is manipulating the list.

"I contacted you the moment she came in. It's fortunate you got here so fast," the guard says as he hands the Talin a collar. "You'll want to put this on before you leave with her. I've already filled out all her paperwork and backdated a medical checkup and decontamination. You're free to take her now."

"Of course." It's hard for Lakin to remain still while a new collar is secured around her neck. It's a pretty sure bet she won't be able to remove this one just by pressing her thumbs to it. To her horror, the Talin isn't finished yet. He clips a leash to her collar and gives it a little tug.

"Come along, female," he says. "I have ground transport waiting for us."

Lakin follows the Talin out, taking in every detail she sees. She's not sure where she is, but it's a planet. She has a vague idea where the Talin homeworld is and there's no way the mercenary made it all the way there in the time they were traveling. This must be another Talin colony that's not Kalor. The greenery and sky don't match that planet.

A colony is good. Often colonies have less infrastructure than homeworlds or stations. That should make it easier for her to escape and evade. If Holian and Dalt can't find her, it'll be up to her to get away and call for help. Without aid her plan is the same as when she was on Kalor: get ahold of an interstellar comm, call in a favor, and wait for pick up.

Feeling a little better, she lets the Talin push her into an automated ground transport. It's a smaller one with only two seats facing each other. She tries to take a seat, but he pushes her to sit on the floor at his feet. Once inside he taps at a display. The doors shut and the transport starts moving.

"You may call me Master Ladian," the Talin tells her.

"Yes, Master Ladian," Lakin chirps, keeping her eyes on the window, noting direction, buildings, and the general layout of the city as it passes. "May I ask a question, Master?"

"Of course," he says with a pleasant rumble.

"Where are we?"

That question gets a surprised rumble from his chest. "Poor little thing, you don't even know where you are. This is Molpa Colony. We're small but fruitful. We're an importation stopping point between the Kilkurn station and homeworld. I'm the leader of our colony's Clan Assembly. I make sure that…"

Lakin nods and pretends to listen to the long-winded Ladian extoll his importance. She's never heard of either Molpa Colony or Kilkurn station, so she can't place this planet on any star charts in her head. But with those names, she can find her place with access to the planet's Unibase.

"… and once that decision is finalized, we'll be even more important. Ah, here we are," Ladian announces with a satisfied rumble.

The transport stops in front of a large, domed building. This must not be a large colony, because it didn't take them long at all to leave the city center and end up on the outskirts. Behind his large home is a vast wilderness, most of it made up of mountain ranges covered in thick greenery.

Getting out of the ground transport, Ladian tugs on the leash. She's already climbing out, so the tug is just annoying. She bites her tongue to keep from snapping at Ladian.

"Come along. I need to get you situated. I have a meeting to attend soon."

Instead of leading her into the domed house, they go around the side to the back. There she sees a single large enclosure, almost twice as big as the ones back on Kalor. Ladian leads her to the gate and opens it up. She steps in without protest, and he unclips the leash from her collar and shuts the gate.

"I'll be back at twelfth mark to check on you. If you need to clutch to something before then, look to Grem." With that, Ladian strides off.

Feeling a strong sense of foreboding, Lakin turns around to find she isn't alone in her new cage. A large human male stands up from where he was sitting on the ground at the far end of the enclosure. He has the palest skin she's ever seen, with blue eyes so light they almost look white. His blond hair hangs down his back, thin but gleaming. Under normal circumstances, Lakin would greet him with a smile, but his expression makes her pause.

"It's about time they got me a female," he says as he takes a menacing step toward her with a smirk. "Why don't you be a good bitch–get in that bed and down and spread your legs for me!"

CHAPTER 21

Lakin

A quick look around the enclosure reveals nothing she can use as a weapon. She isn't one to engage in hand-to-hand fighting, but that doesn't mean she doesn't know the basics, especially if facing down another human.

Standing tall, she stares him down, only letting confidence show on her face. One of the fastest ways to be a victim is to look the part. In several prior situations she's faced down opponents with only her bravado to back her up.

"I'll rip you apart if you try to touch me," she says, proud when her voice comes out even and strong.

He walks forward until he's covered half the distance; then he stops, cocks his hip, and crosses his arms over his chest.

"Ladian likes his humans submissive. Sounds like you need to work on that," he comments. "But I guess they take what they can get here, and I'm sure I can teach you how to be a good little girl."

"I don't think you need to teach me anything," she spits out. "But I bet I could teach you a thing or two."

"Tough talk." He gives her a big predatory grin and nods in the direction Ladian walked off. "Ladian brought a guy in here because he was worried that I was lonely. Borrowed him from another clan. Nice enough guy. It only took me a few hours to teach him how to get on his knees and present. Then he took it in the ass well. Never even whimpered. I was really sad to see him go back to his clan."

Lakin works to keep the fear off her face. That answers one question Lakin's been wondering about. Not all the humans the Talins own are well-adjusted and kind like those on Kalor. This guy is the typical abusive bully.

"You're disgusting."

Taking a threatening step toward her, Grem brings a fist up. "I'd be friendly to me if I were you," he warns her. "I've gotten good at hurting people in ways the Talin don't see. And you can whine all you want to Ladian. He won't believe you."

"Because he trusts you so much?" she asks.

"Because he doesn't believe any of us," Grem retorts, taking another step.

"You got hurt, didn't you?" Lakin asks, making an educated guess. "Someone abused you, and he wouldn't listen to you."

That stops Grem in his tracks. His face flashes from taunting to haunted. But the change is brief, and then his lips twist back into a cruel sneer.

"All these Talins are the same. They think we're dumb as dirt when they're the ones who don't understand anything. Ladian thinks he's so important, but he's just a minor politician on a backwater colony. I bet he had to bribe someone to get you. But I'm glad he did. It's been a while."

"I'll fight you," she warns him. "I'm not some scared girl you can bully."

He's too close now, almost within reach, and she runs through tactics in her head. Duck down, punch to the groin, roll away. If the punch to the groin doesn't work, step back and kick at one of his knees. She's going to need to keep moving because he's bigger and stronger than she is. Her only hope is to stay out of his reach.

"Good," he says. "I'm bored. If you fight, it's a bonus for me."

"New human!" an excited voice exclaims as a rattle of excitement sounds loudly behind her.

Lakin moves sideways so she can see the new arrival but also keep Grem in view. It's a female Talin wearing a gem-encrusted ornate pouch dangling off a wide, elaborately decorated belt.

"Hello," Lakin says hesitantly, bouncing her gaze between this new Talin and Grem.

"Hello, Mistress Umella," Grem says, dropping his gaze down and rounding his shoulders a little. The change in him is startling. A moment ago he was all testosterone and aggression, and now he's the image of submission.

That tells Lakin two things. One, Grem wasn't exaggerating when he said Ladian liked submissive humans, and two, she's in for a world of hurt if she doesn't act the part.

Dropping her gaze, she mumbles out, "Hello, Mistress Umella." Meekly she looks up through her lashes at this Talin, who's still rumbling with happiness.

"You're so pretty," she says and unlocks the door to the enclosure. "Come here, I want to play with your lovely mane. We've never had a female before. I keep telling Ladian we need to visit the slave markets more, but he says no quality humans can be found there."

Moving to stand in front of her, Lakin muffles a gasp as the Talen grabs her wrist in a harsh grip.

"I know I should put a leash on you, but I'm too impatient to go find one. We'll need to hurry before Father sees that I'm taking you out."

Ladian didn't appear old enough to be a father to this adult Talin, so Lakin guesses Ladian and Umella are adult siblings still living with their parents. Lakin jogs to keep up with Umella as the female tells her all about how important it is that Lakin be an obedient human.

By the sound of it, she's now owned by some Traditionalists. If that fact isn't enough to spur her toward escape, Umella's next words make getting away before nightfall a priority.

"I can't wait for you to have pups. With Grem as the sire, they'll be so handsome.

Leading her into the domed house, Umella doesn't let up on her strong grip. Lakin notices they don't have many security measures. The domicile door doesn't even lock. There aren't any perimeter fences around the property, and so far, she's only seen one servant who jumped to do Umella's bidding. Once she's out of the enclosure, running away will be easy.

Grabbing her roughly by the waist, Umella sits and pulls Lakin into her lap. "You may clutch me," Umella says.

Hesitantly, Lakin turns sideways on the Talin's lap and wraps her arms around the woman's neck. It feels awkward and uncomfortable, but Umella either doesn't notice Lakin's discomfort or doesn't care.

"There now, don't you feel better? Poor little human," Umella coos, running her hand down Lakin's back with more force than necessary.

How can Umella think this is soothing at all? Thankfully, a servant appears with a tray full of items, distracting the Talin before she rubs the skin off Lakin's back.

Setting the tray down on a nearby table, the servant bows his head deferentially. "As you requested. Cook is preparing a bowl of human feed for your new pet. I'll bring it as soon as it's ready."

"Very good," Umella says as she tugs at Lakin's arms. "You need to unclutch now."

Relieved to take her arms out from around Umella's neck, Lakin gives a little squeak of surprise when Umella easily picks her up and unceremoniously drops her to the floor.

The squeak turns to a grunt of pain as her backside hits the floor hard. Before she even has time to process, Umella is grabbing her hair and tugging her backward so she's forced to scoot between the Talin's spread legs.

The entire process is painful and unnecessary. All Umella needed to do was tell Lakin where she wanted her, not drop and drag her. Biting her lip to keep from snapping at the Talin, she moves a little to get comfortable on the hard floor. There's no dignity in being the pet of this woman.

Unfortunately, the discomfort isn't over.

Umella brushes her hair with long powerful strokes, uncaring that she's ripping hair out as the brush meets tangles. Lakin hisses in pain, and Umella pauses.

"You're rather unkempt," she states with mild condemnation in her tone. "If you took more care of yourself, this grooming wouldn't be so difficult.

Every nice thing Lakin thought about the Talins caring for humans vanishes. She almost feels bad for Grem. He might be an abusive asshole, but she's got a strong suspicion that circumstances among these casually hurtful Talins probably helped shape that part of his personality.

When the servant comes back carrying a bowl, Umella puts down the brush and addresses the servant. "See if you can find a wrap to fit her," she orders. "This one smells. And see if you can find a set of wrist and ankle adornments. We're the first family here to have a female, and I want our crest to be very obvious."

Nodding, the servant hands her the bowl of food and hurries off. To Lakin's relief, Umella hands her the bowl instead of trying to feed her by hand like Dalt does.

With Dalt, being fed feels affectionate, like something a lover would do, not an owner. Having this female Talin feed her would just be degrading. And probably messy.

The bowl is full of dark porridge. It's bland but hearty, and Lakin swallows it down quickly. She could easily eat another bowlful, maybe a third. It's been a while since her last meal, and a lot has happened in a short time.

"Could I have another serving?" she asks, keeping her eyes downcast and slumping her shoulders a little. Like Grem did earlier, she tries to look appropriately subservient.

"Later," Umella declares as she pulls her Ident Cube off her belt and taps at it. A holo projects up, showing rows of Talin words and some symbols in a grid pattern. "We're going to a small gathering now. I can't wait to show you off. I'll be the envy of all the eminent families here."

Great, now she's going to be paraded around. The good news is that the longer she's with Umella, the more time she isn't in the cage with Grem. And if Umella takes her anywhere, it will give her a better lay of the land for when she escapes.

"I believe I've found everything you requested," the servant announces as he hurries back into the room, his arms full of items. Umella stands and almost kicks Lakin by accident as she meets the servant halfway across the room.

Snatching a deep green wrap out of his hands, she shakes it out and holds it up. "This should do nicely," she declares and then gives an annoyed rattle when she sees Lakin's still sitting on the floor next to the chair.

"Come here," she orders, her tone cross. Scrambling to her feet, Lakin hurries over to Umella and the servant. Without another word, Umella unties the wrap Lakin is wearing and nearly rips it off her. Gasping, Lakin instinctively starts fighting.

Umella cuffs her on the side of the head, making her see stars. The servant makes a distressed rattle when Lakin staggers a little. Dropping the rest of the items he's holding, he grabs Lakin's arm to steady her.

"Behave," Umella orders as she finishes pulling the wrap off her. The servant's touch is gentle as he helps Umella put on the new wrap. It's a little big, but clean and warm. This planet is colder than tropical Kalor, and she's thankful for the heavier fabric of the new wrap.

"Perhaps I should fetch an omnie," the servant suggests after Umella's done knotting the wrap closed at Lakin's waist. It takes Lakin's translator a moment to unpack the word omnie, but an image of a long-sleeved coat-like wrap that reaches almost to the floor fills her head.

The servant continues when Umella doesn't respond. "And maybe another bowl of food. She seems a little underweight. Her previous owners probably didn't know how to care for her. Not like you do, Citizen Umella."

A rumble of pleasure sounds from Umella at the servant's words. "You're probably correct about the former owner. And I'm an excellent owner. You need to fetch an omnie and another bowl of food. She looks cold and underweight. I'll finish putting on the adornments."

She gives those orders as if she thought of them herself. The servant doesn't react except to bow his head respectfully. He gives Lakin a little reassuring squeeze with the hand still holding her arm before he lets go and leaves. It looks like she's got one Talin in her corner here. He might be a servant, but he knows exactly how to manipulate Umella.

Not that it's hard. This woman is transparent and narcissistic. Those kinds of individuals are easily manipulated to a certain extent.

Standing perfectly still, Lakin watches Umella pick up the items the servant dropped on the floor. It's not until she's securing the first one to Lakin's wrist that she realizes they're restraints. It takes a great deal of will power to keep from pulling away as the Talin puts cuffs on her wrists and ankles.

They're wide, made of a leather-like material, and encrusted with small gems on the edges. A stylized image of a planet with written symbols inside has been etched into the material. Although Lakin's never seen a set so ornate, she recognizes these kinds of restraints.

The clasps not only lock the restraint around the wrist or ankle but can also be locked together. With a press of a digit, Umella could lock her wrists to each other, or her wrists to her ankles, or her ankles to each other. Thankfully, only two can be locked together at a time, so she can't end up hogtied with all four limbs locked together. Still, Lakin isn't thrilled with this new development.

She can only hope the day doesn't get worse.

CHAPTER 22

Lakin

"Her mane is so lovely," a Talin says as she grabs a fistful of Lakin's hair. With her wrists secured behind her back and Umella holding her by the shoulders, she can't pull away from this new handsy Talin. Even if she could pull away, there's no place for her to go. Seven Talin women and one man surround her, all chattering together and rumbling. Hands touch her face, chest, back, and torso. One hand even runs all the way down to her backside.

She jerks at all the unwanted touches, but that just makes the Talins around her rumble out laughs.

"She's not very well-trained," one comments and tugs at her heavy omnie, trying to draw her away from the Talin with a fistful of her hair.

"We just got her today," Umella explains. "There's no paperwork on her background. She probably belonged to one of those Reformist families. Humans don't do well if they're given too many liberties. They need structure more than anything."

"And you say she was found wandering around a derelict space station?" the male asks.

"That's what her paperwork says," Umella replies.

"We should breed her to my Hova," another one says. "He's got a lovely curly dark brown mane. Their cubs would be adorable."

"Hova's too old," the female with a handful of Lakin's hair argues. "My Romi is young and fit. I'm sure they'll get along well and be quite fruitful. The female he was paired with back on Meno Colony had several sets of twins before we got him. None of your males are proven breeders like he is."

"Oh no, she should be bred with my family's male. If her young has his lovely dark eyes and her dark mane, they will be stunning."

"We have Grem," Umella announces. "I don't need any of your males." Several of the women rattle with displeasure at Umella's announcement.

"You're not going to put her in with Grem. Are you?" the male asks. "He's much too brutal."

"She'll be fine," Umella says with confidence as she pulls Lakin away from the crowd. The one holding her hair only lets go when Lakin makes a sound of distress. The one holding on to her omnie tries to follow Umella for a stride. But when Umella lets loose with an irritated rattle, she backs off.

"Still, I'd put them in separate cages next to each other for a few rotations, just to be on the safe side," one of them murmurs. "It's what my brother does back on Talarian, and he's well-known for his skills at breeding and raising humans."

"I'll think on it," Umella says and takes a seat. Lakin stands for a moment, unsure what to do. Then Umella makes a small rattle of annoyance.

"Floor," she says and points to a piece of ground next to her right foot. With her hands bound behind her back, Lakin isn't graceful as she sinks to the floor and several of the women make unhappy rattles when she finally hits the ground with a small sound of discomfort. Her poor backside's going to be bruised by tomorrow.

"Can I hold her?" the man asks. "I've never met a female before."

"I'd like to pet her too!" another one says with an excited rumble. A few others voice their desires, and Umella rumbles with pleasure at the requests.

"You can all take turns holding her," she declares with a gracious sweep of her hand at Lakin. Before Lakin can even start struggling to her feet, the man steps forward and plucks her off the ground. Sitting on one of the many backless chairs in the room, he settles her on his lap and hugs her to him.

"Can we not release her hands?" he asks with a dissatisfied rattle. "I wish her to clutch to me if she wants to."

Umella makes a rattle of irritation. She's forced to lean far forward to reach Lakin, but with a quick press followed by a beep, Lakin's cuffs detach from each other. Pivoting on the man's lap, she throws her arms around his neck and whispers, "Thank you."

Fighting anxiety the entire time Umella had her hands secured, Lakin was finding it harder and harder to stay calm in this situation.

Letting her emotions get the better of her won't do any good. She needs to keep her wits about her and focus on an exit strategy, but Umella has done a good job of upsetting her calm at every turn.

"You can clutch to me as tightly as you need, little female," the man whispers back with a soothing rumble. "I don't mind."

"Is she upset?" a woman whispers, sitting next to the two of them. Umella is talking loudly about her skills with humans and isn't paying any attention to them.

"A little," the man responds.

"Do you think we can go to the Colony Assembly and get her removed? Grem was almost put down last solar for what he did to Manliean's human. The poor thing almost died, and he was a male of almost equal size to Grem. This female is much smaller than him. We need to do something."

"Nothing can be done for at least a rotation," the man says grimly. "Umella and her family should have never been granted a second human, not with the violations they have on record. I bet someone was bribed."

"I have no doubt," the woman agrees.

This is all interesting information, but Lakin needs them to talk more about the colony port, security procedures, and whether they have a communal trans-universe satellite or if each community or family supports their own smaller link-up satellite. A trans-universe satellite is more powerful. It can send and receive data quickly but will be more difficult to access because it's communal property and will have set colony-wide protocols. If each family maintains a personal link-up satellite that communicates with a nearby station to transmit long distances, the process will be slower but easier to gain access to. Some families might not even have security attached to their link-up, and theoretically, Lakin could just sneak into a domicile and access it through any information square belonging to the family.

As a pet, how does one causally start asking these questions about satellites and security?

"Are you hungry…" the woman begins and then makes a frustrated rattle and looks to Umella. "What's the name of your new pet?"

A rattle of surprise comes out of Umella, and she drops her gaze from the woman to Lakin and then back to the woman.

"Tiny," Umella declares and Lakin's lips curl in disgust. Really? This Talin just named her Tiny?

"That's certainly fitting," the woman says with an amused rumble. "She is one of the smallest humans I've ever met."

I'm not even that small, Lakin thinks. Her arms are getting sore from holding on to the male, so she pulls them out from around him and sits back, dropping her hands into her lap.

"Are you well, Tiny?" the male asks with a worried rattle.

"Are you hungry?" the woman asks again. But before she can answer any questions, another set of hands grabs her and she's lifted and set onto a new lap.

"It's my turn," a new voice declares. Lakin cranes her neck back to take in the Talin who grabbed her. It's the one who held on to a fistful of hair.

Predictably, this Talin plays with her hair. It wouldn't be so bad, but her scalp is sore from Umella's harsh brushing earlier. All this attention reminds her of children with a new toy. There must not be much in the way of entertainment on this colony if everyone's so enamored of her.

If she was someone else, she might enjoy all this attention. Her childhood friend Mellena would thrive on this. Ignored by her own family, Mellena loved being the center of attention and was all about touching and hugging. A human like her would do very well as a pet among these people. Large, tough, energetic, and attention seeking. Mellena would flourish here.

Well, maybe not owned by Umella and under danger of being housed in the same cage as Grem, but other than that, this would've pressed all Mellena's buttons. Especially the petting. Someday, when she's free, she needs to visit home and see if she can find Mellena. That woman needs to be introduced to the Talins and all their touching.

Right now, Lakin's sick of the petting.

"Tiny appears to be fatigued," the man says to Umella loudly enough to get Lakin's notice. The Talin holding her stiffens and grabs Lakin's chin to force her head up.

"Yomian is correct," she declares and lets go of Lakin's face. "Perhaps a refreshing beverage?"

"That's a good idea, don't you agree, Nomian?" Yomian asks the woman sitting next to him.

"Absolutely," Nomian agrees. "I can take her to the kitchen for refreshments."

It looks like the only guy there, Yomian, is on her side as well as Nomian, the female Talin sitting next to him. After studying them for a moment, Lakin's sure they're siblings.

"No," Umella responds sharply.

"She also might need to use the elimination facilities," Nomian points out blandly. "I'll escort her and make sure she's sufficiently clean before bringing her back.

"Take her," Umella says quickly, making the two-pieces of-over-ripe-fruit-being-smashed-together rumble of disgust. "If she's soiled her wraps, send word to my household so they can bring new ones."

Soiled her wraps? Only years of training keeps Lakin from voicing a scathing retort.

"We have wraps also if the need arises," Nomian comments as she stands up and pulls Lakin off the lap she's sitting on. The woman holding her lets go with a displeased rattle. Nomian holds her securely but gently and strides out of the room.

"There now," Nomian says as she rumbles out a purr. "You're safe for the moment. My brother will do his best to talk Umella into keeping you separate from Grem until we can get the Colony Assembly to remove you from her care."

Walking into a food preparation room, Nomian sets her down on a high clean countertop and starts rooting around. Pulling a drinking flask out of a cooling box, she hands it to Lakin.

Unlatching the top, Lakin drinks greedily. She's finished off the entire flask in a few long swallows and wipes her mouth. "Thanks."

"Are you well? Do you have any pain or injuries?" Nomian asks, taking the empty flash out of Lakin's hands.

"Nothing too bad," Lakin admits. Her scalp is sore, and her butt hurts, but neither is what she'd consider a true injury. "I just don't like so many strangers grabbing and touching me. I'm free-born. I don't belong here."

"Free-born humans are out there waiting to die from all kinds of avoidable things. That means you very much belong here," Nomian counters, and Lakin sees her chances of convincing Nomian to help her escape drop to zero. "But you don't belong with Umella and her family. You should be owned by those who will treat you as a beloved pet, not a possession to make others jealous."

"Your brother's right, you know," Lakin says, deciding on another tactic. "Ladian bribed the official to get me. I saw him pass something off to the guard in charge of me."

"I wish I had more proof than the word of a pet," Nomian mutters. "That family engages in all kinds of disreputable acts. They skirt the law as if it has no meaning for them." She sounds a rattle of frustration and sets the drinking flask down on the countertop with more force than necessary. "I'm sorry, Tiny, but you're probably going to need to be with them for at least the rest of this rotation. Yomian is on the Colony Assembly and he should be able to get an oversight committee to look into your situation."

"What does that mean for me?"

"Because of Grem's history, I know they'll take you away from Umella and Ladian. Then you'll be taken back to the reclamation center," Nomian explains. "Umella and her family's claim on you will be revoked, and you'll be offered to the next family on the receiving list. We're on that list, but I'm not sure where we rank. It's kept a secret to keep families from disputing with each other."

"He's going to hurt me," Lakin says, thinking about Grem. "That Grem guy. They'll put me in with him, and he's going to hurt me."

What she doesn't say is that if Grem tries anything, she'll hurt him right back. She might not win because he's a good deal bigger than her, but he won't come out of their battle unscathed. But Nomian doesn't need to hear that. She needs to hear Lakin sounding helpless and scared.

Nomian folds her arms around Lakin. "I'll see what I can do," she promises, rumbling out a soothing purr. She makes Lakin miss Dalt's rusty purr. "If I have to spend the night standing next to the cage to keep you safe, I will."

Good to her word, when Nomian takes her back to the group, she doesn't let go of Lakin. Instead, she sits down close to her brother with Lakin in her lap.

"Hand her to me," the woman sitting next to Umella demands. "It's my turn."

"I'm sure Umella would rather the human rest for now," Nomian says, eyes focused on Umella. "She's overwrought from all this attention. Perhaps I could put her in our enclosures here until you're ready to return home? She could even spend the night. As you know, our enclosure is empty so she can acclimate to the colony's climate in quiet solitude. I read that's helpful for some humans."

"Don't be impertinent, sister," Yomian says with a warning rattle that doesn't sound harsh to Lakin's ears. "I'm sure Umella already knows that Tiny will need to be left alone for a full sleep cycle."

"I'm terribly sorry, Umella. I should've realized that was your intention when you brought her here, even though you only gained ownership of her today," Nomian says with an apologetic rumble. "I shouldn't have questioned your knowledge of human needs."

Figuring she needs to appear tired and overwhelmed, Lakin draws up her knees and curls herself into a ball, hiding her face in Nomian's neck. Then she has to fight the urge to void her stomach when Nomian's smell hits her. The Talin doesn't smell bad. She just smells wrong. Cedar should fill her nose, not soapy-citrus.

Swallowing down her nausea, Lakin concentrates on breathing through her mouth to keep her stomach settled. She listens to the brother and sister team effectively box Umella into a corner. These two are smart and ruthless. By the time some of the group rise to leave, Umella has agreed to let Lakin stay with the siblings for the evening.

Silently, Lakin applauds this dynamic duo but doesn't show any outward sign of triumph when Umella and the last of the group leave.

An audible sigh of relief comes out of her when Nomian takes the wrist and ankle cuffs off.

"There's no reason to wear these," she mutters as she tosses them into a corner. "It's nothing but hubris to bind a pet like that. A collar is more than sufficient to signify ownership. One doesn't need a pet dripping in crests."

Walking into the room carrying a bundle of something, Yomian makes an approving sound to see the restraints in a discarded pile on the floor. "Umella and her family are constantly trying to prove they're better than they are."

"You speak truthfully," Nomian says to her brother and then addresses Lakin. "How do you feel, Tiny? We have a healer coming to assess you, and a member of the Committee of Pet Welfare is due to arrive this evening to appraise the legality of your sale. You need to be well-behaved for both of them." Without waiting for a reply from Lakin, Nomian turns to her brother. "I'm due at the port. I must leave."

"I'll take good care of her, sister," Yomian assures his sibling. "I brought a nice kneeling pillow for her to rest on while we wait for the healer."

Smacking her chest hard enough to make a loud thump sound, Nomian rumbles with affection. "You're a good brother. We'll find a human of our own soon."

"Perhaps we're next on the list, and this one will be ours," Yomian says with a hopeful rumble. "We're a much better family to care for her."

"Perhaps," Nomian says. "But don't let your expectations elevate. There's a very good chance another family is next on the list."

"Probably," he says, but Lakin can tell that his hopefulness isn't deterred by Nomian's words. Purring, Yomian leads Lakin out to the garden as Nomian gathers a few things to leave. Once outside, Yomian sets down the giant fluffy pad next to a hard stone bench and urges her to sit down on it. He pulls his Ident Cube off his belt, taps it, then reads something. He's engrossed and she can't read Talin, so Lakin makes herself comfortable. For the moment, there's no reason not to relax and get a little rest. She's safe. There's no chance of escape while Yomian sits right next to her, and the garden is a pleasant place. She learned long ago to rest when she can, and she's caught naps in much more uncomfortable locations.

Curling up on the kneeling pillow, Lakin drifts off to sleep.

CHAPTER 23

Lakin

When opportunity presents itself, Lakin isn't one to hesitate. That's why the moment the man from the Committee for Pet Welfare left her unattended, she ran.

The timing couldn't be more perfect. Not only did he leave her in the transport alone, but right next to her is a bag of supplies Yomian insisted go with her to her next home. Then, to cement the opportunity, the man stopped the transport right on the edge of the jungle and got out, disappearing into a nearby dwelling with an admonishment for her to "stay put and out of trouble."

Snatching up the bag of goodies, Lakin sprints for the dense green on the other side of the empty roadway and quickly disappears.

She doesn't feel even remotely bad about abandoning the man who collected her from the sibling's house. She's gotten good at reading Talin body language, and she knows for certain that the stop he made isn't on his schedule. She has a strong suspicion she was about to be traded for a bribe. This colony seems to have issues with bribery.

At first, she runs full tilt through the jungle, but once she's far enough away that she can't hear the sounds of the small town any longer, she slows her pace. Thankfully the thin slippers seem surprisingly sturdy and are providing good protection from the uneven and sometimes spiky jungle floor.

Stopping in a small clearing, she crouches down to rifl through the bag. There's a change of clothes, more slipper-shoes, some food, a weird fluffy pillow, but no tools. She needs to get this collar off before they use it to track her down.

Setting the bag aside, she explores her collar with her fingers. It takes some time and more than a few cuss words before she finally pries off a small plate next to the locking mechanism with a thin-edged stone. Then she bashes at the collar with the same stone until she hears the distinct sound of delicate electronics dying.

The collar will probably need to be cut off but at least it can't be used to track her. Tossing the useful stone tool into her bag, she stands up and scampers up onto a boulder to peer at the horizon.

The plan is simple; hide in the jungle for a few days until they stop looking for her. It won't be comfortable but with the food and extra clothing in the bag, it shouldn't be horrible.

Once they give up on finding her, she can sneak back into the town and "borrow" what she needs.

An important part of the plan, probably the most important part, is not to get lost in the jungle!

She can see a tall mountain range looming in the distance. If she can make it to the foothills she should be able to find her way back by following the ships coming and going from the port.

With the mountain acting as an easy destination, Lakin picks her way through the jungle until she starts getting tired. It's been a long couple of days.

"I need a break!" she mutters. Finding a convenient rock, she settles herself down and looks at the bag, realizing there's one fatal flaw to her plan.

"I'm going to need some water," she declares grimly to the bag. The mountains aren't high enough to have snow at the stop so she isn't guaranteed any rivers or streams. The lush jungle around her indicates it rains regularly, but how regularly? Will it be enough to keep her alive?

She's debating the merits of heading back to the town to liberate more supplies when a sound gets her attention. It's not any of the normal sounds she's grown accustomed to in the short time she's been running loose on Molpa Colony. She's not sure what it is, but she knows it's significant.

Snatching up the bag, she dives into a nearby bush and goes still.

Dozens of four-toed feet appear in her field of vision. They walk around the area and even climb up on the rock she'd been sitting on.

"I can't find any markers of where she went from here," one man tells the others. "There's a clear trail up to here. Now it's obfuscated. Either she was picked up and carried off by something or she somehow left no trace of her path."

"A raxic could kill and carry her," a female voice volunteers. "From the image you showed me, she's rather small, easy prey for even a juvenal raxic."

Raxic? Crap! Sounds like if they don't capture her, she's going to need to find a defensible place to hide tonight. Maybe figure out some kind of weapon.

"If Osian wasn't such an idiot, she'd have a tracking collar we could use. He's supposed to change out the collars every solar, not keep them until they're in such poor condition that they fail moments after getting a location."

Sounds like she disabled the collar just in time!

"She might have done something to it. Some of these humans can be rather clever."

"I doubt it." That's the voice of the man who collected her this morning. "Humans are a stupid species. Not good for much at all. Only bright enough to be obedient pets, nothing more."

Some of the others agree as they move around the area. When one of them contacts someone and asks for search bots to be sent out, she knows she can't stay there any longer.

Slowly, she eases herself back. She's only moved a few inches when she snaps a branch and all the talking stops.

"Do you think that was a raxic?"

"Or maybe the human?"

"It came from right over here."

"You two go first. If it's a raxic, your weapons will wound it. Try not to shoot the human. Females are so scarce out here."

"I'll try."

Should she make a break for it and try to outrun them? Her small size in this dense forest might give her a slight advantage. She debates when to jump up and run as two sets of feet get closer and closer to her spot. They are veering off to her left slightly. If she's patient, they'll get themselves tangled in the brambles over there, giving her precious seconds when she maneuvers herself into a better hiding spot.

She never gets a chance.

A big hand closes over the back of her wrap and lifts her clear out of the bush. "Got her!"

She only gets a second to register the group of mostly unfamiliar Talins all making happy rumbling sounds at the sight of her when a blur suddenly charges and the hand holding her lets go. She lands awkwardly, twisting her ankle and ending up in a heap on the ground.

While she sits helpless on the ground, a fight between the group of pursuing Talins and a figure wearing black pants, a black tunic, and a black cowl rages.

The newcomer is one hell of a fighter, moving with incredible speed and disabling two of the Talins before anyone can even raise a weapon.

Most of the group are taken down without much effort from the cowled fighter, except for two. When he attacked, they backed off and let the others wear him down before they approached.

"Are you from the Remoro Clan?" one of the two remaining wheezes out as he and the stranger exchange a few blows.

"I can give you asylum here," the talkative one continues. "We're a very new colony and don't have enough workers in any trade. You could have your pick of work. You don't need to sink to mercenary work or thievery."

The offer is obviously a ploy, an attempt to distract the black-clad stranger so the second Talin could get into position. They attack the hooded male as one, but he's much too skilled to be caught.

With movements too fast for the eye to follow, the stranger knocks one of the remaining men senseless and then watches the last one run at top speed back into the forest, presumably to get help.

Now the cowled figure is the only one standing. Chest heaving from exertion, he methodically examines each Talin on the ground to make sure no one's getting back up any time soon.

Stumbling to her feet with a wince of pain from her ankle, she grabs a nearby vine covered tree to steady herself.

By the time she's standing, the figure has finished checking the unconscious Talins. She tries to take a step toward him, but her ankle isn't a willing participant and folds under her weight. She goes down, but the male in black is there, grabbing her up before she can hit the ground. She wraps her arms around him and hugs tightly.

"It's about damn time you got here, Dalt," she whispers. "I was worried about you."

"How did you know it was me?" Dalt asks with a shocked rumble as she pulls the cowl down to reveal his face. He sits down on the nearby boulder, cradling her on his lap.

"You do realize humans aren't dumb. Right?" Lakin teases and grabs ahold of his clawless right hand and holds it up. "No claws? No quills? That's hard to miss."

Dalt's completely silent for a moment, staring at her hand holding his, and then he rumbles out a laugh. "I might be the stupid one."

"Just stick with me," Lakin says with a grin. "I'll do the thinking for both of us."

"I very much intend to stay with you," Dalt agrees as he looks around them. "It's good to hold you again, but we need to move."

"Right, good idea, let me just," she moves off his lap to grab the bag of supplies but ends up stumbling a few steps when her ankle protests.

"Damn, that's bad," she mumbles, leaning against a tree. Dalt hauls her into his arms again. He cradles her high on his chest and she holds her injured foot up so both of them can see her rapidly swelling ankle.

"You're injured," Dalt says, worry clear in his voice.

"Looks like," Lakin agrees grimly. "If you can find the right-sized branches, I can use them as crutches or—" She stops talking as Dalt tightens his hold on her.

"No," he says simply. He leans over, holds her with one arm as he plucks up her bag and throws it over a shoulder. Then he jogs off into the forest, obviously intent on carrying her to their destination.

"Or you could do that," she states wryly.

Leaving the unconscious Talins to the mercy of the forest, Dalt carries her through the wilderness at a brisk pace, impressing her with his endurance and strength. "How did you find me?" she asks as greenery flies past her.

"Tracked your collar to this planet," Dalt tells her simply. "But got here too late and found Holian's collar in some trash. Next I looked through the facility records. I was heading to the family you were given to, only to run across a group organizing a search party. I followed them."

"That would explain your excellent timing," Lakin states with admiration. "I knew you'd find me."

"You did?" his voice is surprised. "You weren't scared?" How is this guy running, carrying her, having a conversation and not needing to breathe hard?

So not fair!

"Maybe a little worried," she concedes. "I had to escape, after all. But not scared. Besides, if you hadn't found me, I'd have just figured out a way to find you."

"Ingenious little human, I know you would've found a way," he answers with a quick purr. She can tell he's sincere and not mocking her.

"What happened after I got myself captured? I feel dumb about that, by the way. I should've been sneakier, but I didn't expect someone to be walking out of the engine room."

"I saw the image capture of you bumping into the mercenary," he tells her grimly. "But not until we took the ship."

"Wait, back up there. You took the ship. That's it?" she asks with an arched eyebrow. "That's all you're going to give me. You took the ship?"

He grunts in response. Then, almost absently, he rubs his scent glands into her hair as he slows to a brisk walk. The smell of cedar fills her nose, and Lakin realizes how much she missed it. All her remaining anxiety falls away as Dalt's bonding oil soaks into her scalp.

"You know, I bet it was a little more involved than that simple sentence lets on," Lakin teases him. "But I'll let you get away with that description for now."

"Hold your breath," is the only warning she gets and suddenly they're in water. Clutching her with one arm, he swims them a short distance. Well, no, he doesn't swim, he walks. It's as if he's so heavy he simply sinks to the river bed and strolls across as if walking on a normal path.

They emerge on the other side of the narrow but deep river. The water is freezing, but to her surprise the omnie gets warm and self-dries within minutes.

"That's handy," she says, rubbing the material between her fingers. "No wonder the servant was so adamant that I needed to wear an omnie."

"It will also self-regulate, getting steadily warmer through the night as the temperature drops," Dalt explains as he start jogging again.

His clothes don't self-dry like her omnie, but they do dry quickly. By the time they reach the spot where Dalt set up camp, he's dry but breathing a little hard. The last section of their travel was up a steep hill.

The campsite includes a small domed shelter made of some kind of fabric, a heating coil set on a rock, and a metallic box. The domed shelter is very interesting because she sees no obvious doors. She's intensely curious about how they'll get in and out of it.

"I came down in a shuttle. It's hidden several darts away. That's far enough that I don't want to try for the shuttle tonight," Dalt explains as he sets her on the ground next to the heating coil. "They'll be out searching, and they could easily spot us. Once it's dark, we'll pack up and head out."

"Good plan," she agrees, assuming he can see much better in the dark than she can. She watches as he sets a few square objects around the small campsite and then taps the Ident hanging off his belt. After a brief hum, a net of energy arches up and covers them completely.

"From the outside, this area will look like part of the jungle," he explains. "It will fool sensors too." Sitting down heavily next to her, he gently reaches under her omnie for a leg and pulls her injured ankle into his lap. He feels around the injury for a bit, making her gasp a few times.

"It's sprained, not broken," he declares with a rumble of relief.

"I could've told you that," she grumbles. "I know what a sprain versus a break feels like. Give it a little time and I'll be fine."

With a rumbled laugh, he reaches over to the metal box and flips open the lid to rummage around. "Here," he hands her a wafer. "Let this dissolve on your tongue. It'll help with the swelling and pain."

With a mental shrug, she leans forward and uses her mouth to take it from Dalt. He makes a slight, gasping, rumbling sound as her lips close around his finger and thumb, but remains still.

He only drops his hand after she's finished sucking the wafer from his fingers and straightens up. But his upper body remains stock still as he stares at her.

"Did I break you?" she teases.

"Would you do that again?" he asks suddenly. "But not with my fingers? Would you be willing to put something else in your mouth?" It takes her a moment to figure out what he's asking, and then she laughs.

"Sure thing, big guy," she says with a grin. "I can put, uh, other things in my mouth. But maybe a little later. I'm kinda hungry right now."

"Of course." Dalt reaches back into the box to pull out a few nondescript pouches. Tossing them on the heating coil, he taps a few buttons and soon the pouches pillow out.

"This isn't human feed," Dalt warns her. "But it's considered safe for human consumption."

"As long as it's not rotting or moving, I'm game," Lakin declares with a grin as Dalt pinches the corner of one of the pouches to pull it off the heating coil. Setting it on the ground, he pulls a small knife out of his belt and cuts it open. Aromatic steam curls up from the opening, making Lakin's mouth water.

Once Dalt has deemed it sufficiently cool for her to eat, he hands her the pouch and shows her how to tip it up and let the food slide out into her mouth.

The flavor of the cubed food reminds her of one of the mild Earth curries her neighbor was so fond of when she was growing up.

"Is it sufficiently bland?" Dalt asks, worry in his tone. Lakin nods eagerly.

"Tastes great," she tells him, happy to be eating something other than the tasteless human feed the siblings gave her. She needs to find some way to get a change of information into the Talin literature about humans. They need to know that humans like flavor in their food. "I wouldn't mind having this again."

"You like it?" His appalled words make her laugh, but then she chokes a little because her mouth is full. Rubbing her back, he hands her a drinking flask and murmurs to her soothingly as she coughs and drinks until her throat feels clear.

"I guess I like it so much I tried to breathe it," she jokes.

"You can't breathe it," Dalt warns her, and she laughs again.

"It's too bad you don't get my humor," she tells him. "Because I'm hilarious."

"If you say so, I'll believe it."

His voice is so staid that she doesn't realize he's teasing her right away.

"Har, har," she comments with a grin.

"Should I pinch your nose shut so you're not tempted to aspirate your food again?" he asks, moving his hand up to place it on her nose. She bats it away with a chuckle.

"Don't you have rations to eat?" she asks.

"I fed on the shuttle before I got here, so I won't need to eat for at least another rotation."

"All the more for me," Lakin says and tips a few more cubes into her mouth.

Once she finishes, Dalt pulls her into his lap and eyes the damaged collar. He puts his finger between the collar and her throat, testing the fit. Then he grabs ahold of it on opposite sides. Carefully, he pulls until she hears the metal protest and then she's free.

"Thanks," she murmurs, rubbing a hand over her naked throat. "I didn't like that collar at all."

With a grunt, Dalt throws it into a nearby bush. "It's an old style, unnecessarily heavy and cumbersome. I'll get you a much nicer one once we're back on Kalor."

To her surprise, the thought of Dalt putting a collar on her doesn't bother her. "I want to pick the style."

"Certainly," he agrees. "Are you still hungry? Would you like another ration pouch?"

"I'm good for now," she tells him. "Maybe I'll have another one later. But right now, could you do two things for me?"

"Of course."

"I need you to join me in that little shelter thingy, and I need you to take off your pants."

He moves so fast she doesn't get to see how the shelter's door opens.

CHAPTER 24

Dalt

Dalt almost rips his pants to get them off. He knows he's being a brute. He shouldn't have asked Lakin to put her mouth on him. That's not something he should ask a female to do. It's considered rude and inappropriate. But after she sucked on his fingers it felt like his brain was hit by a live current of electricity.

Not only wasn't she offended by his request; she was even amenable to it.

And now, even though it would be easy for her to pretend she never offered, she brings it up and pushes him into action. Blood is already filling his member, inflating and causing the tip to emerge from its protective pouch.

"This is so different from a human," Lakin murmurs as she runs her hand over the head of his mating shaft, then dipping her fingers into the tight space between it and the pouch. "I like it."

"It's evolution," he mumbles, unsure how to respond to her admiration. On the rare occasions Talins have sex it's treated like a race to climax. Lakin isn't in a hurry and seems content to spend time admiring his body.

It's such a different experience that Dalt has no frame of reference for it.

"It's fascinating," she continues, rubbing her soft fingers against his trapped mating shaft. "It's like velvet inside here. And then it springs out, like it's eager to meet me. It's kinda adorable."

She has admired his strength and skill but never said she found him visually appealing.

"I'm adorable?"

"Have I not mentioned before how cute you are?" she asks as she leans over and brushes her lips across the very tip of his mating shaft.

That touch makes his shaft finish swelling causing the mating pouch to snap back and his erection bounces free. Fully engorged, it bobs in front of Lakin's face, his seed sack hanging heavily below.

"Well, hello there!" she announces. "I've missed you."

"Are you…are you speaking to my mating shaft?" he asks. "If you are that is fine, but you should know it's not like the tentacle on a Hamlershin. It doesn't have a separate brain from the rest of me."

For some reason his explanation makes her giggle and whisper, "I don't know, it might be a primary brain. I've met plenty of males that let their dicks do all their thinking for them."

Her giggle and words cause warm air from her mouth to waft over his shaft, making him shudder at the sensation.

"Is dick the human word for mating shaft?" he asks, trying to focus on her instead of the demands of his body.

"It's a nickname," she explains, never taking her eyes off his throbbing shaft. It's almost as if her gaze has weight and he can feel her eyes stroking him. How is that possible? Is this because he's scent bonded? It's no wonder his ancestors wrote long pieces of literature about the dangers of bonding. It's intoxicating.

"…cock, pecker, peter, johnson, and trouser snake," she says and he realizes he missed the beginning of her comment. "Anyway, I've always liked calling them cocks or dicks. The others all sound too weird to me."

"You can use any word you like for my mating shaft," he says, hoping it's the correct response.

He watches as she wraps a slim hand around his mating sha–no, dick. That appendage is a dick or cock now. He's determined to use the words she likes!

She strokes up and down a few times with a touch so light it could be a brush of clothing. Even that slight pressure is electrifying.

"Such a pretty cock," she whispers before reaching up and swiping a hand across his cheek. He can feel his over full scent gland release bonding oil. She gathered most of it in her hand, only leaving a little to trickle down his face.

"I love this smell," she says, rubbing his bonding oil over his shaft. "Your oil makes a perfect lube."

"It..uh..it's meant to," he stutters out. It's hard to talk while she strokes him. "Female Talins produce oil in their scent…uh, glands and their–"

A firm squeeze pushes all the air out of his lungs. "By the ancestors, Lakin, don't stop!"

She makes a soft sound of humor. "You like that?"

"Very much…much! You can make it engorge any time you like," he assures her, giddy at the idea of Lakin touching him often. "You are free to treat my body as if you own it."

"Does that mean I can put a collar on you?" she asks with a little laugh. He adores her laugh. It never fails to lighten his heart. He's sure that if her laughter could be bottled, no one who bought it would ever suffer the Fading.

"If you wish," he agrees. "You can put a collar around my throat or my member."

He's thrilled when his comment makes her laugh again. "Kinky," she says.

"Kinky," he repeats, testing out the unfamiliar word. When his translator draws a blank. "Is that good?"

"Right here and right now it is," she assures him.

"Then I'm highly kinky," he agrees. "How should I be kinky for you right now?"

"All I want you to be is still for right now," she tells him as she pushes against his chest. She wants him to lie back, so he falls backward on the bed mat. This temporary domicile is one of the nicest that credits can buy and includes a built-in bed on the floor. He hopes it is soft enough for his delicate human.

"I can be still for you," he says as she runs her hands up his thighs. Her delicate little hands leave a trail of fire as they stroke his skin. He's never paid much attention to the sensory information he receives from his dermis. Except for heeding the warnings it gives him about heat, cold, or pain, he's never really thought about what things feel like. If someone told him before this that his dermis could respond to delicate contact, he would have mocked them.

But he would've been wrong to do so.

When she scrapes her blunt fingernails lightly just below his seed sack, he shutters and fights to keep from moving. The sensation is both wonderful and horrible. The skin of his pouch tightens at the base of his engorged member, becoming almost painful. When her fingers finally start feeling around the base of his member, he just about levitates.

"Did that hurt?" she asks as she lifts her hand away. His involuntary movement must have startled her.

"Good!" he gets out past his tight throat and addled brain. "Much good."

"Then I guess I'll keep going," she murmurs softly.

He's rumbling out a purr so loud that if anyone gets close to their campsite it won't matter if they can't see it; they'll hear him. He needs to calm down. He needs to get himself under control. He needs—

Her warm mouth closes over the tip of his member, and all thoughts leave his brain. He's nothing but sensations. Every part of his brain is taken up with processing the most amazing thing he's ever experienced.

He's heard about human-Talin sexual interactions. He's seen the product of those unions, giggling and playing in Holian's mansion. He's watched other human-Talin couples cuddle and lip-press, heard humans give their adorable little moans and even smelled arousal coming off them occasionally. But none of what he knows prepares him for this absolute loss of higher brain function he's experiencing with Lakin.

Their one time before this at his cabin was phenomenal. The intimacy they shared in his bed was well beyond his expectations, entering into the realm of transcendence. He never knew anything could be better than burying his member into the sweet heat between her legs.

He was wrong.

For the first time in his life, he's glad his claws and quills are missing because otherwise he might accidentally damage little Lakin as his body no longer listens to his demand for stillness. Letting the tip of his member pop of out her mouth, he looks down just in time to watch her run her soft, flat human tongue up the length of him. Then she gets her knees under her and wraps both hands around him and sucks the tip back into her dainty mouth.

Her hands and mouth never stop moving as she works on him. It doesn't take long before he realizes his climax is imminent.

"Lak—" He tries to say her name, but he can't even make his brain work well enough for that. Desperate to keep his human from experiencing anything she might consider unpleasant, he tries again. "Lakin, I'm—"

Raising her head, she gives him a quick glare. "Keep quiet. I'm busy here," she tells him and then goes back to lavishing attention on his throbbing shaft. A sound he's never made before in his life issues from his chestbox, along with the purring. He's never made two sounds at once, but a strange rumble builds and soon it's so powerful it's rattling the temporary domicile. This new sound is much too aggressive for a rumble, which is used to display softer emotions such as surprise, pleasure, or approval. This rumble is wild and savage. It's the rumble of a man succumbing to his base instinct.

No, not just succumbing, reveling.

His climax hits him hard, also like a blow. He cries out, his rumbles crescendo, and pleasure spikes through him. Undaunted by the fluid flowing out of him, Lakin keeps licking and sucking until she wrings everything out of it. Only when his member deflates and pulls back into the protective pouch does she let go.

With the loss of his erection, his thinking brain comes back online and he realizes he never did anything to make sure Lakin enjoyed herself.

Deep shame fills him as he sits up, only to watch as she withdraws her hand from between her legs, the lower folds of her omnie falling back into place. Her face is flushed, and she gives him a content, lazy smile as she crawls forward and falls to the mat at his side. "That was great," she murmurs, closing her eyes and snuggling up against him.

"You pleasured yourself?" he asks, as he reclines and then draws her against him. Her skin is flushed, and her breathing is rapid. "While you cared for me, you brought yourself to culmination also?"

"It was easy. Listening to you come was hot," she says.

"You enjoy servicing me?" he asks cautiously, realizing he might not have ruined anything with his selfishness.

"Sure," she says. "I liked it. I liked what we did back on Kalor. And I'm sure I'll like a lot of other stuff we do together."

"You're a kind and generous human, Lakin," Dalt tells her, overjoyed to find that not only isn't she upset with him, but she is open to repeating her action in the future. His words make her giggle.

"And you're easily impressed," she tells him. "Now I want to take a nap and I demand snuggles."

"Snuggles after," he insists.

Her brows furrow. "After what?"

"After you climax again so I know you're truly satiated!"

"No I–"her words are cut off when he rolls on top of her.

"Mine!" he growls. "I care for what is mine." Her legs part and he settles between them. Her omnie and wrap rise up high.

Kneeling between her legs, he reaches down and tugs the wrap and omnie up until they're both bundled at her waist. He'd should take the time to tug the garments off, but the need to taste her is too strong.

Dropping his upper body down, he puts his face close to the curls hiding her sex. He could already smell her sweet slick. With a single finger he opens her slit, entranced as her wet delicate flesh is exposed.

"Human women are like flowers," he breathes with renewed wonder. "Beautiful and full of sweet nectar."

"That's the most–oh!"

Her words are cut off when he puts his mouth to her and licks from her hole to her clit. She tastes as good as she smells.

When he teases her little human clit by only licking at it lightly, she makes an aggravated sound.

"I swear, Dalt. If you don't start getting serious I'm going to do something drastic!"

He sucks the nub into his mouth and she gasps. Her hips raise, trying to push against his face. Grabbing her hips, he forces her back down and holds her still as he sucks, licks and rubs bonding oil all over her clit and inside of her slit.

Slick weeps from her and their scents combine, activating something primal deep in his mind. He needs to hear her come and it needs to be loud!

He pulls his face away only far enough to speak a few words. "Tell me how much you want this. I want your every gasp, groan, moan and scream!"

"Aren't you insistent," she quips. She's about to say something else when he slides a single digit inside her. One of her legs pushes down, as if to push him away while the other curls around his body to draw him closer. He understands exactly because her mouth on him had been sweet torture also.

He fits his mouth back onto her clit as he works his finger in and out of her. She's hot, wet, and tight. Unable to resist, he moves his finger so he can press his tongue inside her.

"Oh! Yes!" she cries out. He didn't expect her to like this so much, but he keeps doing it and soon she starts whimpering and thrashing against him.

It's awkward but he gets a thumb and finger around her clit and starts massaging it, gently at first and then with greater pressure. All the while he's stroking his tongue inside her, licking her juices from her core.

He loses himself in her sex. Time disappears and he's reduced to a creature of need. He'll never get enough of her juices in his mouth or the sound of her pleasure in his earholes.

Her heels press down his back and he's thankful there's no sharp plating there to accidentally hurt her.

"Dalt!" she screams, her back bowing and her body going stiff. She tightens around his tongue and slick floods from her into his mouth. He swallows and licks until she's sobbing and her heels pull up and push against this shoulders.

"Stop," she begs. "No more."

It's only with great reluctance that he does as she asks. He takes a moment to use his tongue and fingers to clean his face, getting every last taste of her in his mouth.

"We will do this again," he warns her.

"That sounds like a threat," she murmurs. Looking up he sees her eyes are closed and her face relaxed. He's worn his little human out.

"A promise," he counters.

She slits her eyes open and looks up at him. Moving languidly, she pats the spot next to her.

"Get over here. I need snuggles."

Assuming that snuggles is the human term for clutching while lying down, Dalt unfurls his body and stretches out next to her. Lakin rolls over and wiggles up next to him. Using one of his arms as a pillow she throws a leg over his belly and an arm over his chest. He's become part of her bed and he adores it.

Soon Lakin's small body is twitching slightly as she dreams, and Dalt holds her carefully to keep any twitching limb from hitting one of the hard plates on his body.

Even in her sleep, Lakin's a danger to herself.

CHAPTER

25

Lakin

Jarred from a deep sleep, Lakin blinks groggily as the side of their temporary domicile is ripped open from both ends and a dozen hands reach in after her and Dalt. With a roar, Dalt launches himself at the hands. Cries of pain and aggressive rattles reach her ears.

Lakin tries to bat away the hands reaching for her, but she doesn't have any weapons, so she's easily held still while restraints are fastened to her wrist and ankles.

"This again?" she shouts in frustration. "Really? This again!"

When a new collar is secured around her throat, she screams with anger. She's not one to flay uselessly when a cool head is almost always the better option, but being woken so abruptly and ripped away from Dalt along with being bound again pushes her reasonable brain beyond her ability to cope.

To make matters worse, she can hear Dalt fighting behind her, and unlike earlier, it doesn't sound like he's winning. Fear for him makes any hold she had on her temper fray and break.

"I'm going to get free," she shouts at them. "And when I do, I'm going to figure out a way to kill each and every one of you, even if I have to travel to the ends of the universe to do it. I'll pull out your damn teeth and wear them as a necklace. None of you will ever be safe from my wrath!"

Her declaration of violence is met with several rumbles of laughter. "She's quite the feisty human," one woman holding her says.

"Would we expect anything less from a human Daltenion would pick?" a male asks as he reaches out to feel Lakin's hair. She bites at him. He pulls his hand back with a rattle of anger, but the woman holding her just rumbles out another laugh.

"You deserved that Tilarin," she says.

The sounds of fighting gets more intense before she hears a weapon being discharged and then suddenly all the sound behind her goes quiet. Struggling to turn her head, she can just see Dalt lying motionless on the ground with at least six Talins around him. Several of the group are on the ground, obviously in pain. One of them is even unconscious. One male is cradling an arm to his chest. In his other hand is a device pointed at Dalt. With an unhappy rattle, he looks up at the woman holding Lakin.

"I didn't want to use it, but we were going to lose," he explains with an embarrassed rumble. "He's so fast. I've never fought anyone with such speed."

"And you probably never will again." There's pride in the woman's voice. "Now hurry, we need to leave."

The few men on the ground get up, testing limbs for soundness. Everyone can walk, and one man hefts the unconscious one over his shoulder. "Ready," he calls after he's taken a few strides to test his ability to carry his cohort's bulk.

"Excellent," the woman says and turns to the other woman in the group. "We need to leave the moment we board."

"The ship's prepared," the second woman assures her.

With a rumble of satisfaction, the woman holding her strides off. Everyone else falls in step around her.

"We could easily take him with us," one of the crew members points out as they walk.

"No, he needs to follow us," the woman in charge counters. "I won't drag him home bound hand and foot. He must walk onto Talarian of his own free will. I can smell him all over this human. He'll follow her. He'll have no choice, and then he can answer for his disappearance."

That makes no sense. The woman's argument is flawed. Lakin's anger means she can't be silent.

"You're an idiot," she blurts out. "If he's chasing after me, he won't be going anywhere of his own free will! You're still forcing him."

"Hush, human, you have no idea what you're talking about," the woman says and then pointedly ignores Lakin to talk to the man on her right.

For the first time in a long time, Lakin feels tears fall from her eyes. She's been helpless before. She's been hurt and abused. A few times she was sure death was imminent. But now, as she catches a last glimpse of Dalt's form, she feels a fear she's never experienced before. His chest is moving, so he's breathing, but how hurt is he? Could a wild animal on this planet kill him while he's defenseless?

"Please," she begs. Threats didn't work, so maybe cajoling will. "Don't do this. I'm a horrible pet. I'm annoying, and I escape a lot. And I bite. And I don't do anything pleasing. Please, don't take me away from Dalt."

The woman holding her doesn't even pause in her long stride as Lakin makes her case. "It's interesting that you threaten at the same time you plead to be left behind," the woman says with a humorous rumble. "I can see why you and Daltenion would make a good pair."

"Daltenion?"

"You don't even know his true name?" the woman murmurs so softly that Lakin knows she's thinking out loud. "Is he so eager to erase his family that he sheds every part of us, even his true name?"

"If you let me go, I'll tell him to get in touch. I promise," Lakin tells her. "I'll even get him to send vids and letters and all kinds of communications. I'll have him sign everything Daltenion. I'll call him Daltenion. I'll have it tattooed on my damn forehead. Just let—"

"Hush, little human," the woman interrupts with another rumbling laugh. "You don't know what you're talking about. Be good and remain quiet."

"I thought I covered that!" Lakin shouts in the woman's earhole, startling her enough to make her stride hitch for a step. "I'm not a well-behaved human. I'm not worth the effort of stealing. Just put me down and walk away. It's best for everyone. You don't want me on your ship. Shit will get broken."

A rattle of annoyance comes out of the woman, and she comes to an abrupt stop. Shifting Lakin around so she can be held with one hand, the woman uses her other hand to capture Lakin's chin and force her to be still.

"You're shouting and crying. You're far more upset than I anticipated." The woman replaces the rattle with a purr. "Poor thing, you've been through so much. I can make you feel better." Everyone else stops when the woman stops, not talking or hurrying her.

Looking at one man on her right, she jerks her head. "Second, do you have any human-grade tranquilizers?"

Those words make Lakin struggle. She knows it's useless, but she can't make herself remain still while the man steps forward.

He holds up a wafer. "It needs to go in her mouth."

The woman's grip on her jaw tightens to the point of pain. The moment she gasps, the man slides the wafer between her lips. Then he helps the women hold her mouth closed.

Just like the pain relief medication Dalt gave her earlier, this one dissolves on her tongue. The drug is fast and makes her feel woozy. She blinks up at the faces around her as tears roll down her cheeks.

Damn it, when did she get so weepy?

"I believe it's taking effect," the man announces as he withdraws his hand.

"Please," Lakin begs again, even as her eyes flutter closed, her lids suddenly too heavy to keep open.

"Rest now," the woman tells her, shifting her weight again. Sleep pulls at her as the woman settles her high against her chest, cradling her like a child. The smell of soapy-almonds fills her nose.

"Wrong," Lakin slurs. The smell is wrong. The arms holding her are wrong. The voice is wrong. Nothing here is as it should be.

"Everything will be right soon," the woman assures her, and then Lakin is asleep.

CHAPTER 26

Lakin

Waking abruptly, Lakin remains still and lets the sounds and smells filter into her brain as she tries to figure out if anyone's near her. It's easy to tell she's on a ship without even opening her eyes. The artificial gravity is unmistakable, and it even feels heavy, as if simulating a little more force than the galaxy standard gravity used on most space stations and ships.

Taking a few deep breaths, she tests the air. The scents added to the atmosphere tell her it's a standard mix, so she doesn't need to worry about suffering from oxygen deprivation. So far, she hasn't heard anything, so she risks a peek and cracks open one eye. She's on her side on a bunk, facing the wall so she doesn't see much. To find out anything more about her surroundings, she's going to have to give up the pretense of being asleep.

Letting her eyes open fully, she turns her head to take in the room around her. She's in an empty crew room, resting on the only bunk pulled down from the wall. The lights are dim, probably in an attempt to help keep her calm, and the hatch to the room is closed.

She's not sure if it's locked, but getting out of the room is the second step. The first step is to get herself out of these restraints.

It takes some rolling around, but she gets her hands out from behind her back with a lot of panting, cussing, and wiggling. Getting her bound wrists past her feet used to be easier, but apparently, she's gotten a little out of practice.

Once her hands are in front of her, she sits up on the end of the bunk and examines the lock on her restraints, delighted when she notices the tech holding them closed. It's a type of bio-print lock that could be fooled.

There's a small storage locker in the room. Hopping over to it, she finds an assortment of random items. One item, a tube of plastifilm, is just perfect for what she needs.

Plastifilm is used to create a thin, protective, transparent layer over anything. But it can also be used to defeat a bio-print lock. Hopping over to the single small table in the room, she opens the tube of plastifilm and spreads a layer on the table. She doesn't give it long enough to harden, only become semi-rigid. Plastifilm has a medium set time so that workers can manipulate it into any kind of shape when doing repair work. Pealing the strip off the table, she hops to the door and presses the strip right where everyone will have put their palm to open the door if it's locked.

When she's sure she has a clear imprint on the plastifilm, she pulls it off and sinks to the floor. She sets it on the floor in front of her and looks at her nails. She'd scratched and bit when they'd dragged her away from Dalt. That meant there are Talin cells under her nails. Using one nail to clean under the others, she sprinkles what's there on the plasti film. She could only hope there was enough.

If this didn't work she'd simply hide the plastifilm on her person and scratch someone the moment they touched her. With a little planning it would be easy to deliberately gather biological material under her nails.

She doesn't pick up the plastiflim for fear of potentially losing the material she painstakingly gathered from under her nails. Instead she maneuvers her wrists until she can press the bio-print lock to the strip of plasti-fill.

After a breathless second, the lock recognizes the print and biological marker on the plastifilm and clicks. The cuff opens.

She repeats pressing the process to each lock and soon she's free. What were they thinking, leaving her in a room with all the necessary tools to get loose?

They must think she's a complete idiot.

No, that's not correct. The fact that she's human makes them underestimate her. To them, human equals helpless. Dalt would never make such a mistake.

Thinking of Dalt makes her heart speed up. She needs to get back to the planet. She doesn't know how long it's been, but Dalt could still be deep in the forest, unconscious and helpless.

Unfortunately, the plastifilm trick doesn't work for the lock on the room door. Tugging her omnie open, she feels around until she finds the long, thin needle-like tool she stole off Dalt so many rotations ago. She's going to have to find out where he got it because she needs to get herself a few more just like it. Since one end is sharp, she's gotten in the habit of pinning it to the inside hem of her wrap, and even now, after so many things have happened, it's still there.

She does something very similar to the display next to the door as she did to her enclosure gate back on Kalor. Just like back on the colony, her ministrations not only unlock the hatch but also render the locking mechanism useless.

It takes her much longer to open up the hatch than to escape from her restraints, and she's feeling some serious anxiety by the time she finally eases the hatch open. The hallway is clear, so she hurries out and starts exploring. Most ships have a similar layout because there are only so many ways to design a spacefaring vessel. She needs to find the engine, electrical, and biosystems rooms, so she heads aft. For being a good-sized ship, there doesn't appear to be much in the way of a crew. She's amazed she hasn't run into anyone yet.

Her luck must be back in working order because she finds her way to the aft area without seeing a single soul. The engine room is locked up tightly, but the electrical room isn't. Sliding in, she locks the hatch behind her. It's common for ships to keep their vulnerable systems locked down while under way, but either someone messed up or no one thought the electrical system could be vulnerable.

On the surface, she can understand their reasoning. The system she's looking at has triple redundancies, and enough fail-safes to keep her from doing any actual damage unless she wants to use some kind of explosive.

But no one's ever truly prepared for Lakin because she knows those fail-safes can be manipulated.

Pulling off a cover, she wiggles her arms in and starts feeling around. It takes three different covers to find what she's looking for, and she ends up with most of her upper body inside the machinery. It's delicate work, looking for the system circuits she needs without accidentally frying herself. At one point she smells smoke. Looking down, she finds her omnie caught fire on an exposed plasma diode. Slapping it out, she takes a few steadying breaths and goes back to work, keeping clear of those diodes.

Once she's done, she puts everything back together and slips out of the electrical room. Now she needs to find a pod and wait. Pretty soon her sabotage will go into action and everyone should be running around in chaos. Then she'll launch in the escape pod, figure out where she is, and head back to Dalt.

That's when her luck fails her.

She rounds a corner just in time to run right into a Talin coming from the opposite direction. With an oomph, she bounces off the woman and falls to the ground in an ungraceful heap.

"What… how?" the Talin starts, but stops talking the moment Lakin scrambles to her feet and tries to run. It's no use though. The Talin scoops her up and restrains her with little effort.

That's it! She's done with the being manhandled by Talins. From now on she's going to make finding a weapon a priority before anything else.

The female doesn't say a word as she carries Lakin back to the room she escaped. With a rattle of annoyance, she realizes the hatch's lock won't engage.

"I don't suppose there's any point in putting those back on you anyway," the Talin says, eyeing the manacles in the corner.

"None," Lakin agrees quickly, and the Talin rumbles out a laugh.

"I'll need to take you to the bridge with me." Her words are accompanied by a soft rattle of impatience.

"You can leave me here. I promise not to leave the room this time," Lakin says.

"I get the impression you like to roam, pet," the Talin says, hefting her up and starting back down the corridor. "Better to keep you close at hand rather than have you find trouble."

Lakin remains silent as the woman carries her through the ship. She memorizes the route as they walk and notes the locations of several emergency pods. This mishap might help her. If she's going to be on the bridge, she'll be able to figure out how far away they are from Dalt. And she might even be able to sew some discord or disable something on the bridge when no one's looking.

The possibilities are endless.

"Why did you bring her in here?" a familiar voice asks. The woman puts Lakin down to face the Talin who drugged and kidnapped her in the first place. She's the one who was in charge of the group planetside, so she must be in charge up here as well.

"Sorry to intrude. I'll just be going," Lakin says brightly and turns to leave, but a wall of Talins stand in her way.

"If she's staying here, she'll need a place to sit. I'll fetch a kneeling pillow," someone says and hurries away as Lakin turns to face her kidnapper.

"I don't know how she did it, Captain Sherianan, but she got out of her bonds and out of the room." This feels like a military ship, so is this captain part of the Talin military, a mercenary, or a rebel of some kind?

"Everything just came loose," Lakin explains, trying to make her face everything innocent and clueless. "I woke up, and they fell off when I moved."

"And the hatch?" the captain asks the woman now standing behind Lakin.

"Nothing obvious is wrong with it, but she did something because it won't lock or even latch."

"I think it was a faulty display," Lakin volunteers. "I just pressed on it a few times, and the door came open for me. I was really hungry and lonely, so I went looking for someone to feed me."

"Did you now," Captain Sherianan murmurs, sounding out a rumble of interest. "I must say, you're rather composed for a human who's been through so much. I'm surprised you're not in tears. You seemed rather upset when we took you away from Daltenion."

"Why would I cry?" Lakin asks, deciding to go for a subservient act. "If you're my new owner, you're going to take care of me. Right? You must like me to go through so much effort to steal me."

A loud laugh rumbles out of the captain. "You are a special one," she comments, grabbing Lakin's arm and tugging her toward the captain's chair. "I can see why Daltenion scent-bonded to you."

Those words make Lakin freeze and then stumble. "I…I don't know what you're talking about."

"I think you know exactly what I'm referring to, Lakin."

They know her name? Who are these people? Time to go for broke.

Straightening to her full height, Lakin meets Captain Sherianan's gaze, letting her face reflect her determination.

"Let me go or I'll destroy your ship." Out of the corner of her eye, she can see a counter telling her Talin homeworld standard time.

"You have three submarks to comply." As she expects, the Talins around her find this amusing. Several of them, including the captain, rumble out laughs at her threat. The Talin who ran off to get a kneeling pillow comes back onto the bridge and drops a large plush square mat on the floor next to the captain's chair. The captain points to the mat.

"Come here and make yourself comfortable. It'll be a few marks until we arrive," she says. Lakin doesn't move toward the pad. Instead, she leans against a nearby wall and braces herself.

"I warned you," she says with an evil grin as she watches the submarks turn over to change the mark counter on the clock. Everyone on the bridge freezes for a moment, but when nothing happens right away, they rumble out laughs again. One of the Talins reaches for her, but just as he's about to close his hand around her upper arm, the entire ship shutters.

So much for dramatic timing. Her count down was slightly off. That would've been amazing if she'd timed it that perfectly.

No sooner does the quaking on the ship stop than several alarms sound, sending the Talins around her into a frenzy as they hurry to their posts and start assessing damage.

"I'm getting several failure readings on engine two," one shouts.

"I see at least three spots of contamination on level four from the fuel supply pipes," another one calls out.

"Hull integrity on level twelve at cross section four is compromised." Before anyone else can call out any more issues, the captain gets their attention with a loud rattle.

"Stop telling me what the alarms are saying and confirm issues with secondary sensors and vid feeds," she orders. With a glance over at Lakin, the captain sounds an annoyed rattle. She keeps eye contact with Lakin as she instructs her crew. "It's unlikely that so many things would go wrong so quickly and at such an opportune time. Look for sabotage with the ship's emergency relay system."

Smirking, Lakin remains still even as the captain stalks over to her with a low vibrating rattle. "What did you do to my ship, human?"

"Are we not friends anymore?" Lakin asks in a childish sing-song voice. "I warned you."

"You will tell me what you did," the captain demands.

"What she did?" one of the crew asks. When the captain looks up to meet his gaze, he continues. "Captain, how can you think this human could be responsible? We have multiple system failures. How could she have wreaked so much havoc? A rebel must be aboard. There's no other explanation."

"And that's why I'm in charge and you're not," Captain Sherianan declares grimly. "Because I know our pets are far more capable than most think." Looking around at the rest of the crew on the bridge, she asks again, "Now, have any of you confirmed the alarms through secondary sensors or vid feeds yet?"

"There's no report of contamination from hallway sensors, only the hatch display sensors," one of them announces, and the captain makes a rumble of relief.

"I thought as much," she murmurs and grabs Lakin by the back of the omnie. "Tell me what you did," she demands, giving Lakin a little shake to emphasize her words.

"I was going to ask for a pod, but now I want a shuttle," Lakin says, working hard on not being intimidated by this Talin. If Captain Sherianan meant her bodily harm, she could have easily hit Lakin instead of just grabbing her omnie and shaking her like a recalcitrant child.

"Stupid little human," Sherianan nearly shouts into her face. "You're making us vulnerable. It could mean death for all of us. Tell me what you did so it can be fixed or you risk dying with us."

"Captain, there's a parasitic ship on us," one of the crew calls out, rattling with surprise and then with fear.

"Again, confirm with another system," Sherianan calls out, but Lakin feels her heart pound.

"You need to check on that," she whispers to Sherianan.

"What?" she asks, pulling Lakin higher so she doesn't need to lean over for them to be the same height. Their noses are almost touching, and her feet are dangling in the air when Lakin speaks again.

"I didn't do anything to the outside alarms," Lakin whispers to her. The two of them freeze, staring at each other. Sherianan doesn't make a sound as she examines Lakin's face, probably trying to figure out if Lakin's lying.

"Second and Carian with me," Captain Sherianan shouts out as she drops Lakin to her feet. She doesn't let go of Lakin's omnie as she turns but just drags her along to a far wall where several other crew members have gathered. A section of the wall slides away to reveal body armor and weapons.

"Prepare for battle," she tells the two who followed her to the wall. "Suril, lock down all corridors and bring up—"

Before she can finish issuing that order, the hatch to the bridge crashes open with a violent scream of metal. Reflexively, Lakin ducks down to avoid shrapnel from the door, but she doesn't get very far because Sherianan still has a grip on her omnie. In one smooth motion, Sherianan swings her around and shields Lakin with her much bigger body.

"Be still," she orders as she grabs a piece of body armor and shoves it down over Lakin's head. The piece is huge so it slides right over her shoulders and traps Lakin's arms at her sides. The bottom edge of the armor drops down almost to her knees.

"This isn't my fault," Lakin says quickly as chaos breaks out around them. "I didn't do this. I didn't touch the outside sensors or the ship's navigation system. I'd never do that."

"We will discuss your penchant for subversion once this is all over," Captain Sherianan growls out. "Until then, stay still and quiet." With that, she pushes Lakin down to the floor. Sherianan and Suril move so they're standing between her and the threat.

That's when she hears Sherianan rumble out a loud laugh as a familiar voice roars, "Lakin!"

CHAPTER 27

Dalt

"Ancestors! Daltenion, what do you think you're doing wrecking my ship?" Sherianan shouts, absolutely unintimidated by his rage.

"Wrecking your ship?" he questions, not bothering to lower his volume at all. She's lucky he hasn't executed every crew member he's come across so far or knocked her out with a neuralization beam like she did to him on Molpa Colony. All in all, she'll be lucky if all she ends up with is some damage to the ship.

"You assaulted me! Stole my human! And then you ran off. You should thank me for not separating your head from your body!"

"That would upset our parents," Sherianan taunts him.

"Do you think I care?" he roars. "Where is Lakin?"

"Dalt?" a voice calls out from behind Sherianan and several of her crew. Uncaring about being gentle, Dalt grabs and tosses bodies out of his way. His sister hits a wall with a loud oomph. One of her men soon joins her. The other one tries to hit him with a tranquilizing agent, but he bats it aside and sends the man crashing into a large display on the far wall. Ignoring the sound of breaking glass panels, he drops to his knees in front of Lakin.

"Are you well? Did they hurt you?" he asks as he tugs the overlarge piece of armor off his little human. She looks confused and annoyed but not injured.

"What the hell is going on around here?" she asks. "Did I hear that right? Do you guys share parents? Is she your sister? Dalt, with family like that, you don't need enemies!"

"With a human like you, my enemy's job is already half completed! Daltenion, order your pet to explain the damage she did to my ship," Sherianan demands, having regained her feet and stomped over. She's standing over them, rattling in annoyance, but Dalt doesn't even glance up.

"She is my sibling, but I don't interact with her or my family," he admits.

"That's why I stole you, Lakin," Sherianan informs her. "Daltenion finally contacted us requesting help only to refuse to see any of us."

"This explains a lot," Lakin says with a small grin. "I love the fact that you Talins think you're more superior than other species. Above petty emotions. But then you all pull shit like this, and I know you're just as bad as the rest of us."

"I don't understand anything you just said," he confesses, and for some reason that makes Lakin laugh.

"Just to be clear, we're not in mortal danger?" she asks in a half whisper. "We don't need to fight our way out of here?"

"Sherianan might go to extreme lengths to force an interaction between me and my family, but she wouldn't deliberately hurt you. Or hurt me beyond reason."

Looking over his shoulder, Lakin frowns at Sherianan. "No hurting him at all. Or I don't tell you how to fix your ship."

"I don't take orders from pets," Sherianan retorts.

Dalt wants to stand up and fling his sister into the wall again, but Lakin stops him with just a hand on his quill-less forearm.

"I've got this," she whispers with an evil glint in her eyes.

Curious, he remains quiet.

"That's fine. You don't have to even talk to me," Lakin says causally as she uses his shoulder to stand up. Once he's sure she's steady on her feet, he stands up also and takes up a flanking position. No one moves any closer to them, but he keeps an eye on them anyway. "And I'm sure you'll figure out what this pet did to your systems eventually."

"Human—" Sherianan starts to say, but Lakin cuts her off.

"*Talin*," she taunts. "This is a negotiation, not an interrogation. Either talk to me as an intellectual equal or untangle it yourself. Oh, and I'd be really careful because there just might be some hidden gems out there waiting to get activated and cause even more problems."

Dalt never really appreciated how devious Lakin could be until this moment. She couldn't have been on this ship for that long, yet she managed to cause utter chaos. Human or not, this female has a penchant for getting loose and causing pandemonium.

Even though he's in the company of Talins he doesn't know, he can't hold back any longer. His scent glands are full to bursting, and his pride in Lakin only makes the impulse more necessary. Stepping up behind her, he wraps one arm around her shoulder and draws her back sharply against his front. Leaning over, he rubs his cheek into her hair. His bonding scent fills the room, and Lakin sighs with pleasure.

"I can't believe you're doing that in mixed company," Sherianan says, her voice full of censure. "You're making it obvious you have no control because you scent-bonded. Don't you have any sense of self-preservation?"

"You're just envious," Lakin says languidly. Her body is relaxed against his, his scent calming them both. "Because Dalt makes me smell good and you don't have a human to rub on."

"You can't know that," Sherianan says, her voice indignant. "I might have many humans at home."

"If you did, there's no way you'd be so uptight," Lakin shoots back, making Dalt rumble out a laugh.

"She has no human," Dalt confirms.

"How do you have this information, Daltenion?" Sherianan asks, her voice quieter and accompanied by a gentle rumble of inquisitiveness.

"I keep track of the family," he tells her. "I couldn't bring myself to see any of you, but I've made sure everything is well. If you ever required me, I would've returned."

"Why did you hold yourself apart?" Sherianan asks, real hurt in her voice. "We care the most about you, yet you have kept yourself hidden away all these solars."

With a wave of an arm, Dalt shows the room his lack of quills and claws. "I'm flawed now. I failed and caused many deaths. I didn't want to put any of you in the position to either refuse my request for a visit or put up with the sight of my deformity."

Lakin smacks her little hand down hard on his thigh. It doesn't hurt him, but she winces at the impact. "Damn it, Dalt. We've talked about this. You're not a failure. And you're sure as hell not deformed."

"In this regard, I agree with the pet," Sherianan says. "None of that matters. Do you think us so shallow to believe such lies? If there were deaths, they were unavoidable. If there was suffering, I'm sure you felt the most anguish. But after the war was over, you hid from us. We sent missives through the command chain, but all we got back was confirmation of delivery, no response."

Grabbing Lakin up in his arms, he hugs her tightly to his chest. Sherianan's accusations are all true. After the war was over, after he finished healing, he ran away to Holian's colony, hid away in the forest with the other soldiers whose families discarded them like so much trash. He couldn't imagine facing his parents or sister. Couldn't imagine surviving their disappointment.

Suddenly he's not on his sister's ship any longer. He's back. Captured. Listening to the screams of others being tortured.

"Easy, big guy," Lakin soothes, placing her hand on the back of his neck and massaging the scar tissue there. "Breath with me. You stopped breathing, and that's a bad idea. In, out, with me."

Her words pierce the memories. Her commands help him come back to himself. The screaming abates, and the bridge around him comes back into focus.

But he's no longer standing apart. He's no longer standing at all. He's on his knees, still clutching Lakin to his chest. Sherianan is on her knees in front of him, purring loudly.

"Daltenion?" she asks, her voice soft.

"Daltenion died," he tells her hoarsely as the last of his memory episode fades away. "He died at that outpost. I'm only

Dalt now, half of what I was. Broken and defective." When Lakin bangs her fist against one of his chest plates, he looks down, blinking in surprise.

"I don't blame you for cutting down that name. Daltenion is a mouthful and sounds way too pretentious for you. But dead? Broken? Defective?" She snorts with derision and wiggles a little so she can cross her arms over her chest while still being held by him. She's staring at him with irritation. "That's a load of bullshit. I've seen you battle. Your speed is incredible, and nothing is wrong with your reflexes. You have flashbacks, big deal. No one gets through life without emotional damage. No one."

"You seem to have survived all your traumatic events without repercussion," he whispers, and she rolls her eyes. At first he thinks she might be suffering a seizure, but then he remembers that some humans do that as a sign of exasperation.

"I haven't," she tells him. "I'm just not one to sit and cry myself to sleep, but trust me, I've got some nice little scars of my own. Someday, when I've had enough to drink, I'll tell you all about them. Then I'll sob, and you get to clean up the mess because once that box gets opened, it's ugly."

"I would hold you no matter how much water leaked from your eyes," he assures her, even though he's a little confused by her short speech. That must've been the right thing to say because she smiles at him and uncrosses her arms and stands up, looming over his kneeling form. Pressing close she loops her arms around his neck. She folds her smaller body around him, making him feel warm and bonded. Their combined scent fills his nose, and it's the most peaceful he's felt since the morning she recklessly climbed onto the Traditionalist vehicle to rescue Holian back on Kalor.

He purrs with pleasure. If he had his way, they would spend the next mark like this.

"I can see why you fought so hard to keep this one," Sherianan comments with a rumble of amusement.

"Shut up," Lakin grumbles. "Can't you see we're having a moment here?"

"Your moment will need to wait. My ship is dead and drifting and needs to be repaired. I'd like to remind both of you, this trouble was caused by this mischievous human," Sherianan says as she gets to her feet.

"This mischievous human would like to remind you, Captain Sherianan, that none of this damage would've happened if you hadn't *kidnapped me!*" The last words are delivered in the loudest voice Lakin can manage. To Dalt's gratitude, she raised her head and looked over her shoulder at Sherianan when she shouted, saving his earholes from hurting. But she's not done yet.

"Oh, and you drugged me! And put me in restraints and locked me in a room. Gee, I'm so sorry I might have messed with your ship a little."

Letting go of Dalt, she turns to face Sherianan, looking up into the face of the captain without fear. "You couldn't just have invited us up for a drink and dinner? Couldn't send a message asking to meet? No, you had to come in force, attack us, and then drag me off. Do you realize I thought Dalt might be dead! That's the reason your ship isn't moving. You don't get to have nice things if you leave someone I love helpless and potentially dying on a backwater colony. Talins who do that get their stuff broken. By me!"

Now everyone in the room is rumbling with laughter, including Dalt.

"She's spirited," one of the crew comments to another.

"And clever," the other responds. "I still can't figure out what she did."

Dalt's not surprised that Sherianan reacts with amusement instead of anger at Lakin's tirade. His sibling knows she was in the wrong but carried through with her actions anyway. In her own heavy-handed way, by attacking him and stealing Lakin, his sister was telling him she still feels a strong sibling bond.

It's both wonderful and annoying at the same time.

"So here are my demands. First, I want this off!" she states, tapping at the collar around her neck. "If you object to me going around with a naked neck, Dalt can put another collar on me, but yours needs to come off. Second, you're going to give me something you value that I can hold for insurance until we're off this vessel. Then, and only then, will I make your shiny ship stop screaming and move again."

"What item of value would you want to hold?" Sherianan asks.

Dalt admits he's curious too. What could Lakin possibly ask for that Sherianan couldn't just take away by force later?

"You're going to key your Ident to me," Lakin says, and Sherianan rattles with shock. A few other crew members rattle with surprise as well. Lakin's not asking for a small thing.

The Identification Cubes Talins hang from their belts are often the key to getting access to just about everything in that Talin's life—their credit accounts, homes, personal data, family information, and so much more. Sherianan could have another Ident Cube created, but it would take time and a lot of effort. All the while Lakin would be accessing and possibly stealing credits or selling information.

And once keyed to Lakin, Sherianan wouldn't have access until Lakin keyed the Ident Cube back over. Without a doubt, Lakin's plan is brilliant.

"That's unacceptable," Sherianan snaps. "Pick something else."

"Your heart in a box," Lakin retorts. "Look, you brought this all on yourself."

"I wouldn't be here, but Daltenion asked for help," Sherianan informs her.

Twisting around, Lakin looks up into his face. "Is that true? Did you go to her for help?"

Uncomfortable, Dalt shifts his eyes to a nearby display. "After you were stolen off the Traditionalist ship, I panicked. Holian wasn't sure we'd be able to track you because it took us so long before we were able to separate the ship and pursue. I knew my parents would have the means to track the mercenary's ship, and they did."

"Our parents contacted me," Sherianan adds. "I hurried to follow. They requested that I try to influence Daltenion into seeing them. I thought taking you into my custody would be the most efficient method."

"And how did that work out for you?" Lakin asks with a raised eyebrow, making Sherianan sound a rattle of displeasure. Turning her attention back to him, Lakin puts a hand on his face, rubbing her fingers gently over his scent glands.

"That means a lot to me," she tells him. "You were willing to ask for help from people you were desperate not to interact with just to get me back. And just so you know, I've got your back too." He's not familiar with that human phrase, but he understands that her statement is a declaration of loyalty and a promise of mutual protection.

"I'd do anything to assure your life," he tells her.

"If we could please refocus on the matter at hand," Sherianan interrupts. Lakin scowls at Sherianan, and then her expression changes. Dalt isn't sure what this arrangement of human facial features means until Lakin holds out her hand imperiously.

"Unlock your Ident and hand it over," Lakin demands. Ah, so this is the expression he's heard described as smug.

"Daltenion, tell your human—"

"Oh, no," Lakin cuts her off. "Don't even try. It won't work. Didn't you just hear what he said? This guy isn't going to make me do anything."

"Daltenion, this is ridiculous," Sherianan appeals.

"I'm sorry, sister, but you've brought Lakin's wrath upon yourself," he answers. "If it helps, I'm almost sure she won't do anything illicit with your Ident as long as you fulfill your part of her request."

"Almost sure?" Sherianan repeats with an outraged rattle. "Almost sure!"

"Captain, my long-range scanning capabilities have been terminated. I have only medium and short-range," one of her crew calls out. "And medium-range is starting to glitch."

Lakin's still holding her hand out with an expectant expression on her face. Rattling with anger, Sherianan unclips her Ident, presses several fingers to it and speaks in old Talarian. The Ident beeps a few times, indicating it's ready for a new voice identity. Sherianan slaps the Ident into Lakin's waiting hand. Lakin holds the cube up to her mouth and speaks.

"Lakin of Develia." Then she says something in a language Dalt's never heard. The best way to keep an Ident secure is to use an obscure language or term. In this room full of so many earholes, both women have managed to keep their passwords a secret.

His sister, the brilliant captain, has met her match in Lakin.

"Now, fix my ship," Sherianan demands, but Lakin shakes her head and taps her collar. Rattling with impatience, Sherianan steps up, presses a finger to the collar, and orders it to unlock. It snicks open, and Lakin takes it off and hands it to him.

"Break that for me," she requests, and he's all too happy to snap the thing in half at the hinge. If Lakin's going to wear a collar, he's going to make sure it's one she can take off and he can track.

Not that he ever plans on having to track her again. Oh no, they're never going to be separated.

Now it's his turn. He turns Lakin to face him and tugs a small energy weapon out of his belt. Placing it in her hand, he leans close so only she can hear. "Tuck this in your omnie. It can fire up to twenty times before needing a new cartridge. It will knock out anyone you hit in the torso or head unless they're wearing armor."

Her nimble fingers take the weapon from him and tuck it away with minimal fuss. He doubts anyone even saw the exchange. Along with always being at her side, he's going to make sure she never goes around unarmed again.

"I'll get you a better weapon later," he promises.

"I knew there was a reason I love you so much," she whispers, and Dalt feels blood rush to his head.

Love. She used the word love. That means a great deal to humans. Especially to a human like Lakin who possesses such character and honor. Humans might not be able to scent-bond, but they do love, and that's just as important to them.

And even more significant, humans choose whom they love. It's not a simple chemical reaction; it's a complex emotional process. She knows all his darkest secrets. She's seen him get trapped in his memories twice now. She knows his faults and flaws, yet this wonderful female has come to love him. She's picked him.

After he left the military, he didn't think he would ever feel such joy again.

CHAPTER 28

Lakin

Lakin gets her first look at Talarian, the Talin homeworld, for about three seconds before she and Dalt are mobbed.

"Oh, she's got a lovely mane. How old is she?"

"Can I hold her?"

"I have a treat. Can I feed it to her?"

Dalt can't rattle to tell them to get away from her, but Sherianan, standing right behind him, can and does. Loudly.

Several of her crew hurry to stand in front of Dalt and Lakin to act as shields. All they did was walk off the shuttle at the city center port. The moment other Talins notice her walking with Dalt they veer toward them.

Even with the warning rattles and the crew standing strong and formidable, the questions don't stop.

"Is she part of a breeding pair?"

"What clan owns her?"

"Do you have a male also? I can offer mine up for stud services as long as we can negotiate about the ownership of the offspring."

"Would you be interested in selling her?"

"I was here first. If he's going to sell her, it will be to me!"

"You've never even owned a human, and your clan won't let you near any of the ones they own. You are too rough, and they know it!"

"You're one of the lowest members of the Cholchian crew. No one will ever sell to you!"

The two arguing start rattling loudly, too involved in insulting each other to realize that everyone else is moving away.

"I thought humans are just pets," Lakin whispers to Dalt. "These guys are acting like I'm some exotic animal."

"You're right on both counts," Sherianan answers for Dalt. "Humans are extremely popular pets but also hard to get. Owners don't sell them."

"Ever?"

"Almost never. When they do sell, they tend to screen the buyers and demand quite a lot. Not just in credits but also in how they expect the pet to be cared for. You're considered quite the prize among us, little Lakin."

"That explains a lot," she mutters.

"And humans are rapidly becoming a symbol of all the dividing issues between the Traditionalists and the Reformists. The Reformists want a lot of fundamental Talin legal and cultural ideals undone, and the Traditionalists want them sealed in stone. Most have nothing to do with human pets, but somehow your species has ended up at the very heart of the conflict."

"I feel bad for anyone owned by a Traditionalist," Lakin says.

"As you should," Dalt agrees. "The way they treat their humans is a helpful insight into what a Traditionalist is. What kind of Talin they are at their core."

"Good point," Lakin says as she wraps her arms around Dalt and buries her head against his neck. She's not one to shy away from conflict, but this crowd is growing at an alarming rate, making Lakin feel more and more uneasy.

"That will work," he grunts. When she makes a confused sound he explains. "Keep your face hidden. If you appear distressed it will be easier to fend them off."

"That's easy," Lakin tells him. "I think I'm a little distressed." That makes Dalt sound a soft rumble of humor.

"I doubt that. How can one such as you be intimidated by a friendly crowd? They have no weapons, no ill intent, and no shackles. There's no challenge here for you."

His humor and confidence makes her laugh and eases the anxiety that was building.

"Good point," she says as she puts her lips on the exposed strip of skin at the base of his neck, deliberately licking that bit of sensitive flesh. His gate falters slightly before his strides even out again. He taps her on the ass.

"Behave," he says with a purr.

"Almost never," she counters.

It takes them some time, but they finally make it to the ground transport. It's large enough to accommodate everyone including the crew. Once they're all loaded and moving, Lakin thinks to ask where they're going.

"My family's compound," Sherianan informs her. "Most of my crew stay with me at the compound on the rare occasion we have a stopover here. All their families are on colonies so they have no one special to visit."

"Captain Sherianan is making it sound like more of a choice than it is. None of us are very fond of Talarian," Carian explains. "Colony families are generally looked down on by homeworld families. No one wants to let us stay at their compound."

"You guys don't have places where you can rent rooms?" Lakin asks.

"Not allowed on Talarian," Carian says. "The expectation is if you're here, your family or employer will provide you with housing. Or you stay on the ship, like my former captain had us do."

"But not Captain Sherianan or her family," Suril adds. "She might be from a well-respected clan and a wealthy family, but she doesn't care if we come from the colonies or don't have a prestigious clan or a credit rich family. She hires us based on talent and skill."

"I hope you're not expecting a raise from all this praise," Sherianan comments dryly, making most of the crew in the transport rumble with amusement. Suril doesn't break eye contact with the captain.

"You know exactly what I expect," he says, and to Lakin's surprise, Sherianan looks uncomfortable. The commanding Talin fidgets a little before turning her gaze to Lakin.

"I got a message from my parents earlier, just before we disembarked the ship. They said some surprise guests are visiting," she says. "All I know is that one member of the party is a high-ranking Talin and I believe he brought his human pet with him." Sherianan pins Lakin with her gaze. "No matter what, you need to be well-behaved. Do you understand? My family and clan might be solidly in the Reformist camp, but we can't afford to be seen as radicals. If you act out, you could put us all in danger. Be polite. Be diffident. Be obedient. At least while the guests are here."

"I'll try," she says with a grin. "But aside from the polite option, I don't have much practice with any of those descriptors." That makes the crew rumble out laughs, and Sherianan rattles in exasperation.

"Do we know who it is?" Dalt asks.

"We don't. Mother was very mysterious. I thought it best to warn Lakin as she tends to speak her mind rather readily."

"I'm not sure if that was an insult or not," Lakin murmurs, thinking through Sherianan's words.

"It wasn't an insult. It's a statement of fact," Sherianan counters and then holds out her hand. "You're off my ship so I'd like my Ident back and rekeyed to me."

The original agreement was that Sherianan would get her Ident back via courier drone after Lakin and Dalt were safely away. But as Lakin and several of the crew worked to get the ship up and running again, Holian was able to contact them. His instructions were concise and without much detail. They needed to get themselves to the Talin homeworld. He'd contact them once there.

That was it. So now they're here on Talarian heading to Dalt's family's compound to wait for further instructions from Holian. And now there's a mystery guest visiting. Lakin is equal parts intrigued and concerned.

Pulling Sherianan's Ident cube out from a fold in her omnie, Lakin murmurs to it before handing it over to Sherianan. With a relieved rumble, Sherianan snatches it back and speaks her code phrase. The cube beeps, accepting its new rekey, and Sherianan clips it on her belt. When she looks up, her body is more relaxed.

"Troublesome human," Sherianan mumbles, making Lakin raise an eyebrow. Sherianan speaks again before Lakin can say anything. "I know. You believe what you did to my ship was just retribution."

"It had nothing to do with retribution and everything to do with survival," Lakin argues. "I didn't know who you were or why you took me. Remember that next time you think kidnapping me might be fun."

"Trust me," Sherianan says with feeling. "I will never have that impulse again. But now I see how you were able to survive out in the universe as a wild human."

The transport pauses to allow a set of ornamental gates to lift out of the way before continuing down a short path to a large majestic dwelling.

"Ah, here it is," Sherianan says, but her voice is tight. Lakin can tell she's worried about the mysterious guest waiting for them.

A female Talin, probably a member of the staff, hurries out of the front of the dwelling and rushes to them, tapping impatiently at the transport's door as the automated system opens. Sherianan and her crew get out first. The last to emerge are Dalt and finally her.

Dalt stands tensely next to her, and the way he keeps flexing his fingers into a fist tells her he's ready to fight. Or maybe run because he keeps looking around as if plotting escape routes. She doesn't know how long it's been since he's interacted with his parents, but she hopes this goes well.

Despite the disastrous way they met and Sherianan's high-handed behavior, she likes Dalt's sister. Lakin can even see doing something similar if she was desperate to get her sibling to interact with her. If she was that worried about the health and well-being of a family member, she could be driven to do something stupid also.

The fact that Sherianan didn't move to strike or hurt Lakin in any way, even after realizing she was the one causing all the malfunctions on the ship, was a true show of character. Other captains thought nothing of abusing their crew and wouldn't even hesitate to strike a lowly human, but Sherianan kept her cool. Lakin admires that.

Perhaps Dalt's parents are as honorable as his sister. One thing's for sure. If they say anything that hurts Dalt, Lakin's going to talk. She doesn't care how important the mystery guest is. She's not going to let anything drive Dalt into a downward spiral of shame.

If she has to, she'll bring down the energy grid to the house or even the entire city center. She'll find any and every way to make their lives inconvenient and vexing. They'll rue the day they hurt Dalt's feelings.

Hmmm, rue the day, she likes the sound of that.

"I'm small, but I'm mighty," she reminds herself.

Dalt must've overheard because he rumbles out a soft chuckle. "I don't think any of us doubt that."

The entire group follows the servant into the dwelling and down a hall, finally passing through a massive arched entrance into a grand room with high ceilings held up by ornate pillars.

If the outside of the estate wasn't proof enough, this room is further evidence that Dalt comes from wealth.

Every wall of the room is covered in shelves full of expensive items and artifacts. She even recognizes a few from species she's dealt with over the years. She eyes a green crystal bowl that costs more than several of the ships she's crewed on. And that's just one item out of hundreds.

Lakin's so busy looking at all the riches, she doesn't notice the group gathered at the far end of the room. At this point Sherianan's crew is being led out a set of side doors, and only the three of them are left to make their way across the large space. Two of the waiting Talins are wearing identical colors and emblems dangling from their wide belts. The emblems match the one Sherianan carries, so Lakin assumes those are the parents. She doesn't recognize any of the others with them, but then a human face pops out from behind one of the Talins.

Lakin makes eye contact with her, and they both smile. For some reason, Lakin feels like she should know this human, but she can't place her.

Without hesitation, the stranger pushes a large male Talin out of her way and steps forward. She's probably right at Lakin's height and maybe a few years younger. Her face is open and friendly with no trace of wariness or fear. Although she wears a collar around her neck, it's covered in jewels and fits loosely, more a piece of jewelry than anything else.

She tries to walk toward Lakin, but the big male she pushed out of her way grabs her and gently pulls her back until she's flush against his much bigger body. She looks up at him with a mildly disappointed expression but no dread.

He rumbles out a purr and leans over to run one of his cheeks along the top of her head before straightening back up to watch them approach. He seems to be paying special attention to Lakin, and she thinks she knows why.

That little exchange gave her all the information she needs to know about the relationship between these two. That and the very slight bulge she can see under the woman's wrap.

"You were in the infirmary," Lakin says with a smile, finally figuring out why the face looks vaguely familiar. "When I first got to Kalor and escaped, you were in the infirmary with Dalt when I ran in there. I'm Lakin."

The woman laughs in delight and nods. "That was me! My name's Sora. And I still can't believe how fast you were. Even hurt, you still managed to climb onto one of those cabinets in no time flat."

"Desperate times and all that," Lakin says with a shrug. She's not interested in reminiscing about past pain. "But look at you. I asked Dalt a couple of times what happened to you and all he'd say was that you went to a better place. I thought you died!"

That makes them both laugh.

"I've heard you're even harder to keep confined than this one is," the Talin holding Sora comments. Sora looks up at him with affection.

"Lakin, I'd like you to meet my Talin, Searin," Sora says as she drops her gaze back to Lakin.

Grabbing hold of Dalt's hand, Lakin holds it up. "Sora, meet my Talin, Dalt."

"You two talk as if you own them, not the other way around," someone mutters with an amused rumble.

"We don't?" Lakin asks, making Sora laugh and everyone else rumble with humor.

"I believe the human Sora might have left out something important," one of the Talins says. "Daltenion, this is Prime Son Searin." The way Dalt stiffens tells her this is important information. She sends a questioning look at Sora, who gives a little shrug.

"Eh, it just means he's in line to be the next monarch."

"Oh, if that's all," Lakin whispers with a roll of her eyes that makes Sora giggle.

"His mom could pick his sister instead," Sora explains. "And the real power of the government is in the assemblies."

"But he is royalty, so should I bow or something?" Lakin asks, casting a sidelong glance at Searin.

"If you want to," Sora says. "But we humans don't do stuff like that. We're mostly seen as really smart dogs."

"What's a dog?" Sherianan asks.

"A dumb human?" someone volunteers, making Lakin and Sora burst out in laughter.

"She's mine," Dalt says, drawing Lakin against him in a very similar pose as Searin with Sora.

"Be at ease, Ground Commander Daltenion, I have no wish to take your human away from you," Searin says with a gentle rumble of reassurance. "The circumstances with Sora were complicated when our paths crossed on Kalor. But I have no wish to acquire any more humans."

"At least not by buying them," Sora whispers to herself as she touches her stomach. That move tells Lakin her earlier guess wasn't wrong. Sora is pregnant, and judging by the possessive way Searin won't let her go, the baby is his.

That's interesting.

Despite Searin's words, Dalt doesn't relax, but Sora's yawn brings all their attention to the human who colors red after she finishes and notices all eyes are on her.

"To bed for a nap," Searin orders and pushes her toward a Talin waiting by yet another set of doors. "Monian has prepared a place for rest."

"But I want to visit—" Sora protests.

Searin's rattle cuts her off. "Sleep for a mark, and then you can visit with Lakin." It's obvious from Sora's face that this is both a familiar argument and one she never wins.

"Fine," she grumbles. "But only if you join me."

"Of course, I'd never do otherwise," Searin agrees. "There's no point in discussing everything until Holian arrives. Then we will sit down and go over the attack and possible countermeasures."

"We'll have a secure space prepared for the meeting, Prime Son Searin," one of the older Talins assures him.

"Excellent," he comments as he leads Sora away.

Looking over her shoulder as they walk, Sora catches Lakin's eye. "I'll see you later, and we can talk."

"Be prepared," Lakin calls after her. "I've got a lot of questions."

Sora's smile brightens. "Great! I'll trade answers for stories."

Once they're gone, the tension in the room noticeably eases.

The two older Talins she assumes are Dalt's parents step forward. He straightens up next to her and takes his arms from around her only to urge her to retreat behind him.

She expects them to berate him for his absence. To demand he explain where he's been and what happened to him.

He's expecting bad things too. The four of them stand stock still, staring at each other for several long moments.

Then his parents rumble out purrs.

CHAPTER 29

Lakin

"Son, present your human to us," his mother demands. That's not even close to what Lakin's expecting. Dalt must not have expected that either because he jerks at the woman's demand.

"Mother, Father, this is Lakin, my human. Lakin, this is my mother, Grander Citizen Ornianan. And my father, Grander Citizen Tuchianan."

"Grander Citizen is a title they give someone who's retired after a lifetime of dedicated service to our people," Sherianan tells her helpfully.

"Hi," Lakin says with a little wave. "I guess I get the title of human? Or, if we were anywhere else, I'd say my title is Electrical Systems Tech Lakin."

"Or Professional Saboteur Lakin," Sherianan mutters.

"Don't be bitter," Lakin whispers to her, making Sherianan huff.

"You're a very lovely looking human," Tuchianan tells her with a purr of his own.

"We're very happy Daltenion acquired you," Ornianan says, glancing over at Dalt. "We've missed you very much, my son. We wish you could've visited us without such extreme measures."

"When you contacted us for help, we were overjoyed," Tuchianan confesses. "Then we realized you wouldn't show yourself to us even if we helped."

"Even knowing that, you still did as I asked," Dalt says thoughtfully. "Thank you."

"Of course we did," Ornianan says, sounding genuinely shocked. "It would never occur to us to refuse you a request. Especially if it's as important as helping to track down a stolen human."

"I had thought…" Dalt begins to say but falters. Lakin knows exactly what's going on in that head of his and leans into his side. Looking down at her, his familiar rusty purr starts up.

"If they're mean to you, I'll make it so this place can't reconnect to the energy grid for at least four rotations," Lakin whispers to him. "I've got your back, Dalt. And no matter what happens here, we've got the cabin waiting for us back on Kalor."

That does the trick. He pulls in a deep lungful of air and looks back to his parents, both of whom stopped purring when he started. His rusty purr quiets a little but doesn't stop as he brings his hand up and taps it against his chest, making a nice loud impact sound. Lakin has seen so many Talins do that same move that it doesn't even make her jump anymore. But still, if she tried that even once, she'd have a bruise!

"I greet you, my parents," he intones with rigid formality. "On my last mission, I failed and we were captured. I was able to gain my freedom and smite the enemy, but not before many were tormented and executed, including most of those under my command."

Tuchianan and Ornianan process his words during several beats of silence. Now they look at him, taking in the missing quills and claws, the scars on his shoulders and marks on his chest plates. All the evidence of his past torture is plain to see.

Lakin hopes they also see how brave he is.

Not one to remain quiet for long, Lakin clears her throat. "Dalt saved me. Not back on Molpa, but before that, on Kalor."

"We are aware you were held and tortured by Traditionalists," Ornianan says gently, grasping on to Lakin's statement. "You must be terribly burdened by the experience. We're glad Dalt was there to rescue you."

"Those guys were long dead by the time I met Dalt," Lakin informs them. "What I mean is that he saved me from hurting myself."

"Humans are wont to do that," Tuchianan agrees, making Lakin grimace.

"Yeah, okay, I walked right into that one," she mutters and then summons up a smile. "I was going to escape Kalor and—" Twin rattles of dismay sound from the parents.

"It's not safe for humans alone," Tuchianan says with a bite of anger. "Foolish female. Humans don't survive without keepers."

"I could spend the whole damn rotation arguing with you about that, or you could let me finish?" Lakin says in an even voice, reminding herself she needs to be nice to these Talins since they're Dalt's family. Well, she needs to be nice to them until they do something that hurts Dalt, then no-holds-barred Lakin gets to come out and play.

"There is nothing to argue, but please continue, human," Tuchianan says with a little rumble of encouragement. Lakin just manages to keep from rolling her eyes.

"Anyway, there's Dalt, watching out for me. I was all set to escape even though I was still hurt worse than I wanted to admit to myself. I was going to run no matter how much more damage I had to do to my feet or the rest of my body. My only thought was escape. They kept caging me, but it never lasted."

"As I well know," Sherianan murmurs.

Everyone ignores her. Their eyes remain focused on Lakin. "But Dalt changed that. Not by force. He didn't brutalize me. Dalt's inherently honorable. He thinks he's broken. That he failed. But that's just because the mission was screwed to begin with. Even though what happened couldn't have been prevented by anyone in his rank, he accepts responsibility. That's the mark of someone who cares and wants nothing more than to care for others."

Tuchianan and Ornianan make soft rumbling noises that are halfway between a purr and the sound Talins make to encourage others to keep talking. It must be their way to try to comfort her and tell her to continue explaining.

"You've said the universe is a dangerous place for a human, and you're not wrong about that. There've been a few times that I was in a bad spot, and usually it was because of someone else's duplicity or poor judgment. That means I don't trust. Ever. But with Dalt, I find myself trusting. I knew he'd fight like hell to find me after I got captured by that mercenary or when Sherianan grabbed me. There was never any doubt in my mind. I wasn't sure he'd find me, but I knew he'd draw on every resource he had and fight any battle required to get to me."

"But more important," Dalt says, interrupting her. "You would do the same for me."

"Without a doubt," Lakin agrees. "If I'm trying to escape now, it's to get back to you."

"And my ship stands as testimony to that," Sherianan comments, causing both parents to sound questioning rattles. Without hesitation Sherianan tells them all the things Lakin did to her ship, and there's definite admiration in her voice. By the time she's done with her tale, both parents regard Lakin and rumble out sounds of appreciation.

"Dalt, what kind of human have you found yourself?" Tuchianan asks with wonder.

"The perfect one," Dalt answers easily.

"Your speech earlier about Daltenion's worthiness was unnecessary, little Lakin," Ornianan tells her after the rumbles quiet. "We never rejected him. We were desperate to talk to him after his return, but no one would tell us where he'd gone. We've always been proud of both our children."

"Even if they didn't follow in our footsteps," Tuchianan adds.

"Can I ask what both of you did to earn the title of Grander?" Lakin asks.

"Certainly," Tuchianan says mildly. "We didn't die."

"Maybe a little more detail than that," Lakin requests with a laugh.

"It's a long story spanning several decades and includes the foundation of the Barvarian Colony, soon to be renamed Sorana," Ornianan says with a dismissive rattle. "But that opens up a request we'd like Dalt to consider. Perhaps Sherianan too if she's willing to take time away from her company."

Dalt's arms around her stiffen. "I'm not fit for any kind of duty, military or civil," he tells them in a tense voice.

"Don't be hasty," Ornianan says quickly as she purrs loudly. "Hear us out before you refuse. Lakin's description of you means you're the perfect one for this role." Looking up, Lakin watches Dalt open his mouth to object, but Tuchianan cuts him off.

"We want to set up a sanctuary on Barvarian Colony," Tuchianan says quickly and then glances over at his wife. She rumbles and reaches for the Ident hanging on her belt. She taps it a few times, waits, and then taps it again. A ping sounds through the room.

Sherianan rattles out a sound of surprise. "Did you just dampen the room?"

"Yes, what we're about to say needs to be kept in the strictest of confidence," Tuchianan states with a sharp rattle. "There are things we've never told either of you. We never planned to. We felt you shouldn't suffer any sense of guilt or self-recrimination because of the choices your parents made."

"Oh wow, this is like an episode of a drama vid," Lakin whispers to herself, entranced by the drama unfolding. "Is Dalt adopted?"

"Your comments aren't helping," Sherianan mutters to Lakin and then addresses her parents. "Please ignore her. She doesn't know how to remain quiet."

Tuchianan and Ornianan look at each other and give quiet rumbles, communicating in the same way Lakin's parents did with a language all their own. Finally, Ornianan looks back to Dalt and Sherianan. "I carried both of you in my belly. We founded the Barvarian Colony so I could have a safe place to give birth. We raised you there and founded a cresh specifically for the two of you. For the first handful of solars, you were the only students. We told everyone that our ship was specially fitted with a facility to produce children because we were going to found a colony, but the truth was we lived by ourselves on the colony for the first solar to keep our secret safe."

"But we were grown at the same time," Sherianan announces with a puzzled rattle. "Dalt and I are the same age. That's not possible with live birth."

"It wasn't common, but it is possible," Ornianan explains. "When I looked far back in my family line, I found females who had multiple babies at the same time. We only meant to have one child to minimize the risk of discovery. But the ancestors must have wanted to bless us because we ended up with two."

"Two children of the same age, one male and one female, meant no one even thought to question us," Tuchianan says with a proud rattle. "And because we founded the cresh, no one questioned us when we took a very active role in your education."

"Or when we took you traveling with us," Ornianan adds.

"I remember those trips fondly," Sherianan says with a soft happy rumble. "I was so small you had to hold me up so I could touch the ship's control console. You taught me how to set a navigation system up from scratch."

"You were only six solars old," Ornianan says proudly. "And by the time we returned from that trip to homeworld and back, you could set up a navigation track by yourself. I was so proud."

"I just thought that's how all parents treated their children," Sherianan says, rattling as realization dawns on her. "When you told us not to tell anyone about it, I assumed you wanted us to be humble. Not to brag about the family's ship. But it wasn't that. Was it?"

"No," Ornianan agrees. "We didn't want to be caught being parents. We would've been shamed and possibly exiled. You would've been enrolled in a cresh on homeworld and forbidden to contact us."

"I knew about those laws," Sherianan says with a thoughtful rumble. "But I never thought about them in the context of my own experiences. It never occurred to me to question the way we were raised. You risked so much for us."

"Well, that's fucked up," Lakin mutters to herself, but she must have said it a bit too loudly because all eyes fall on her.

"I'm unfamiliar with your phrase," Tuchianan says.

"Oh, uh, it's a term used when something is wrong," Lakin tries to explain, flushing with embarrassment. "It's wrong that you had to hide being a parent. Hide that you wanted to love each other and your children. I remember my parents before a bad air filtration in their domicile biosystem killed my dad and made my mom sick for a long time. We never had much, but there was always laughter. I'll never forget the sound of my mom laughing or my dad's deep voice as he teased her. You guys have a messed-up society if stuff like that is against the law."

"Perhaps," Tuchianan allows. "But we are a successful species nonetheless. Unlike humans who have no political power, no inhabitable homeworld, and exist on the fringes of other species territories."

"Ouch," Lakin mumbles. "Good point, but low blow." Looking up at Dalt and then over at Tuchianan, she tilts her head and asks, "But is the success worth it? I've been told about the Fading. About how Talins sometimes succumb and die, but humans can keep that from happening because we can fall in love with you guys. But you could love each other too, not just rely on finding a human pet for affection."

"This is true and why there are Reformists," Ornianan says with a sharp rattle. "You judge us harshly, Lakin, but we are slowly undoing those traditions. Many are coming to the realization that the toll of our strict laws regarding emotions and bonding are outdated, unnecessary, and potentially harmful."

Contrition fills Lakin. "I'm sorry I got judgey."

"You had a very different childhood than a Talin would have and it shows," Ornianan says magnanimously. "Our ways should seem foreign and abhorrent to you, or any human raised with a loving dam and sire."

"And that brings me to our need for your help, my children," Tuchianan says. "Barvarian Colony is nothing right now."

"What happened? And I thought you said you were changing the name to Sorana?" Lakin asks.

Tuchianan speaks up. "We are wealthy but we don't possess the kind of credit needed to create an entire successful and self-sustaining colony. We didn't allow other investors so it was only us on the planet until we left and returned to Talarian. It's been sitting empty since then."

When he pauses Ornianan begins talking. "Prime Son found out we still own the planet and suggested we sell it to him. He's willing to turn it into a thriving colony that will also act as a sanctuary for humans and Talins."

"You're going to sell?" Dalt asks.

"We've sold three-quarters of our claim on the planet, but the last quarter is for you and Sherianan. If either of you ever need a safe place Sorana Colony will be there for you. It's on the edge of our Empire and far from any other Talin colony or stations. The closest civilization to Sorana is Delorta."

"It you're talking sanctuary than the Delorta are a good species to have close at hand. They're some the sweetest people I've ever met!" Laken exclaims.

"Indeed," Ornianan says. "That's one of the reasons we picked that planet."

"That explains the dampener," Sherianan says with a short burst of rattling, a sign of her releasing tension. "This is so illegal it feels as if the mavins should appear out of thin air to take us into custody."

Tuchianan sounds a purring rumble. "I trust you both to keep our secrets no matter what you decide. Come now, it's time for the evening meal. Let's all sit together and talk as a family should."

"Do you know about Holian?" Dalt asks before anyone can turn to leave.

"Commandant Holian, from Kalor Colony?" Sherianan asks. "What about him?"

"He's like the two of you," Tuchianan tells her. "His mother created Kalor Colony so she could birth and raise her son."

"Damn, no wonder you guys have so many colonies. You had to found and build whole damn colonies just to have kids," Lakin says quietly, amused by her humor, but the Talins all rattle in disagreement.

"That's not why most colonies are built," Tuchianan assures her, and Lakin holds up her hands.

"I was joking," she says quickly.

"Ah, you were trying to be humorous by willfully stating an egregious error as fact," Sherianan says with a rumble of comprehension. "I'm sorry, Lakin, but misinformation is not considered funny among the Talin."

She sighs and feels Dalt vibrate against her. Glancing up at his face, she can see he's trying hard not to rumble out a laugh at her expense.

"After they've spent more time with you," he assures her, "they will find you amusing."

CHAPTER 30

Lakin

"Do not touch the water," the servant tells her for the fifth time as they walk past a stone pond, very similar to the artificial hot spring on Kalor Colony. "It will hurt your delicate skin. It's for Talins to soak in and soften keratan so we can better remove old bits of plating. If you try to swim in it, the water could cause burns."

"That means I shouldn't dip my toe in?" Lakin asks, knowing the Talin won't hear the sarcasm in her tone.

"As I've said, that would be unwise," the servant tells her. "It'll burn your appendage. There'll be pain, and a healer will need to be called. Should I set up a barrier?" he asks her anxiously, suddenly stopping and turning around. "Do you think you might forget and try to bathe?"

"I'll keep her away," Sora says, emerging from an ornate section of the garden. "You can leave her with me, and I'll make sure she doesn't get close to the water."

"Sora," the servant says with a delighted rumble. "You're looking healthy and well. You seemed out of sorts earlier."

Aggravation flashes across Sora's face. But then the smile is back.

"I was just overly tired," she tells the servant. "I'm sorry if I caused a fuss. Searin made sure I got plenty of sleep earlier, so now I feel fine."

"I'm sure Prime Son Searin is a good master to you," the servant says with a cheerful rumble. "His mother is renowned for her collection of human pets, so I know he must have good training. But I couldn't ask you to watch over another human. That seems ill advised."

"But we like to socialize with each other," Sora argues. "I'd be sad if I didn't get to talk to Lakin. Or groom her mane."

"Groom my mane?" Lakin mouths at Sora with a quizzical expression. Sora makes a slight gesture that either means she'll explain later or she's going to cut Lakin's head off. She hopes it's the former.

"Oh yes, that's true," the servant says with a rumble of agreement. "If you stay in the ornamental section of the garden, I'll have some treats sent out to you."

"That would be wonderful," Sora enthuses as she steps forward and takes Lakin's hand. "We'll stay right over there. I promise."

"Very good," the servant says and hurries away. With the servant gone Sora leads Lakin into the section of the garden that's densely packed with vegetation in full bloom. The smell of the flowers is almost overwhelming, and the colors are vibrant. Lakin's impressed.

"One of the servants collects rare plants," Sora explains. "And this is her pride and joy. She's worked for this family her entire life. Her husband died not long after they married, but because they already had children in a cresh, she never bothered to enter into another marriage contract. Her life revolves around serving here."

"That all sounds so cold," Lakin says as she joins Sora on a plush blanket set up in the very middle of the ornamental garden.

"Welcome to Talin society, where both the disease and the cure are illegal," Sora says with a sad shake of her head.

"Excuse me?" Lakin asks, not following.

"Oh sorry, I forgot you're pretty new to the Talins," Sora says with a chuckle. "I'm talking about the Fading. Searin almost died from it. Then he almost died from the Ending. I've got to keep an eye on that guy. He keeps trying to off himself."

"You're morbid!" Lakin says with a chuckle. "I like it. You might be a good person to ask a few questions. Otherwise, I'd have to wait until I'm back on Kalor and ask Maddy."

"Ask away," Sora encourages. "Talins tend to be pretty closed mouthed. I'll tell you what I know."

"How do you know if a Talin is scent-bonded to you?"

"It's pretty obvious," Sora answers with a chuckle of her own. "You smell like them all the time, and they have a compulsion to rub their scent glands on you."

"It's not just a self-soothing thing," Lakin clarifies, and Sora gives her a worried look.

"No, it's not. I mean, it's soothing for them to do that, and I find it soothing when Searin does it to me, but they don't feel a compunction to just do it randomly. Scent-bonding is a very big deal. It leaves a Talin vulnerable."

"How vulnerable?" Lakin asks, feeling a strange dread in her chest.

"If Dalt has scent-bonded with you and you leave, he dies," Sora says bluntly. "That's what Ending is, and it's a nasty way to die. Did you ever see someone who was addicted to Black Ice have to go off of it suddenly?"

"Yeah, it got popular about a year before I left Develia station," Lakin says, remembering how devastating the highly addictive drug was. "Our neighbor's teenage son got addicted. He died while they were trying to get him off it."

"I've seen that. The colony I grew up in on Staverious was one of the first places Black Ice showed up. Anyway, when a Talin is separated from their scent-bonded partner it's like that. They go through what amounts to really bad withdrawal that very often kills them."

"Shit," Lakin mutters. "I knew they didn't like to be separated from scent-bonded partners, but I didn't realize it was that bad. Now the laws and customs make more sense."

"I understand why they did it to begin with, but they don't need to make it so strict anymore. That's why Searin and his family are working so hard at changing everything." Sora looks grim.

"But it's slow, and there's some violent pushback," Lakin murmurs.

"Yeah," Sora says with a sigh.

The information about Dalt doesn't bother Lakin. She's already made up her mind to stay. This only cements it.

Dalt needs her. And these Talins need her too.

She gives Sora a big grin. "Don't worry about Dalt. I'll take care of him."

A relieved expression crosses Sora's face. But before she can say anything a servant is there, setting a tray with two steaming bowls on it between the two of them.

"I included a few sweets," the woman, says pointing to a corner of the tray. "You two need to share those. Only one each. I've been told too many can be detrimental to humans."

"Those are my favorite." Sora eagerly reaches for one right away, making the servant chuckle.

"Be good, little humans," she calls out as she walks away.

"Eat the sweets, but don't touch the soup," Sora advises her around a bite of the chewy candy. Picking up her bowl of soup with the other hand, she dumps it into a nearby bush and then sets the bowl back down with a little click and a grin.

"Yeah?" Lakin asks, taking a bite of her own sweet.

"It's horrible! Most Talins buy these bags of human feed," Sora explains with a grimace. "They're full of these hard balls. They take those, grind them up and add them to hot water to make our soup. If you've ever had old e-rations, you know what it tastes like."

Winkling her nose in distaste, Lakin eyes the steaming bowls. "Why?"

"Supposedly it's nutritious, and the humans who grow up eating the stuff don't mind it. But you and I know what good food tastes like."

"And the mane thing?" Lakin asks, touching her hair absently. Sora chuckles.

"Talins are a little obsessed with our hair. They call it a mane, and a lot of them like grooming it. I think they're under the impression that we spend a lot of time grooming each other as a way to bond."

"That's just weird," Lakin says, but Sora shakes her head.

"It's because parents groom their kids' hair," Sora says. "There's a whole section in one of their instruction guides dedicated to human grooming. It says grooming our manes daily is good for our health and will help us bond to our Talin owners."

"That explains Umella," Lakin says, remembering the Talin's rough treatment of her hair.

"Umella?" Sora asks.

"It's a complicated story, but I ended up on Molpa Colony," Lakin starts to say as she shifts positions a little to get more comfortable. Something pokes her in the waist. Distracted, she feels around and pulls out the needle tool she forgot was there.

"Hold on," she says to Sora, putting the tool between her lips to hold it while she reties her wrap.

Sora makes a little choking sound. "Why do you have an Atonement Needle?"

Pulling the needle tool out of her mouth, Lakin regards it curiously. "Is that what this thing is called? An Atonement Needle?"

"You didn't know?"

"I stole it off of Dalt a while back," Lakin explains. "It's so useful that I've gotten fond of it. I keep meaning to ask him about it but I forget or get distracted."

"Useful?" Sora asks, her expression both appalled and amused. "Useful for what?"

Lakin holds it up with a big grin. "This thing is perfect for breaking locking displays in ways no one can figure out. I used it to break an entire ship. I love this tool! And it's really easy to hide, watch." Lakin flips a section of her wrap open, threads the needle through the hem near her waist, in a way that won't poke her this time, and smooths the dress back out. "See, perfect tool!"

"I guess so," Sora says and Lakin gets the feeling she's trying not to laugh.

"What's so funny?" Lakin asks, feeling a little exasperated by Sora's poorly disguised amusement.

"So, ah, that's an Atonement Needle," Sora repeats.

"You said that. How about telling me other things about it, like what it's used for."

"Atoning," Sora manages to say with a straight face and then bursts out into laughter at Lakin's vexed expression. "Sorry! I couldn't help myself. Right, so those needles are an old-school part of Talin culture. Everyone carries them around but it's rare to use them anymore."

"They're ceremonial?" There aren't many things you could do with a ceremonial needle and Lakin is internally cringing when Sora nods. "Tell me the rest."

"Let's pretend you insulted me in some way and you wanted to make it up to me. If it was bad enough, you would kneel in front of me and offer the needle to me. Now I can do one of two things. I can take the needle and break it in two and hand you back one half. That means I've accepted the apology and the broken needle is a symbol of destroying the bad feelings between the two of us."

"That's not so bad," Lakin comments. "Why do I get the feeling the next option isn't so pleasant?"

"Because you've spent enough time with the Talins to know better," Sora replies. "The second option is that I don't take the needle. I don't accept the apology. Now you're required to show me that you're willing to go to great lengths to atone, so you pierce your tongue with the needle."

Lakin winkles her nose in distaste. "That's brutal."

"It gets worse. You have to stay kneeling with the needle in your tongue until I take it out and break it in two. I read an article about the history of the Atonement Needle and just a few years ago a woman knelt for three rotations before her parents forgave her and took the needle out of her tongue."

"I think that's taking tough love a little too far," Lakin mutters.

"Your turn. Tell me why you stole an Atonement Needle and then why you had to go around using it to break things," Sora insists.

"Ah, well, let me tell you a tale of great adventure," Lakin starts with a big smile. "It all starts with an electrical systems tech and Leemrons chasing the ship she's on."

"This sounds like it's going to be a good story!"

"It is," Lakin assures her. She spends almost a full mark telling Sora the story of her captivity, ending with a few marks earlier when Dalt got called in to talk to his parents alone so she was invited to tour the gardens and found Sora. "And that puts me here with you."

"I'm impressed," Sora says with a shake of her head. "And I'm envious of your skills. I never learned anything that useful in the ten years I was a slave."

That sobers Lakin. She knows a little about Sora's past but not enough. She always felt lucky that she remained free while many humans were forced into indentured servitude and sold into slavery by poverty-stricken and desperate families.

"Tell me about it," Lakin requests. "If you're comfortable sharing.

"My story isn't half as interesting as yours," Sora assures her. "But it has a happy ending." She breezes over her years as a slave and spends most of her time talking about Searin and the Prime Family.

Lakin's only a little envious as she learns about the part Dalt played in Sora's life.

After she's done talking, Lakin starts laughing. "Poor Eranan," she says between fits of laughter. "No wonder he's so frustrated. Between the two of us, we made his life so hard!"

"I do feel bad about that," Sora admits sheepishly. "Keeper Eranan is a nice Talin. Dalt is nice too. I'm glad you two are together. I feel like you two are a good match."

"Me too," Lakin agrees, thinking about Dalt and all the ways he respects her as an equal.

"Your owners are requesting your presence," a servant says, interrupting their talk. "I know the two of you are having fun, but be obedient and follow me."

Both women get up as the servant looks at Lakin's full bowl of now-cold soup.

"Bad pet," she admonishes. "You should've finished your meal. Humans can't go too long without sustenance. Your systems are much too delicate for that."

Lakin just manages to keep from snorting at that comment, but she does see the little smile Sora gives her as the two of them follow the servant back into the house. Soon they're in a room with Dalt and his family, Holian, and Searin. Sora heads straight to Searin and curls up in his lap while he purrs. Lakin looks over to Dalt and gives a little mental shrug before doing the same thing.

It's cool inside compared to the warmth of the garden, so it's pleasant to be surrounded by Dalt's warm and solid body.

"Missed you," he whispers in her ear. In response, she nuzzles her face against that sensitive bit of skin at the base of his neck. His rusty purr vibrates his chest.

"The information you gave us led us to a small conclave of Traditionalists," Searin tells them. "We just got the final communication from the ships I sent out. Somehow, they found out that we were coming. That means we raided an empty compound. But they didn't have time to clear out all the data so we've found some fragments we might be able to put together into something useful with a little time." Searin looks to Holian and makes a rattling sound of frustration. "We still don't know their true plans. It's obvious they want to eliminate Searin as a threat and having Holian's knowledge would help with that. But that doesn't give us much to work with.

"You know, there's another reason to kidnap Holian besides his knowledge of the Prime Families security protocols," Lakin murmurs thoughtfully.

"Yes?" Searin asks with an inquisitive rumble.

"Well, let's think about this in a slightly different way," Lakin says, sitting up on Dalt's lap. "Both you and the monarch visited Kalor. That could make the Traditionalists to believe Holian has become a major player among the Reformists. That might lead them to believe he can give them important insight into how strongly the monarch and Prime family are aligned with the Reformists. And who else is closely aligned with them."

"Everyone knows we are Reformists already," Searin argues with a soft rattle.

"But they don't know how strident you are," Lakin counters. "I bet you've been pretty circumspect about changing anything."

"How can you possibly know that?" Holian asks, his tone telling her he's incredulous but not being accusatory.

"Because that's how politics work just about everywhere. You can't change anything too quickly. Most species don't handle change well, and the way the Talins are all about their ancestors, I'm thinking they're like that too." She looks up to Dalt for confirmation, but Searin answers her unspoken question.

"You'd be correct," he says with a sharp, displeased rattle. "It took many generations for our species to start growing all our children in artificial wombs and raising them in creshes. It will no doubt take just as long to reverse those laws and traditions. You're an observant and cunning human, Lakin."

Before she can respond to Searin's compliment, Holian speaks. "You think I was targeted because the Traditionalists want to know how vehemently the Prime Family believes in the Reformist agenda? Not just because of my involvement with the protection of the Prime Family?"

"Exactly! They need to know if it's just a passing interest or if it's a passionate crusade," Lakin agrees enthusiastically. This scenario reminds her a lot of what was happening among the Cari a couple of years ago. Except their factions weren't so strictly delineated, but it still boiled down to something very similar— opposing political beliefs regarding the advancement of their own society.

Before it was all over, the Cari almost wiped themselves out. Lakin doesn't want that to happen to the Talins.

"Do you have any siblings?" she asks Searin, and that brings the discussions around her to an abrupt halt.

"I have a sister," he answers. Lakin realizes everyone is staring at her and several are making rumbles of curiosity.

"I have a plan for you," she tells him with a smirk. "I know how to find out who the Traditionalists are. And the best part is those Traditionists will be falling all over themselves to do it."

CHAPTER 31

Dalt

Dalt listens to his ingenious human describe a plan that would make the Traditionalists out themselves. The basics of the plan are simple. Let the Traditionalists believe Halieni, Searin's sister and potential next monarch, can be recruited to their side. As she lays out the steps to achieving the end goal, Dalt marvels at Lakin's talent for intrigue.

Ships are not the only thing Lakin can artfully destroy. Insurrections are on that list as well.

"The most brilliant part of this whole plan is that neither Scarin, nor Halieni need to be put in danger," Holian tells her.

"Exactly. If you guys do this right, they should be begging for Halieni's attention and doing anything they can to prove themselves to her," Lakin agrees. "Searin is a nonissue unless the current monarch suddenly dies."

"That's not likely," Sora assures her. "She's hale and hearty."

"The timeline is the most problematic part of your plan," Sherianan says with a frown.

"I know," Lakin agrees. "You're going to need to work fast. Find a few Talins you trust who aren't associated with the military. Merchants maybe?"

"I know several who might be useful," Tuchianan comments. "I'll send missives to feel them out."

"Give me their names so I can have checks done on them also," Searin commands.

They continue to talk, ironing out the plan until a servant hurries in to interrupt. "I'm very sorry, Grander Citizen Tuchianan and Ornianan, but there is a communication link request for Commandant Holian."

"From Kalor?" Holian asks as he stands. He doesn't rattle or rumble, but Lakin can tell he's concerned.

"No, Commandant, from a newly arrived ship," the servant says. "They didn't ask for you by name. They asked to speak to whoever owned the human female Lakin."

That makes Lakin give out a little gasp and jerk in his arms. "My crew!" she breathes out, excitement on her face. She scrambles off his lap and grabs the servant by the wrist, narrowly missing getting a handful of quills. "Where can I connect the link?"

The servant rattles with surprise and consternation but doesn't move. He looks up at Holian. "Sir? Your pet is touching me."

Moving swiftly Dalt stands and grabs Lakin up in his arms. "You can't be sure it's your old crew," he tells her as Holian directs the servant to lead them to a private room.

"I know it is," Lakin says, full of confidence as Dalt follows Holian and the servant out of the meeting room, down the hall, and into a smaller room dominated by a large display on one wall. The servant taps the display a few times, and a link activates.

"Captain!" Lakin shouts out the moment the face appears on the display. The servant hurries out with the door latching soundlessly behind him. Lakin wiggles and Dalt knows it's because she wants to be put down. He slowly lowers her to the floor. He doesn't want to let go of her. They might be in a secure room on the Talin homeworld, but Dalt feels like Lakin is about to be snatched away from him.

"Greetings," Holian says. "I'm Commandant Holian. This is Ground Commander Daltenion, and I believe you know Lakin, our pet." The captain's face on the display twists in disgust as she takes in Lakin's collar along with Holian's words.

"We're contacting you because of Lakin," the captain replies. "We wish to purchase her back. She's a valuable member of our crew. What is your starting price?"

"Captain, you don't—" Lakin starts to say, but Holian cuts her off.

"Quiet," Holian barks at her, startling her. After serving under Holian's command for years, Dalt's not surprised at his sharp tone, but it catches Lakin off guard. Blinking, she takes a half step back and bumps into Dalt, who wraps his arms around her.

"Where is your ship located at this moment?" Holian asks the captain.

"We are in stable orbit waiting for permission to land a shuttle at your city center port," the captain replies, looking suspicious. "We have full permission to be in Talin-controlled space as well as up-to-date registration numbers."

"Remain in orbit and do not land a shuttle. I'll be contacting you regarding the human," Holian says and then shuts down the link before the captain can say anything more. Turning, Holian lets off an aggravated rattle and stares down at Lakin. "This doesn't please me."

"Let me talk to them," Lakin offers. "I know I was given to you because I was in bad shape when the authorities found me, so you aren't out an initial cost of purchase. But I'm sure I can get some credits to pay for the healing and medications. Heck, I'm owed a ton of back pay. I might even be able to pay you back myself." Lakin's attempt at humor falls flat as Holian makes an irritated rattle. That surprises Dalt. Holian is normally a very self-possessed Talin, rarely making any rumble or rattles that reveal his emotions. Could the idea of Lakin being taken away by her old crew be upsetting the commandant as much as it upsets him?

"I'm not concerned about wealth," Holian tells her, his voice harsh. "I will not let you go back to serving on that crew. It's unnecessarily dangerous. I don't even want to think about what would've happened if you hadn't been brought to me after being discovered in the mercenary's ship. And then you threw yourself into danger again to help me. And no sooner are we safe than you volunteer to go into yet another dangerous situation. You have no sense of self-preservation. None!" That last word is almost a roar.

Wide eyed with surprise, Lakin opens her mouth but then closes it with an audible click. Her face goes blank, and she looks over her shoulder at him, but there's nothing Dalt can say. When she doesn't speak, Holian continues. "I'll talk to your crew first and make sure they understand that there are no circumstances where you will be returning to serve with them. Then I'll arrange to file paperwork so Dalt officially owns you. Then I'm going to find some place to rest because I'm very tired of humans running around trying to get themselves killed!" Holian takes a deep breath, stops rattling, and addresses Dalt.

"Dalt, do not let this one out of your sight. Do you understand me? I don't care how much she whines, wheedles, begs, or cries. You will be with her every moment of every rotation. Even in the elimination facilities. Everywhere!"

At Dalt's nod, Holian makes one last frustrated rattle and swings his gaze back to Lakin. "You will not run away!"

With that, Holian storms out of the room, slamming the door behind him.

Dalt has only seen this kind of display of emotion from Holian once when he was frantic to save some of his men. It comes from a place of fear and Holian being terrified someone under his watch is going to die.

He's afraid for me, Dalt realizes. *He knows I scent-bonded with Lakin. Without her, I'll suffer the Ending.*

Holian is going to do his best to keep Lakin with Dalt by refusing her old crew access to her.

His family is doing their best to keep Lakin with Dalt by offering up Barvarian Colony. He has no doubt the colony does need help, but many others could serve there. They don't need him.

But the efforts of Holian and his parents mean nothing if Lakin doesn't want to be with him.

"Damn, I just wanted to say hi to all of them and make sure everyone's doing okay," Lakin mutters, crossing her arms over her chest and glaring at the door. "I wasn't going to help them invade the capital or anything."

"I don't think that was Holian's worry," Dalt says.

"Could you open the link back up?" Lakin asks. "I want them to know I'm fine."

In that moment Dalt makes a decision. Rumbling out a purr, he rubs his scent glands into Lakin's hair. No sooner has he emptied both scent glands than she's rubbing her fingers through it and distributing the oil onto her scalp. The scent changes slightly, and both of them breathe deeply.

"That's the best smell," Lakin murmurs, snuggling into him.

"I'm going to re-establish the link to your old ship," he explains to her while still holding her tightly. "Then I'll leave the room so you can talk to them in privacy. Don't be afraid. No one will be monitoring."

Lakin gives him a confused look. "Thanks, but you don't have to leave."

"It's for the best," he tells her. He can't bear to listen to the conversation where she plans her departure. Plans on leaving all of Talin and him behind.

He taps the display a few times, finding the last uplink, issues a relink request, and then leaves. Just as the door shuts behind him, he hears Lakin exclaiming with happiness at whoever appears on the screen.

He stands in the hall for a moment at a loss. Death is looming. His life without Lakin is no life. They call it Collapsed Scent Disease, but most just call it Ending. The pain will start in his head, radiating out from his scent glands. The pain in his head will eventually become so intense he won't be able to handle opening his eyes in daylight or moving with any speed. Then it will start affecting the rest of him. His muscles will start to seize up intermittently and unpredictably. When the intermittent part becomes constant, his body will no longer let him walk, and eventually, he won't even be able to breathe.

Some suffering from Ending can survive if they get medical intervention. Medical intervention isn't illegal, but it's frowned upon because those who disobeyed the laws and scent-bond "deserve" the pain of Ending with no relief or life-saving measures.

It's a harsh view, but Talins aren't known for being a tender species—except with their human pets.

When the Ending starts taking effect, should he stay here at his family's compound or go back to Kalor? Should he die in his little stone cabin or see if his parents wish to try and extend his life?

Wait. Why is he thinking like this? Why does he need to be without Lakin? Just because she plans to leave with her crew doesn't mean he can't go with her. They wouldn't even need to pay him. They would be getting two crew members for the price of one. And having a Talin on board would pave the way for them at many stations. There's no way they'd refuse that advantage.

Determination fills him as he strides off to the room assigned to him and Lakin. Pulling an old travel bag out, he fills it with necessities they've been given since arriving. He'll want to buy more things before they set off, but some of the most important things he might need to have custom-made. Lakin should have protective clothing when on board a ship. And she should have weapons specially designed for her much smaller hands. He's going to make sure that after today, they're never separated again, but even he has to admit that Lakin would be a formidable opponent if armed and trained appropriately.

He's going to take great pleasure in training her.

The bag is full, and he's just tightening the straps when Lakin walks into the room. Without hesitation she jumps into his arms, a big smile on her face.

"They made it out with all the refugees!" she tells him excitedly. "And even found a safe place to let them off. They're in the Jeka system. Both slavery and indentured servitude are illegal there. That means their former owners can send as many petitions as they want, but they'll never be handed over."

"That's good," Dalt says as he sits on the large bed and cuddles her in his lap.

"I'm so relieved. I've been worried about what happened to them after I sabotaged the Leemrons' ship. I didn't know if other ships were out there, but now I know it all worked out." She gives a happy laugh and pulls her head back enough to give him a quick lip press right on his mouth. He loves those human lip presses. He didn't understand why the humans did that until now.

Now, he can't imagine his life without lip presses from Lakin.

"Are you packing?" Lakin asks, noticing the bag on the floor near his feet.

"Yes," he says, wondering how to tell her that he's going with her. He hopes she doesn't get too upset.

"Give me more here, big guy," she says in her familiar teasing tone. "Are we going back to Kalor already? I was hoping we could stay for just a bit longer so I could hang out with Sora again."

"We can stay until you're ready to join your ship," Dalt agrees.

"My ship?" she asks.

"The ship you served on," he amends.

"Right," she says slowly, eyes narrowing. "And despite what Holian said to them earlier, you're just going to let me waltz off and put myself in all kinds of danger."

He can't help it. He starts purring. Loudly.

"No, I can't let you just dance away from me," he agrees. "I'll be going with you. If you need to serve on that ship to be happy, I'll make that happen. But I'll be standing by your side the entire time."

"You'd do that?" she asks softly. "You'd pull up stakes and just join me? Even though we do really dangerous stuff sometimes? Even though we both might die? You're still willing to go with me?"

"There's no other choice," he states firmly. "What you want, I want. Where you go, I go."

Suddenly she wraps her arms around his neck and clutches at him so tightly he imagines he could stand up and her arms would remain around his neck, her feet dangling in the air. He lets the embrace go on for several moments but then tugs her away.

"We must leave soon," he tells her. "Holian will stop us if we wait too long. Even after he transfers your ownership to me, he still could stop us. He's a powerful Talin."

"We aren't leaving," Lakin tells him, making Dalt rumble in confusion.

"We aren't?"

"I was never going to leave," she explains. "I decided a while ago that I'm staying here. Some humans are kept by Talins who don't deserve them and might be abusing them. We've got to get them to families who will treat them right. But most of all, we need to take the Traditionalists down. Searin, Holian, Sherianan, all of you need me. You need more than just me. We need to find more humans like me—humans we could loan to families to get information and spy for the Reformists."

He's speechless, poleaxed by the fact that not only does Lakin want to stay, but she wants to do more than help them plan out how to defeat the Traditionalists. In true Lakin style, she wants to join in the fight.

Cupping his face with both of her hands, she meets his eyes with her beautiful golden human ones. "I'm here for good, ready to help you guys fight the good fight," she whispers. "Because no matter what, I love you, Dalt. You're mine."

"I'm your Talin," he agrees quickly. "And you're my human."

"Always," she agrees.

EPILOGUE

A SOLAR LATER
(ABOUT 1.2 YEARS IN OLD EARTH EQUIVALENT)

Lakin

The human colony on Develia station hasn't changed much since Lakin's childhood. As she makes her way down a familiar corridor of the crowded station, various smells assault her nose. The environmental controls in this section are old and not kept in good repair so the place always stinks. Most get used to it. Lakin didn't even realize it smelled bad until she left and came back for a visit.

Sliding her eyes sideways, she catches Dalt rubbing his nose. He doesn't complain about the smell, but it's obviously bothering him. Thankfully, this should be the last time they need to visit her old home. Her mother, sister, and brother have all relocated to Talin territory, now owned by the Tavani Clan on Talarian. Closely allied with Prime Son Searin, the Tavani Clan are both Reformists and familiar with humans. Well, as familiar as Talins are if all they do is read their own literature. But it didn't take long for Lakin's family to set them straight on exactly what humans need to be healthy and how they want to be treated. Her young, spunky sister is a favorite of the family with her open affection and blunt mouth.

For their part, the Tavani have even hired a cook who can prepare both Talin and human food. No disgusting pre-prepared human feed for them. Lakin's family is living a secure and safe life among the Talin.

And for the first time in her life, Lakin feels no guilt when she leaves them.

Now she's back on Develia station, hopefully for the last time. Armed with information from her brother, Lakin finds the apartment she's looking for and presses the door display to ask for entrance. A familiar face appears on the display. Lips part and eyes go wide at the sight of Lakin.

"Lakin?" Mellena gasps. Her face disappears, and the door slides open with a creak. It catches halfway, but Mellena just smacks the edge, and it finishes opening.

"Lakin!" she shouts and grabs Lakin up in a bruising hug. Mellena's always been big and strong. According to Lakin's sister, once she got a job working on the station stabilization thrusters, she went from strong to formidable. With the amount of muscle Lakin can feel as Mellena hugs her, Lakin knows her sister wasn't exaggerating.

"I heard you were here a while back, but I missed out on seeing you!" Mellena says as she swings Lakin back and forth a little. Lakin's feet are off the ground and dangling in the air. Mellena's grip isn't painful, but it's not entirely comfortable either. Before she needs to tell Mellena to let her go, big hands grab Lakin and pull her out of Mellena's hold.

"No," Dalt says simply, and Mellena gapes at the big Talin. She lets go of Lakin and steps back, fear evident on her face. Dalt doesn't put her down and keeps her cradled against his chest, probably afraid Mellena will try to sweep her off her feet again.

"Shit, sorry," she mutters as her gaze bounces between Dalt and Lakin. Lakin can tell the exact moment the collar around her neck registers with Mellena. "Ah, shit, I'm sorry, Lakin." Then she pales and looks up to Dalt. "I'm sorry, sir. Can I speak to your slave?"

Rumbling out a purr, Dalt nuzzles the top of her head with his cheek. This last trip to Develia station is hard for Dalt. Unable to bring any weapons on board, she knows he's feeling vulnerable.

Last time they came here, they were accompanied by a whole slew of Holian's men. But this time it's just her, Dalt, and the siblings Yomian and Nomian from Molpa Colony.

"It's not what you think," Lakin tells her as she snuggles against Dalt's broad chest. The scent of cedar fills her nose as Dalt's oil saturates her hair.

Absently, she touches her collar. Dalt had it specially made for her. Not only can it be tracked, but it also has secrets. Dalt had it crafted so once she takes it off, there are a few slim tools on the inside she can pull out to manipulate circuits and other electronics. She still keeps the atonement needle she stole off Dalt hidden on her person, but the collar tools make her feel even more secure.

When he gave it to her, it was better than receiving precious stones.

But Mellena can only see a collar, not all the hidden meanings it represents between her and Dalt. "I'm not a slave."

"Ah, right, sure," Mellena says, her voice heavy with disbelief.

"Can we come in?"

"None of us are here to hurt you," Yomian says with a loud purring rumble as he steps out from behind Dalt. "We just wish to speak to you. I have an offer for you."

"Sure, come in." Stepping back, Mellena lets them file into her small domicile. "An offer? I do all right working here. I'd need to see the contract before agreeing to another job somewhere else."

"It's not a job," Lakin tells her with a wide grin. "It's a whole new life."

Looking thoroughly puzzled, Mellena edges back against the wall. The three Talins seem to take up most of the space of the tiny one-room living quarters. "Maybe you guys should sit."

Without further prompting, Dalt makes himself comfortable on the end of a small bunk while Yomian sits on the only chair. Nomian slides down a wall to sit on the floor.

Probably because Mellena is standing next to Yomian, he holds out his arms and increases the volume of his purr. "You may clutch and cling to me if you wish."

Blinking, Mellena looks over to Lakin who just starts laughing.

"He means you can sit on his lap and hug him, but don't worry about that. Just sit here next to me for a minute, and I'll explain," Lakin tells her.

Mellena relaxes a fraction at Lakin's easy attitude but remains standing. "I think I'm good here."

Yomian rattles out a quiet disappointed sound and drops his arms into his lap. "Please let Lakin argue my case," he begs Mellena. "You're a beautiful human. Strong and robust. I wish you to consider me for your owner. I'll take good care of you."

"We both would," Nomian agrees. "Our colony is small, but we're rapidly growing, and both of us have excellent jobs and status. As the colony grows, our status will grow also. You'll be treated very well. And one of us will always be home to care for you."

"Owned! What the hell, Lakin?" Mellena nearly shouts and turns an accusing expression on Lakin. Lakin doesn't notice because she's too busy scowling at Yomian and Nomian.

"What did I say on the trip here?" she asks them with exasperation. "What did I tell you guys to do?"

Chastised, Yomian sounds an embarrassed rumble. "Wait until you finished speaking to Mellena on my behalf."

"Give you time to explain everything to Mellena," Nomian says at the same time.

"Exactly. Now sit and be quiet," Lakin orders.

Mellena edges toward the door. "What's going on here?"

Lakin sighs and pinches the bridge of her nose. "You don't need to run. No one's going to kidnap you or anything like that," Lakin assures her. "I'm not a slave; I'm a pet. But really, I'm his scent-bonded partner." Lakin gestures with her thumb over her shoulder at Dalt.

Although Mellena doesn't seem soothed by Lakin's words, she no longer looks like she's going to bolt either. Taking it as a good sign, Lakin pats the bunk next to her. "Please, come sit and let me explain everything. After that, you can think about it. We can stay docked for the next rotation to give you a little time to consider."

"Consider what?"

"As I said earlier, a whole new life," Lakin repeats, her wide smile returning.

It takes a while, but Mellena listens to everything she has to say. By the time she's done explaining, Mellena's moved closer to Yomian and is hesitantly touching the large Talin. Patiently, Yomian lets Mellena run her fingers over the keratin plating on his shoulder, down his arm, and finally to explore his quills.

When he unexpectedly pulls her into his lap, she makes a small, startled sound but doesn't struggle. She remains still when Nomian edges close and joins them. Soon Mellena is sandwiched between the two Talins. As they both hug her, she mumbles, "So strong," and tries to burrow down into their embrace.

When both siblings start purring loudly, Lakin almost doesn't hear Mellena's awed, "Oh, so nice."

This is the Mellena she remembers—a woman who thrives on touch and interaction. Yomian doesn't realize it, but his next words pretty much sell Mellena on the idea of being owned by Yomian and Nomian.

"If you come back with me, my family will adore you. I'm not sure they'll be able to give you a moment of peace. When I mentioned I was coming here, they all started buying things for you. Everyone now has a human bed installed in their room just on the chance you'll agree to spend the night with them. No one even bothered updating the outside enclosure. There's no reason. You'll always be with one of us. Both our parents, our aunt and her family, as well as several cousins from my father's side of the family all live at the compound."

"They're all so excited that I think they bought out any stock of human items on the whole colony," Nomian tells her. "The entire family is eager to meet you. Hold you. Cuddle you. Please come back with us."

For the extroverted, attention-starved Mellena, there's only one acceptable answer to the siblings' proposal. With a heartfelt sigh, she wraps her strong arms around his neck, puts her lips to his earhole, and whispers, "Yes."

Dalt and Lakin slip out as Mellena, Yomian, and Nomian cuddle and talk. "That went well," Lakin comments as Dalt carries her back to their ship.

"As you knew it would," Dalt replies with a purring rumble of his own.

"Now that the Reformists are gaining the upper hand, I have no problem with bringing more humans to live with the

Talins. As long as they're owned by the good ones, like you and Holian."

"You're one of the reasons we gained the upper hand," Dalt points out.

"You're the reason I even care about what's happening to the Talins," Lakin counters.

"And you're the reason I bother breathing and eating," Dalt tells her softly as he climbs the short ramp to their ship.

"Breathing, eating, and other things," Lakin murmurs. She kisses the strip of exposed skin on Dalt's neck and feels him shiver. Touching there never fails to get a reaction.

"Yes, and other things," Dalt agrees.

Running her fingers over the scent glands on his right cheek, Lakin lets out a sigh as the smell of cedar fills the air. "Let's go do those other things while we wait for everyone back on the ship."

"All the other things," Dalt agrees.

BONUS CAPTER

MOLPA COLONY

Tani

"Here's your new home, little Tani," Saminous announces jovially as he walks into a large fenced area and gently lays Tani down on a thick pad under a leafy tree.

"Saminous!" someone shouts and Tani looks over in time to see a large human come running out of a little hut-like building in the center of the fenced-in area. The guy is at least two hundred pounds, adorably chubby, and flushed. He has a giant grin as he rushes up to Saminous and grabs him in a hug.

"I missed you!" the guy says.

"I missed you also, Dasom," Saminous answers, returning the hug and purring loudly. "It's almost time for a large transport ship to leave our port. Do you want to watch?"

Another human appears from the hut, walking much more leisurely toward them. He gives Tani a curious look as he addresses Saminous.

"He's been talking about the launch all rotation, as if it doesn't happen all the time," he says, then gives a little wave to Tani. "Hi, I'm Kal and that's my brother Dasom."

"Um, Tani," Tani mumbles, pointing to his chest. While he wasn't scared of the large exuberant Dasom, this male looks far more intimidating.

"Can you look after Tani while I take Dasom to watch the launch?" Saminous asks Kal. "He's wild-caught and has hurt his leg. Healer Felgorum will be here soon to look after him."

Kal's beautiful dark blue eyes go wide and he takes a half step away from Tani. "Wild-caught?"

Tani almost laughs. Kal is as tall as his brother without the roundness. Like Dasom, Kal is pale with light brown hair, but that's as far as the similarities go. Kal is nothing but muscle and probably outweighs Tani by a good sixty pounds. Kal's reaction is downright hilarious, or it would be if Tani isn't so scared.

"He was found wandering around a derelict station, starving," Saminous explains. "But he's calm and well-mannered. There shouldn't be an issue with his transition to pet."

"Sure, I guess," Kal agrees but doesn't look convinced. The fact that Kal is wary of him gives Tani the courage to smile up at the gorgeous male.

"I don't think I can even walk right now," he admits and points down at his swollen ankle.

Kal winces. "Oh wow, that looks like it hurts. Healer Felgorum will sort it out. He's really good."

"Ship launch!" Dasom reminds them in a loud, excited voice. "We're gonna miss it!"

His childish tone and the unique shape of his eyes clues Tani into what is different about Dasom—Down's syndrome.

When Tani was growing up, there was an older child with the same genetic anomaly. He'd been the sweetest kid and Dasom seems to have a very similar personality.

"Yes, of course, Dasom," Saminous says with an amused rumble. "You two converse. We'll be back in a few marks."

Saminous takes Dasom's hand and leads him out of the large enclosure. The excited man skips at Saminous's side.

Dasom calls back to them with a little wave as the gate swings shut. "I'll meet you later Tani! 'Kay?"

Yes, that sounds just like something his childhood friend would've said and it makes Tani smile.

"That'd be great," Tani calls back, even though he doesn't think Dasom heard him.

Kal sinks to the grass in front of Tani and crosses his legs. "My brother's a little different, but he's really sweet."

"Down's syndrome?" Tani asks.

Kal gives him a curious look. "Is that what your people call it when there's an extra chromosome?"

"Yeah. You don't?"

"The Talins have some kind of fancy name for it," Kal explains. "But they don't care. I think Saminous loves my brother even more because he's childlike." Kal frowns and runs a hand through his long, gleaming hair. "When I got older all they wanted me to do was pair off with a woman and start having babies. But I'm not into girls so then my previous owners weren't sure what to do with me. When Saminous offered to buy me I refused to be parted from Dasom so they sold both of us. I think Saminous might've blackmailed my other owners somehow, but I'm thankful. I like this place. Saminous spoils us and he's always taking Dasom on adventures. They never parade women around me or demand I fill a cup with semen. It's great I–"

Tani is listening intensely, finding everything Kal is saying fascinating. He isn't prepared for Kal to suddenly stop talking and flush red. Is there something seriously wrong with the pale man?

"Are you okay? Should I call for help?" Tani asks.

Kal drops his head into his hands and groans. "Only if Healer Felgorum has a cure for death by embarrassment. I can't believe I told you all of that! We only just met and I'm talking about cumming in a cup!"

Tani laughs. "If it helps I had to cum in a cup once and I'm gay too." Then it's Tani's turn to be embarrassed as he starts blabbering. "I mean I'm gay, but I'm sorry if I assumed wrong about you. You said you didn't like women, but that could mean you're demi or ace, not necessarily gay. Um, and I wouldn't do anything to you. Like force you or anything. Unless you want me to and then I'd do anything you asked because you're the prettiest guy I've ever met."

Did all of that just come out of his mouth? Mortified, he slaps both hands over his lips before he says anything else!

To his relief Kal bursts out laughing. "Tani, you're perfect!"
"I'm glad you think so," Tani agrees with a grin. "You're probably the only one."
Getting control of his laughter, Kal scoots a little closer. "Want to put your leg up on mine? Your ankle must be throbbing and elevating might make it feel better."
Shyly, Tani nods. "That'd be nice, thanks."
With gentle hands Kal moves Tani's leg so his calf is resting on Kal's thigh. That little bit of contact makes Tani feel flushed and he pulls a nearby small pillow into his lap and pretends to rest his elbows on it.
"So you've been a pet all your life?" he asks, then almost smacks himself. As an opening for conversation it's dumb. He might as well ask a slave if they'd been born into slavery!
"I was born a pet on Talarian," Kal says without hesitation. Maybe it wasn't such a dumb question. "Talarian is the Talin homeworld. Were you really on a derelict station?"
Tani grimaces. "No, I was working on Tomora station and was kidnapped, then sold here."
Kal's mouth drops open. "You worked?"
His shocked question confuses Tani. "Of course I worked. How else would I house and feed myself? I'm a recormu engine tech."
"But we don't work," Kal sputters. "We're meant to be cared for and adored, not labor."
"*We* as in humans?" Tani asks, feeling as shocked by Kal's response as Kal must've been by his declaration of employment.
Kal's surprise turns to laughter. "Of course humans. We're small compared to almost every other species out there and we don't have a homeworld. It's obvious we can't survive on our own in the universe."
Tani thinks about that for a moment before answering. "It's true we're smaller but that's not a bad thing. I'm good at my job because I can fit into spots even repair bots have a hard time with. A lack of a homeworld makes things harder, not impossible. Every human I knew worked until I was brought here."
Kal looks pensive. "You must think I'm helpless."
"No! Not at all," Tani says quickly. "I think you're amazing. Your loyalty to your brother is wonderful and I envy this life. I was scared at first but maybe it won't be so bad."

Kal looks down and then slides his eyes up to meet Tani. "I hope you like it here because I think I like you."

Tani can't imagine this Adonis being attracted to him. "Because I'm the only gay guy available?"

Kal's frown is fierce as he looks up to meet Tani's gaze directly. "There are four other guys on this colony who're gay or bi. If I asked, Saminous would let me visit them as often as I like. Don't get me wrong. Two of them are fun but I'm not interested in a relationship with any of them. I've been here for four solars and you're the first guy I've met who I immediately want to get to know better." He gave Tani a little grin. "A lot better."

"Greetings, human Kal!" a voice calls out before Tani can think of a response. They both look over to see a Talin wearing a knee-length, dark green tunic accompanied by several wearing light green tunics.

"Hi Healer Felgorum," Kal says, then points to Tani. "Tani's ankle is hurt. Could you fix him please?"

"Of course," the healer says with a purr as he walks in followed by the other two Talins. They're all carrying cases and they gather around Tani but don't make Kal move.

"Don't worry, Human Tani," one of the assistants says. "We'll make you feel all better soon and then you can have some sweet treats."

The healer takes in their position. "Kal, why don't you move behind Tani and cuddle him to make him feel better while we assess and treat him."

Kal looks at him with a raised eyebrow and Tani nods his head. Moving slowly, Kal lifts Tani's leg, sets it on the ground and maneuvers around and behind him onto the pillow.

"You can lean back against me," Kal whispers. "I've got you."

Tani relaxes against Kal. The man wraps his arms around Tani's chest and loosely links his hands together.

He's so distracted by Kal's body against his that he doesn't even notice when the healer starts handling his leg until he squeezes on the ankle. Pain shoots up his leg, making Tani flinch.

"Oh, owwww!" Tani cries under his breath, fighting the urge to pull his foot away.

"I'm sorry Human Tani," Felgorum says. "The discomfort is only for a little longer. Then we'll give you pain abatement medication. It'll make you sleepy, but Kal can hold you while we work."

Tani likes the idea of no pain but is a little worried about being out of it.

"You're safe," Kal murmurs near his ear. The man's warm breath against his neck makes Tani shiver. "I won't let anything happen to you. You're safe here, I swear."

There's no reason for him to trust Kal so completely after only knowing the guy for a short time.

Could there be such a thing as love at first sight? If there is, this might be it.

"I believe you," Tani whispers back. Kal gives him a little kiss on the shell of his ear and then one of the assistants is holding a round wafer to his lips.

"Let this dissolve on your tongue, Human Tani. You'll feel much better."

Tani accepts the wafer without hesitation and falls into a dreamy state where Kal keeps telling him that everything's going to be fine and he'll never want for anything again.

Melpa Colony - ten rotations later
Tani

Cuddling against Kal, Tani wakes from a sound sleep. He's not sure what pulled him from an amazing dream where he and Kal were making love on a soft cloud high in the sky. Not that their regular lovemaking isn't spectacular, but in his dream the buoyant cloud was a nice touch.

"Hi, Tani," a familiar voice whispers. "I told you I'd come back."

It takes him a moment before he can see the outline of the small figure in the darkness of their hut. On the opposite side of the room Dasom is laying on his back and snoring loudly. He can feel Kal's slow steady breathing, indicating his boyfriend is still asleep too.

When a larger, Talin figure steps into the room, Tani's eyes go wide.

"What's going on Lakin?" he asks. "Who's that?"

"That's Dalt. He belongs to me and we're here to rescue you," Lakin explains. "Do you think these two other guys want to go with you? I can give them the reversal of the sleep aid I dripped in their mouths."

That explains why neither of them woke up despite how not quiet the conversation they are being.

Tani wiggles out from Kal's arms and gets off the bed. Holding out his arms, he offers Lakin a hug.

"It's good to see you alive and well," he says.

"Same," Lakin agrees with a little laugh. "After that guard was so rough I was worried about you."

"I had a soft landing," Tani says, pulling away from Lakin to look over at Dalt. "It's nice to meet you."

Dalt grunts, then speaks to Lakin. "We need to hurry. The alarm delay is almost done."

"I know exactly how long it will last. I'm the one who set it," Lakin responds tartly, then regards Tani with a questioning expression.. "Well, do you guys need to be rescued? I can get all three of you to Ocorma station and give you some credits to get back to Tomora station."

"No!" Tani says quickly. "I want to stay here! This place is great. I think Kal might be, um, I don't know, but something important."

Now that his eyes have adjusted to the dim light he can see Lakin's expression soften. "It's okay to say the love of your life. I'm staying with the Talins too because of this guy."

She uses her thumb to indicate Dalt behind her.

"Then I guess we're both good," he concludes. "I hope you didn't hurt anyone getting in here. Everybody who works for Saminous and his family is nice."

"They might be nice but they're not great at their job," Lakin comments. "Which means we didn't need to do anything to anybody."

Relief makes Tani blow out a breath. "Good. That's good."

Lakin fishes around inside her wrap and pulls something small out. "Here, take this. It's an untraceable beacon. We'll be able to track it, but no one else can. If anything happens, activate it and try to keep it close to you. We'll get to you as fast as we're able."

Tani accepted the coin-sized disk. "Thanks, Lakin. It's nice to know I've got options if I ever need them."

Lakin gave him another hug. "Always."

Dalt tugs at Lakin's sleeve. "We must go now."

"Bye, Lakin," Tani says as she lets Dalt pull her away. "Maybe you can come back and visit officially next time."

"I will," she promises and then she's gone.

Going back to the bed, Tani wiggles into Kal's embrace. Even drugged, the large, handsome man pulls Tani close and sounds a content sigh.

Tani knows exactly how he feels!

Dear Readers,

Thank you for reading *Escaping Captivity*. I hope you loved Lakin's antics as much as did. She will aways be one of my favorite sassy FMCs! If you want more **Human Pets of Talin** the next book is ready for you to read: *Negotiating Captivity*.

There is also a second series with human pets: **Origins**. This series is set in the same universe but several hundred years earlier. It traces the beginning of human pets among the Talins.

I hope you enjoyed *Escaping Captivity* enough to leave a review! As an indie writer without the support of a publishing company, I need all the help I can get. Your good reviews keep me writing.

If you have any questions, comments, or suggestions feel free to contact me via email: author@rk-munin.com

Want some free novellas? You can find the links for them and much more on my website:

www.rk-munin.com

Have a fruitful rotation,
Rye

Other books by RK Munin

-SCIENCE FICTION-

Hissa Warrior Series
Rescuing Halin (Mian and Halin)
Buying Tiran (Mara and Tiran)
Tempting Selon (Lara and Selon)
Defying Kilan (Deena and Kilan)
Healing Mavito (Raleen and Mavito)
Claiming Yopin (Mouse and Yopin)
Teasing Woken (Safena and Woken)
Defending Revin (Kamaril and Revin)
Trusting Warik – Coming soon

Human Pets of Talin Series
Loving Captivity (Sora and Searin)
Escaping Captivity (Lakin and Dalt)
Negotiating Captivity (Nalia and Derani)
Fighting Captivity (Zia and Palforma)
Tender Captivity (Jinna and Holian - This is a novella you can get
for free by signing up for my newsletter)
Craving Captivity (Lasha and Tamerin)
The Twelve Nights of Halloheen: A holiday mashup novella (Isla
and Tisuran)
Stealing Captivity (Kasi and Ignatias)
Redeeming Captivity – Coming soon

Origins (A Human Pets of Talin Series)
Creating Captivity (Ari and Bazium)
Gossamer Chains (Rain and Hesarium)
Golden Cages – Coming soon
Purring, Presents, and Parties – Coming soon

-Paranormal /Urban Fantasy-

Ours Evermore Series
Two Wolves for Soren (Soren, Kalli, and Quinn)
A Hacker, Vampire, and Chimera Walk into a Bar… (Tobias, Briar, and Memphis)
When Darkness Meets Dawn (Imani, Lex, and Mac)
Tag, You're It (Novella)
Kidnapping Their Third (Cora, Pike, and Kimble)
Pastries on a Plate and Blood in a Mug – Coming soon

Alpha Series
Alpha Mage (Emma and Kade)
His Alpha Mage (Avery and Jason – Novella)
Alpha King (Cathleen and Lazlo)

New Clan Series
Stray Wolf (Steph and Eli)
Lost Lion (Maeve and Cyrus)
Reluctant Cervid (Tavi and Donovan)
Broken Thorn (Sabina and Theodosius)